*USA Today* Bestselling Author
# DALE MAYER

# Silenced in the Sunflowers

Lovely Lethal Gardens 19

SILENCED IN THE SUNFLOWERS: LOVELY LETHAL GARDENS, BOOK 19
Beverly Dale Mayer
Valley Publishing Ltd.



ISBN-13: 978-1-773366-51-7
Print Edition

## Books in This Series

Arsenic in the Azaleas, Book 1

Bones in the Begonias, Book 2

Corpse in the Carnations, Book 3

Daggers in the Dahlias, Book 4

Evidence in the Echinacea, Book 5

Footprints in the Ferns, Book 6

Gun in the Gardenias, Book 7

Handcuffs in the Heather, Book 8

Ice Pick in the Ivy, Book 9

Jewels in the Juniper, Book 10

Killer in the Kiwis, Book 11

Lifeless in the Lilies, Book 12

Murder in the Marigolds, Book 13

Nabbed in the Nasturtiums, Book 14

Offed in the Orchids, Book 15

Poison in the Pansies, Book 16

Quarry in the Quince, Book 17

Revenge in the Roses, Book 18

Silenced in the Sunflowers, Book 19

Toes in the Tulips, Book 20

Lovely Lethal Gardens, Books 1–2

Lovely Lethal Gardens, Books 3–4

Lovely Lethal Gardens, Books 5–6

Lovely Lethal Gardens, Books 7–8

Lovely Lethal Gardens, Books 9–10

# About This Book

A new cozy mystery series from *USA Today* best-selling author Dale Mayer. Follow gardener and amateur sleuth Doreen Montgomery—and her amusing and mostly lovable cat, dog, and parrot—as they catch murderers and solve crimes in lovely Kelowna, British Columbia.

Riches to rags. … Hearts start to heal. … Friendships start to grow, … just not for everyone!

Doreen knows her relationship with the police captain has always been on thin ground. She has helped them solve a lot of cases, but she's quadrupled their work and constantly gets in their way. So no one is more surprised than Doreen when the captain stops by and asks for a personal favor, concerning a cold case from his own childhood.

Slowly recovering from his injury, Corporal Mack Moreau learns that the captain has stopped by Doreen's house, asking for a moment of her time. Curious, Mack's even more stunned to hear the details about his captain's visit. Mack wants to help, but investigating a case from forty years ago doesn't leave much behind to go on.

Doreen knows that failing to solve a case has to happen sometime. But she'd do a lot to not have that happen here, not when the captain had personally asked for her help. So, with her critters in tow, Doreen is off and running, … leaving Mack watching—and worrying—in her wake.

**Sign up to be notified of all Dale's releases here!**

https://geni.us/DaleNews

# Chapter 1

***Early September***

IT SEEMED LIKE days had whipped past since that last chaotic scenario at Doreen's house. Today she sat at the creek, a cup of coffee in her hand, Nick on one side and Mack on the other. She turned toward Mack. "How's physio going?"

"Better. Apparently I escaped a pretty ugly shoulder injury."

"Good." She hesitated and then asked, "And how about the two guys who showed up here?"

"Rodney has stitches in a region no man should ever have stitches," Mack stated, shuddering, "but should make a full recovery."

"And the other man, Wilson?"

"He'll have long welts for quite a few more days on his back and head," Mack told her. "What I want to know is how you trained Thaddeus to drop bird poop on your attackers like that?"

She winced. "I didn't train Thaddeus. He did that all on his own."

Mack just shook his head, as he considered the bird.

Doreen watched Thaddeus, even now wandering in front of them on the pathway, standing on rocks, hopping off rocks, looking totally harmless. Meanwhile, Goliath and Mugs lay basking in the sun, also just being the heroes they were.

"You know what? I've seen these animals respond in more ways with you than I ever thought possible," Mack stated. "Yet I had no idea they could do what they did this last time."

"Neither did I," she replied. "And I mean it. It's all about loyalty. And, for whatever reason, I've been blessed to have their love *and* their loyalty. And I try hard to never do anything to damage that."

At that, Nick patted her on the shoulder and stated, "Not just *their* love. A lot of people in town love you too."

She gave him a sad smile. "But apparently a lot of people in town also don't love me," she admitted, "so it's been a mixed blessing."

Nick smiled. "Eventually you will find a lot of people on your side versus the other side."

"I suppose," she agreed. "It just takes time."

The two brothers nodded.

"And I need to get the captain back on my side," she added. "I'm not exactly sure how to do that though."

"It's not that he's *not* on your side," Mack argued cautiously. "He just needs you to stay out of our cases when it comes to the legal stuff, so that he can get a case nailed down and so that the criminals don't walk because of problems with the collection of evidence." He sent her a knowing look.

"Right," she said, "all that legal stuff."

"I get that the legal stuff isn't a big deal for you," Mack cautioned her, "but we don't want to do all this work and have these guys go free."

She nodded. "I could be very good for a few days," she suggested. "Maybe he'll forgive me then."

"Nothing to forgive, just keep a low profile," Mack stated.

"Right. I might do that." Doreen studied Mack for a moment. "You're off the rest of this week. How about we try paddleboarding again? If your physio allows it ..." She turned toward Nick. "I don't know where we'd get a board for you," she added, "but, if you want to come with us, that would be awesome."

"That sounds great." Nick nodded, raising his coffee cup in agreement.

Mack faced her and asked, "So will you be off cases for a while now?"

"I hope so," she said, "at least I really hope so."

And, just when the guys were getting up to leave, a vehicle drove up, and she said, "*Uh-oh.*"

"What's *uh-oh*?" Mack asked.

"That's the captain's vehicle."

"Ooh." Mack walked out to talk to him.

Doreen stepped out on the front porch and asked the captain, "Problems?"

"Not so much problems," the captain began, "but I wondered if I could talk with you."

She looked surprised and replied, "Absolutely."

"*Uhm,*" the captain added, "and possibly alone, if I could."

She looked over at Mack, who shrugged. "We were just leaving." At that, Mack and Nick got into their vehicle. Mack made a sign for her to call him later.

She smiled and nodded and led the captain into her

house. "Do you want a coffee?"

He hesitated and then nodded. "If you wouldn't mind. I kind of …" He hesitated again.

"Am I in trouble?" she asked immediately.

He looked at her and then smiled. "No, you're not. Yet, because of the trouble you *do* get into, I have a favor to ask."

She frowned. "Okay, sure. What can I do for you?"

"It's a cold case."

She beamed. "I would love to work on another cold case."

"It involves my cousin. He was killed several decades ago. In fact, he was shot in the garden."

"In a garden?" she asked, liking the idea already, but careful to keep the smile off her face.

"Yeah, in the sunflowers," he added.

"Ooh," she replied, "the *Silenced in the Sunflowers* case."

He slowly nodded. "I guess, if that's how you want to look at it."

She nodded. "That's how I want to look at it. I need details, details." Doreen clasped her hands together to keep from rubbing them with glee, as she shot him a look. "And you'll forgive me if I solve this?"

He laughed. "Nothing to forgive. It's because of your unique viewpoint and your way of coming at things that I'm here right now. If you can help me with this case," the captain stated, "believe me. I'll be in your debt."

"*Silenced in the Sunflowers*, here we come," she cried out.

At that, Mugs barked, Goliath howled, and Thaddeus repeated her words in joy.

# Chapter 2

### *Saturday Morning*

DOREEN STARED DOWN at the phone and repeated, "I know it's crazy," she said to Mack, "but the captain really did want me to look into a case that he's personally involved in. I don't have all the details yet. I just know what he told me. And since I've already told you what he told me," she said in exasperation, "I don't have any other information to offer."

Silence came on the other end. Finally Mack replied, "It's better than what I thought he wanted to say."

"You and me both," she said, with feeling.

She sat on her back deck, the late-afternoon sun shining down on her. Mugs had stretched out beside her, as she absentmindedly rubbed his belly. Goliath was similarly situated atop the table on the deck, lord of all he surveyed, and Thaddeus was just wandering around the grass, plucking at various items. One particularly shiny rock seemed to have caught his attention, and he kept picking it up, dropping it, and picking it up.

"I mean, I gather this is something that's really bothered him," Doreen added.

"You and I both know what it's like to have a bad memory in your history. If you don't know how to even proceed, it's not something you can do anything about. And, with all his resources, if he hasn't gotten any answers up until now …"

"Meaning," she said, "why would he think that I can get answers?"

"I'm not saying that," Mack replied cautiously. "But this was what? Forty years ago?"

She thought about that and then slowly nodded. "Yeah," she agreed. "So what are the chances anyone's left to prosecute?"

"It was a drive-by shooting, so somebody at least had a driver's license. Therefore, they must be at least fifty-six today—if they were sixteen back then. And the captain's cousin was just a kid. Who'll hate on a ten-year-old kid so much that they kill him?"

"I'm not sure there's any age requirement to hate on somebody," she noted softly. "Unfortunately the world's pretty messed up that way, and we're seeing younger and younger criminals, thinking that they should take matters into their own hands."

"And I see that time and time again," Mack confirmed. "Back then I don't think it was quite so prevalent."

"Or … it wasn't as well publicized," she said. "And maybe they were never caught just because nobody ever thought real justice would happen."

"All of which is quite true too," he noted. "It'll be interesting to see the case file when the captain sends it to you."

"I'm just afraid I won't get the full file," she said. Again came that odd silence from the other end of the call.

"In what way? Are you thinking he might withhold information?"

"Well, usually when you give me access to something, you don't redact names and places and statements. But the captain might to protect somebody."

"Then he wouldn't have come to you. And, if you don't trust him, don't touch this."

"Of course I trust him," she replied. "I just also have to trust that he might be concerned about other parties involved."

At that, Mack laughed. "Okay, that's a good point too. Did he say when he would send it?"

"He said later today. He did try to tell me that he's not really expecting the investigation to go anywhere."

"No, of course not," Mack said. "Like anybody else, with a cold case like this, you don't really plan to have it solved. Yet you just hope that somebody finds some answers somewhere along the line."

"Exactly," she said quietly. "And, in this case, I think we have a murder that's been unsolved for far too long."

"Yeah? What will you do about it?" he asked in a teasing voice.

"I'll have to work on it, just as if it were the others," she stated.

"You know that, one time, you'll come up against a case that you can't solve."

She winced. "I have to admit every once in a while, I do have a nightmare about a case that I can't solve and somebody I can't help. And I already feel terribly guilty about it," she murmured. "Let's hope it's not this one. I was trying to get onto the captain's good side. I've pissed him off enough times lately that I don't know if that's even doable."

Mack chuckled. "The captain doesn't have anything

against you," he said gently. "That all these cold cases are getting solved is a good thing. They also increase our workload, and the department is getting a lot of the credit because you're trying to stay in the background. But that's also upsetting the captain because he would like to think that we could solve all these cases too, but we just don't have the manpower. We're busy trying to keep our heads above water with the current cases."

"Which is another reason why you want me to stay out of your current cases," she said, chuckling, "so that you guys have something on your books to close yourselves."

"Hey, that's not fair." But Mack laughed too.

"How's the shoulder?" she asked.

"Same as it was ten minutes ago," he replied affectionately. "And I am really looking forward to paddleboarding tomorrow. And to convince you to try again."

"And your brother will be joining us this time."

"Yep, he is," Mack said.

"But now you're probably not healthy enough to go out there, after getting shot," she added in a scolding tone.

"Actually," he countered, "it's probably good for me. I'm supposed to use those muscles and not let it get stiff."

She thought about the movements needed when they were out on the board. "You at least stay on your board. So, as long as you don't keep falling like I do, it might be okay." But she wasn't all that sure about it.

He chuckled. "And again we're back to how you're more worried than I am."

"*Somebody* should be worried about you," she stated in a serious tone of voice. "If you had your way, you'd be back at work by now."

"I would, indeed," he agreed, "and I am going back on

Monday."

She stopped and stared down at her phone. "Why didn't you tell me that earlier?" she cried out.

"Because I knew it would upset you."

"You should be off for several more weeks."

"Maybe, but I know we're also very short-staffed."

"So what will you do then? Are you restricted to desk duty?"

"I'll go back to work, as usual, and I'll try to be very careful," he replied.

She frowned at that because, of course, his version of being very careful and her version of his being very careful were two very different things.

"Stop worrying," he ordered through the phone.

She sighed. "It won't do any good to tell me that, you know?"

"I do know—and now you know how I feel every time you get hurt."

"You don't get to turn this around on me," she argued.

"I already did." He laughed. "So you'll try paddleboarding again?"

"I can try. It'll just be even more embarrassing with you *and* your brother there, both seeing me fall so many times."

"He's also planning on going back to Vancouver on Monday, so this will be his last chance to do something with me."

"Right," she noted. "Okay, fine. I'll come. At least then I can be the voice of reason."

Mack burst out laughing. "Like that'll be the day," he teased. "You need to look after yourself better, before you get a chance to sit there and tell me what to do."

She grinned. "Yeah, but you do understand how this

may never happen again, so I have to milk this as far and as much as I can."

"Ha. … How about tomorrow morning?"

"Tomorrow morning what?" she asked.

"Paddleboarding."

She winced. "That fast? Don't you just want to go paddleboarding with Nick?"

"Yeah, that fast," he declared. "So you don't get a chance to change your mind. So I can go paddleboarding with you *and* Nick."

"Fine, but, if I get all this information from the captain later today, that might change things."

"You still need to go out and have time to enjoy yourself," he told her.

"Okay, okay. And then lunch?" she asked hopefully.

He snorted. "You and food. Either we can take lunch down with us or we can go for lunch afterward."

"Yeah, that's easy for you to say," she replied in mock horror. "You will be dry. I will be soaked."

At that, there was no holding back, as his laughter filled the line. "No, that's a good point. A picnic it is. I'll arrange it."

And, with that, he hung up.

# Chapter 3

*Sunday Morning*

DOREEN WOKE UP the next morning and, from her bed, checked her emails, but she still had nothing from the captain. Disappointed, she got up and dressed for a morning on the lake. Which really meant a bathing suit because, of course, she would end up soaking wet. She tossed a couple changes of clothes in a bag—in case they went back out into the water again later. With her bag packed, she headed down to the kitchen, ready to feed her furry and feathered crew.

She looked at the animals and noted, "Mack didn't say anything about whether you guys were coming or not." She quickly texted him and asked if she could bring them. She got an immediate *yes* back. She grinned. "Look at that, guys. You're part of that inner circle," she murmured. "Mack gave the okay for you guys to come."

At that, Mugs woofed, and Thaddeus just cocked his head, as if there were any doubt. Doreen wasn't so sure about Goliath; he hadn't been impressed last time. She looked at him. "Should I leave you at home?"

He sauntered toward her, as if he understood, wove between her legs, and didn't say anything. She hemmed and hawed over it all, as she made her breakfast. By the time she finished her second cup of coffee, she heard a honk out front. She walked to the front window to see Mack and Nick sitting in the front seat of Mack's vehicle. She waved, grabbed the leashes and harnesses, and, with the animals and her bag, she locked up the house and walked down to Mack's truck.

She loaded up the animals in the backseat, then clambered in behind them. "You're sure about this, *huh*?"

It was Nick who laughed. "Mack told me that you're not a big fan of paddleboarding."

"Did he also tell you why I'm not a big fan though?" she asked, giving a pointed look at Mack. "Because that's the real reason."

"There's always a reason," Mack agreed, "and nobody likes doing what they're not good at. But they'll never get any better, if they don't do more of it."

"Sure, but the process to getting better," she noted, "is very uncomfortable."

"No, just a little wetter." Mack chuckled.

She sighed and looked over at Nick. "See what I mean? He just thinks it's a big joke."

"Not a big joke at all," Nick replied. "It's good to see you out doing things."

"You mean, outside of solving crimes?" She nodded. "I don't get a ton of exercise, which is one of the reasons why I'm coming."

"What? So now you think you need to add exercise to your day?" Nick asked her.

"Well, there's that theory about staying healthy means you need to physically go out and do things." She reached down and grabbed a light bulb to stop it from rolling into the front seat floorboard. "I've never been much of a gym buff, not sure that that would work for me," she admitted. "I'd probably find somebody had murdered somebody in the middle of it all. However, this is a beautiful area, and I enjoy that part, and it's well-known for its paddleboarding."

"That's because the lake itself is stunning."

She looked over Nick. "And how come you don't live here?"

"I'm still considering moving back again," he muttered. "It's been really nice to have family around again."

"No girlfriend?"

He shook his head. "Nope, no girlfriend." He grinned at her. "You got any girlfriends? My age, not Mack's?"

"No, that I don't." And then she raised both hands. "Mack thinks it's funny, but I never seem to manage to make a friend I get to keep."

"Why is that?" Nick asked.

She shrugged. "I keep getting them thrown in jail."

Nick stared at her for a shocked moment, and then he burst out laughing. "Oh my, and even those who aren't being thrown in jail, I guess it keeps the rest of them away, doesn't it?"

"Sure does," she muttered in a heartfelt tone. "The only people I get to see at all are Mack and Nan and sometimes some of Mack's friends."

At that, Nick nodded. "And Mack's got a good set of friends."

"Sure, but they're all law enforcement," she pointed out, "so that keeps other people away from me too."

"I suppose. Never thought about it that way," Nick admitted.

"As a lawyer, then you probably get the criminal kind," she stated immediately. He turned and glared at her. She shrugged and smiled. "It's a well-known fact. Lots of lawyers are crooked."

"It's a well-known fact that lots of lawyers *aren't* crooked," he replied, narrowing his gaze at her.

She just beamed at him. "So you just keep believing that."

At that, Mack sighed. "No pissing off my brother," he stated in a severe tone.

"I wouldn't do that," she replied. "He's working for me for free."

"I *was* working for you for free," Nick corrected in a threatening tone.

She burst out laughing. "See? You guys have a great sense of humor."

"Why can't I find any women like that?" Nick asked his brother.

"You're looking in the wrong place maybe?" he suggested.

"Maybe they're not looking for you," Doreen suggested.

"It's not really as if I'm looking either. It's just, you know, it's people that I kind of cross."

Mack tsked-tsked and called out, "Children, children, play nice."

The two of them settled down until they got to the beach. She stared out at the open water. "See? It looks beautiful." She pointed to other paddleboarders. "And they look incredibly graceful, like they're one with the water. It's just such an awesome thing to see, but, when I'm out there, that's a different story."

Nick frowned at her. "Do you really think your paddleboarding is that bad?"

"I can't hold my balance," she explained. "It just reminds me of all the things that I can't do, and this became yet another *told you so*."

"It's not that you can't do it," Mack corrected. "You just need to practice."

"Easy for you to say." She glared at him. "That's because you do it effortlessly. Now the trick will be whether your brother can do it quite the same."

Nick shrugged. "I used to paddleboard all the time," he noted apologetically. "So I'm really not expecting it to be hard."

Immediately her shoulders slumped. "Darn. … I was hoping you'd be as bad as I am."

He grinned at her. "Come on. Buck up," Nick replied. "Just think. It can't be as bad this time."

"Yeah? You know what? I've heard that a time or two," she noted in dark tones. "I think people lie."

But gamely she grabbed her board, and, with the animals in tow, she walked down to the water's edge. As soon as Goliath realized where they were going, he immediately turned on her and walked back up to the grass. "Even Goliath has deserted me," she announced.

Mack laughed. "What about the other two?"

"Well, they don't want to swim with me," she noted, "so they'll have to go with you.'

He called Mugs over. Mugs immediately hopped onto the board, walked to the far end, and lay down. He was no lightweight, so the board tipped ever-so-slightly.

At that, Nick looked at her and asked, "The animals go out on the boards?"

"They do with Mack because they trust that they won't

end up in the water."

Nick burst out laughing again, and the grin stayed on his face, as he hopped onto his board, and, from a standing position, pushed himself off the shore.

She stared at him. "You can do that?"

He looked at her. "Do what?"

"Start from here on the beach instead of starting out there from the water."

"Well, it can be hard to get on out there." Nick turned toward his brother. "Didn't you think so, Mack?"

"Maybe." Mack faced Doreen, who looked out at the water. "Why don't you try it?"

"Is there a reason why you didn't give me that suggestion earlier?"

He nodded slowly. "Yeah, there is."

"And what's that?"

He explained, "Because, when you fall closer to the shore, your chances of feeling the fall are much greater than if you fall while you're farther out where the water can cushion you. If you land here, you'll hit this rocky shoreline."

She frowned, stared at the rocks, and then replied, "Good enough." And, with that, she knelt on the board and proceeded to paddle her way out into the water.

When Thaddeus—sitting on her shoulder—realized she was now on the water, he squawked, "Help! Help! Help!"

She straightened up, still kneeling, and looked at him. "Really? Really?" she cried out. "That's not fair."

She heard the two brothers laughing, and very quickly Mack came up beside her and held out an arm.

Thaddeus, looking as if jumping on a life raft, hopped onto Mack's arm and then walked up to his shoulder. As he landed there, he spread his wings, fluffed them, and announced, "Thaddeus is here. Thaddeus is here." As if he were some reigning champion.

She glared at him. "Loser."

Immediately Thaddeus cocked his head, looked at her, and repeated, "Loser. Loser. Loser." And the men burst out laughing.

Glaring at the bird, Doreen slowly managed to stand on her board, using her arms to help balance her. And, this time, Nick stayed close by and gave her some tips. She looked over at him and asked, "Has Mack done very much of this?"

Nick shrugged. "Not as much as I have. My friends were all into this when I was growing up."

She nodded. "And is this like the bicycle thing? Once you learn how to do it, you will always remember?"

"I think after a few times, yes," Nick confirmed. "Something about the whole balancing act makes it the hardest. Once you get a handle of how to stand and how to hold yourself," he explained, "I think you'll find it much easier."

"Maybe," she muttered.

As they moved on ever-so-slowly, she did find it a lot easier.

About thirty minutes later, when she was still standing and hadn't wiped out, she turned to Mack and said, "It's much better today."

He nodded. "But watch out for that wave coming up."

As she turned back to look, she lost her balance, and down she went. As soon as she broke the surface, she glared at him. "You know that I'd have been fine, if you hadn't said that."

He just smiled at her, but Thaddeus was laughing at her

in his big raucous cackle.

"You better stop that," she warned the bird. "Otherwise no treats for you."

And surely it was coincidence, but he immediately shut up and looked at her, with a side glance. She sighed.

"That bird understands words way too much," Mack noted.

"He really does, doesn't he?" Nick asked in astonishment. "It's freakishly amazing."

"I think he does," she agreed. "Just not enough to always be nice about it."

Mack chuckled. "And I shouldn't laugh at you. You've been doing fantastic."

She snorted. "Sure, as long as you didn't want to get anywhere today."

"I'm not going anywhere," Mack noted. "I'm just out here, spending time with my brother."

"And me," she added immediately.

He smiled at her gently. "That goes without saying."

She rolled her eyes at that. "How's your mom doing?" she asked Nick. "I'm sure she's delighted to have you home."

He nodded. "She really is. It's another reason I'm considering a move back here again."

"She can't last forever," Doreen reminded him. "And I can't tell you how grateful I am that I still have Nan right now, so that we can work on having that relationship I never really got to have before." She shook her head. "Too often we dismiss older people as having nothing to offer, but, wow, she puts a smile on my face all the time."

Both men nodded in understanding. "I think people just get really busy in their lives," Mack suggested. "And then we forget that they're even there. But, for them, the days are long, and, without visitors or without any kind of contact, I think it's much harder on the seniors."

"I'd agree with that. I see Nan, not every day and maybe I should, but Nan's just as likely to push me away because she's lawn bowling or dancing or something." Doreen chuckled. "But I do try to see her every few days. And almost always she's there, more than ready to see me. Sometimes she calls me up and hauls me down there just because she needs a hug."

"And that's very understandable." Nick looked over at his brother and added, "And you're right. I should be moving back."

"Only if you've got the business here," his brother stated, focused on Nick. "I know you went to school for a lot of years to do this. I don't want to see you give up that dream."

"I don't think I'd have to," Nick replied. "Kelowna has grown a lot. I haven't checked into joining any partnerships here." He cocked his head. "I could always set up my own business."

"You could," Doreen agreed, looking at him. "I'm not exactly sure what kind of law you do, outside of divorces."

"I do family law, but I have a couple specialties as well," he added. "I'm not too sure I'd have competition from very many attorneys here, so I'd probably be able to keep the business going."

They paddled for another hour, and, by the time they made it back to shore, she crashed on her towel, Goliath right beside her. He'd apparently spent the whole time entertaining himself in the park. She'd been relieved to see him there when she came back. She'd kept an eye on him from a distance, but, when she wiped out, it was a little hard to see anything. But the men had informed her that Goliath was doing fine.

And, oddly enough, the beach was still mostly deserted. "I guess that's one thing about coming early, isn't it? We don't have to worry about crowds."

Other paddleboarders had gone out and left their gear as well. The joys of small-town living.

The two men smiled at her. "And that's very true," Mack added. "Plus, we do have a picnic lunch to look forward to."

She looked up at him and beamed, and then she realized it was only 11:00 a.m. "But you'll probably want to wait, won't you?" she asked.

"No, and you probably only had toast for breakfast, didn't you?"

She frowned at him. "What's wrong with toast?"

"Just carbs, no protein, no sustenance, and you burn right through it, which is great in terms of initial energy, but after that?" He shrugged. "You go downhill pretty quickly."

"Well, that's the story of my life," she replied, chuckling.

And when Mack pulled out a thermos and handed it to her, she looked at him and then snatched it up. "Coffee?" she asked, with a big grin.

He nodded. "If there's one thing I know to bring you, it's coffee."

"You're right," she agreed, sighing happily. "This is lovely." She looked over at Nick. "Did he bring enough food for you too?"

Nick burst out laughing. "Maybe not. Apparently you eat a lot."

She winced. "You didn't tell him that, did you?" she asked Mack in horror. "That's hardly ladylike to eat a lot."

"It's hardly ladylike to starve yourself either," he declared. "The good Lord knows you've been doing plenty of that."

She glared at him again and poured coffee into the lid.

As she sipped it, Mack asked, "You going to share that?"

She immediately shook her head. "Nope, you insulted me, so I don't have to share anything."

He sighed and looked over at his brother. "See what I have to put up with?"

Nick was grinning at her. "She's all heart."

"Exactly," she agreed, looking over at Nick. "I'll share with you."

"Why is that?" he asked.

"You're trying to get that ex out of my life," she replied.

He nodded. "And, by the way, I got another counteroffer."

"Did you?" she asked. "I'm surprised. I never in my life thought that Mathew would negotiate. And that's because he's an all-or-nothing kind of guy. And how much of a negotiation did he do?"

"He came up a little bit, but it really won't be enough to make anybody happy."

She looked at him and nodded. "That would be what I'd expect."

"Maybe," Nick replied. "So I will send back a response that won't have much movement on my side and a message to see him in court."

She shuddered at that. "You know the last thing I want is to go to court, right?"

"I know, but sometimes we have to do what we have to do."

"I suppose," she muttered. "How quickly would a court date be? And would I have to go?"

He shook his head at that. "Not sure about the date. And, yes, you'd have to appear in court as well, unless I can get a dispensation to represent you."

"Right," she murmured. And she sat here quietly.

Mack reached over, placed a hand on hers, and added, "It'll be okay."

She looked up at him. "Do you think so?"

"Yes," Mack agreed, "and the court's not a big deal. This stuff happens all the time. It means that you can't come to a reasonable middle point on your own, so the judge will step in."

She nodded. "And you think that that'll be in my favor? Even though all the stress it'll put me through?"

He looked at her seriously, his gaze steady as he nodded. "Yes, I do."

"And you don't think that my life will be in danger as we get closer to that court date?"

Nick's gaze widened. He looked at Mack, back at her, and stated, "If you're serious about that, if you think that is a potential in this case, I can ask for you to appear by video."

She considered it. "I don't know how much money we're talking about. I just know that he's very, very against sharing."

"I got that impression already," Nick noted. "I've looked at the paperwork that his lawyers have sent back, and they don't seem to think that he should share at all."

"Exactly."

He pondered that for a moment. "We still can't just let him get away with this."

At that, Mack handed her something wrapped up in tinfoil. "Chew on this and not on that," he stated succinctly.

She glared at him. "Do you really think you can just

keep shoving food at me, and I'll stop doing the stuff you don't like?"

He grinned at her. "At least you will for the moment."

She unwrapped the parcel in front of her and then stared at it in delight. "Oh, my gosh, this is a meat pie, and it's still warm," she crowed.

Immediately she unwrapped the tinfoil, so she could access the treat, and took a big bite. She sat here quietly, with her eyes closed, and chewed. Maybe Mack was right. Maybe she could be satisfied with just food. But she did know that she didn't want anything to do with her ex, especially not showing up in the courtroom and having to face him one-on-one. She'd do a lot to get out of that.

# Chapter 4

LATER THAT AFTERNOON the guys dropped Doreen and her animals off at her house, and she ordered Mack to go home. "You've been trying to hide the fact that your shoulder's killing you," she noted quietly. "Go home and get your painkillers and rest.'

He leaned over, kissed her gently on the cheek, and said, "Got it." He walked back to the truck.

She ushered the animals inside and headed for the coffeepot. The coffee they'd had at their picnic had been a long time ago. They'd spent the afternoon just visiting on the beach, swimming, and having a grand old time. Mugs had thoroughly enjoyed himself, as had the others. She opened up the rear kitchen door for Goliath to wander through, and he headed straight for the garden and threw himself down under a rosebush.

She stared at him. "Of all the plants that you can go to, why one with thorns?"

But his tail just switched in answer. She propped open the kitchen door and went back inside. She didn't need food, but coffee would be nice. She checked her email on her phone and realized that the file from the captain was there.

Excitedly she turned on her laptop and downloaded the file. It would take her a bit to go through it, although it was mighty slim. She hated that. And, of course, that's also why nobody had a chance to solve anything because they couldn't get any information to start investigating.

As she flicked through the material, she realized it was missing things, like witness interviews and detective notes. She quickly sent the captain a text message, asking about that.

When he called her a few moments later, he explained, "That's part of the problem. I was the only witness. It was a drive-by shooting, and I couldn't even tell you now what kind of truck it was," he admitted. "Just that a truck came up, someone shot at the two of us, and took off."

"Ouch. Shot at both of you?"

"Yes."

She added, "You didn't tell me that. Did it hit you?"

A heavy sigh came on the other end of the line. "Yes, I took a bullet in the arm, but the other bullet killed Paul. So I understand if there's absolutely nothing you can do," he stated, "but I'm the only witness to that shooting. And I couldn't even tell the cops anything important back then. It happened so fast."

"Right," she noted. "Let me go through this file, and I'll get back to you if I have any more questions." And, with that, she hung up.

Knowing it would be easier to read, she quickly printed out the dozen pages in the file. With that done, she took her first cup of coffee and headed out to the deck, along with a notepad. As she read through the information, she realized once again why Paul's murder had never been solved.

Outside of the two kids, nobody—supposedly—had

seen anything. The boys were in the front yard, where there was a large garden of sunflowers. The kids had been playing in the sunflowers when the vehicle had pulled up. A handgun had appeared out of the open window on the driver's side. Two shots were fired. Both kids went down. One died; one did not.

She also understood the captain having a horrible sense of guilt because he had survived. There was absolutely no cognitive way to make him feel any differently, and she also knew that survivor's guilt was a real thing. Sometimes people could come to terms with it, and other times it was just almost impossible. Still, Doreen didn't want that to be the case for the captain. He'd done a lot for her, and he'd looked the other way many times, when maybe he shouldn't have.

After the shooting, Henry Hanson, now known as the captain, started screaming right away. Adults had come running, but it was too late to save Paul. The captain had been rushed to the hospital and questioned by the police, but he didn't have much to tell them. And she could understand that. The viewpoint from an eleven-year-old versus an adult looking back on the case, must have been pretty traumatic.

And so he would also want somebody else to look into it. But had he reviewed the case in all these subsequent years? She had to believe the answer to her question was a yes. Anything else didn't fit the man. But that also begged another question. Had anybody in the precinct looked at it? Did anybody have any updated information? She checked the dates of the entries within the file. The last note stated it had been looked at fifteen years ago by Cold Case Division, and they didn't have any new information.

She knew that was often the case. Things would sit there and wait, until somebody had something to add to it.

Otherwise the case required manpower that they didn't have. It bothered her to think that these cases were going cold and that people were not doing anything about it.

Only to realize that wasn't quite true. "That's what I'm doing."

And this was definitely one that interested her, partly because the captain's life had been affected, and she could easily see how it had put him on a path to law enforcement and how frustrating to be on that path and yet still not solve this crime.

That pressure, the guilt, the sense of failure, in a way, all that would be hard to come back from.

Her heart went out to the captain, and she knew she'd do everything she could to solve this. The trouble was, there was absolutely no information. As she sat here pondering it, she sent Mack a text. **He sent the file.** Expecting a phone call right away, she was surprised when there wasn't one. She waited and waited but still no answer. Then realized he was probably busy or maybe visiting with his mom and his brother.

She wasn't exactly sure what would delay him, but it's not like he could be at her beck and call just because she had texted him. Still, it felt off. Hating that, she decided to get up and to do something different to help her brain process this meager set of information. Still, she wanted it to shake around in her brain for a bit.

She made note of the cousin's name—Paul Hephtner. She had trouble pronouncing it because it looked like some extra letters were in the name. Nevertheless, it was Hephtner. "H-E-P-H-T-N-E-R," she reiterated to herself.

When her phone rang, she was pretty sure it was Mack, so she just called out, "Hello."

But it was Nan.

"Hey," Nan answered.

A certain amount of fatigue filled her voice that immediately had Doreen sitting back down again and asked, "What's wrong?"

"Oh, nothing, nothing. I'm fine. I've just been doing too much."

Doreen frowned at that, her mind cataloging everything that she could imagine Nan getting involved in, and asked, "Are you sure?" she asked cautiously.

"I'm fine," Nan replied in a more convincing tone.

Doreen sagged back slightly. "I hope so," she noted worriedly. "Maybe you just need to take a couple days to relax."

At that, Nan laughed uproariously. "You forget. That is what I do."

"Oh, I know you say that," Doreen replied, "but then, if that's the case, how can you be so tired and sounding so rundown?"

"We had a tournament this morning," she explained. "And I ended up playing to the end, which is more than I normally do."

"Are we talking lawn bowling?"

"No, pool," she corrected.

At that, Doreen looked down at her phone in shock. "You play pool?"

After a moment of silence, Nan chuckled. "My dear, I've been playing pool for a very long time."

"Of course you have." Doreen sighed, pushing her hair off her forehead. "Silly me," she muttered. "I wouldn't even know what to do with the game, but here you are, probably already a pool shark."

At that, Nan burst into laughter. "Oh, I do like talking

to you," she said. "You have such a fresh innocence on the world."

Doreen winced. "You mean, I'm naïve," she stated bluntly.

"No, I don't mean that," Nan disagreed firmly. "I called to see if you wanted to come down and to have a cup of tea."

"Absolutely," she stated, particularly as she didn't like how Nan sounded so tired. "When?"

After a moment's pause, Nan suggested, "I was thinking about right now, unless you're busy of course."

"Nope, not busy at all." Doreen looked back at the pot of coffee and added, "I do still have a little bit of coffee left in the pot though."

"And that's fine," Nan agreed. "Maybe make it in an hour then? Have your coffee and then come on down for a visit."

"Won't that be around your dinnertime?"

"I'll pick up dinner and bring it here," she offered. Then she laughed. "In which case, I'll pick up enough to bring for both of us. I'll see you in an hour for dinner and tea." And, with that, Nan hung up.

An hour would give Doreen just enough time to have another cup of coffee, sort through her notes, and see if she could come up with a plan of action on this cold case for the captain.

# Chapter 5

WHEN IT WAS time to go see Nan, Doreen got up, grabbed the leashes, and immediately both Goliath and Mugs came running.

"Good day, huh, guys? Two outings in one day."

Mugs just barked. She looked at him and asked, "You want to go to Nan's?" And he started to go nuts—jumping around, jumping on her, definitely a yes answer.

She looked over at Goliath. "What about you?" she asked him. He'd seemed a little bit off today, but then he'd spent most of the morning in the sun at the beach. Yet he appeared to be equally enthusiastic about going to Nan's and equally unenthusiastic about a leash. As soon as Doreen approached him with the cat harness, he raced toward the creek and the pathway. "Okay, I guess no leash for you."

She sighed. Definitely Goliath had an awful lot more say-so than she did. She knew that people would laugh at her for that, but it wasn't such an easy thing when you loved your animals and when you knew that really the leash was a good idea but not necessary. Then it became more of an option, and, if an option, well, Goliath balked. She could only imagine that's what kids were like too.

Once something was deemed an option, then they would take *no* option.

She smiled at that, and, with Thaddeus rising from a nap beside her, where he'd fallen asleep on one of the rose branches, she walked over and asked, "You want to go see Nan?"

He squawked, fluttered his wings, and then gently hopped on and walked up her arm. And, with that, she trooped down to the creek. She stopped to admire the water and the birdlife. Just even the rocks and the way that the light played on them made her smile. It was such a beautiful location. And even though her house was old and probably needed a lot of work, it was still home, and that made it very special for her.

She wandered slowly, enjoying the day, enjoying the view, just finding a certain sense of peace in herself. She was about to embark on another case, but that wasn't necessarily this moment's worry. She took several deep breaths, feeling some of the tension unwind.

After her last case, she was a little more cautious. Mack had been badly hurt, and, for her, that would never be okay. And in a previous cold case, Nan had been hurt, and that had been even worse. Doreen didn't want anybody to get hurt again. She hadn't realized—until watching how bad it was when the other two were hurt—how awful it was to be the observer and to not be able to do anything to help them.

She wasn't sure that being more cautious was an answer because she didn't see that she was being careless. It just seemed that some of the evilness of people around her was directed differently. It wasn't a cop-out, wasn't an excuse; it was just something that she needed to be aware of. With the animals moving just as slowly as she was, they meandered down toward Nan.

When she got to the Rosemoor parking lot, she stopped, once again taking a long look where Mack's shooter had been waiting in his vehicle.

With a headshake, she muttered, "I hope you rot in jail, buddy." And, with that, she stepped forward toward Nan's place.

A gardener worked off to the side. He raised his head, stared at her, and asked, "What are you doing?"

"I'm walking to my grandmother's apartment," she replied, pointing at Nan's patio.

He glared at her. "I've heard about you." He shook his little hand tool at her. "You're the one who doesn't stay off the grass."

She stopped and stared at him. "Do you see these blocks?" she asked.

"The stepping stones?"

"You know, the ones that are for, *ah, gee, stepping*?"

He straightened up and placed his hands on his hips. "Yeah, but the animals aren't."

She looked down to see Goliath wandering through the bushes. "No, Goliath doesn't really listen to anybody," she admitted, "but he's hardly hurting anything."

"Maybe not," he admitted, "but, if that dog leaves evidence of his passing someplace on Rosemoor grounds, you make sure you clean it up."

She immediately pulled out the poop bag she carried with her. "I have his bag right here," she assured him.

As she got closer to Nan's, Doreen looked back over at the rude gardener to see him still watching her. She gave him a bright smile, but he only glared at her. Her shoulders sagged. As she neared Nan, her grandmother stood outside on the patio, chuckling. Doreen shook her head at Nan, as she stepped over the last little border wall. "How can they find such cranky people to work here?" she muttered to her grandmother.

"I don't know, but the gardeners always seem to have a problem with you, don't they?"

"I wonder if it comes as part of the job description," she muttered.

At that, Nan burst out laughing, finding that uproariously funny.

Doreen glared at her. "It's not that funny. I don't want to stop bringing the animals."

At that, Nan faced her. "Oh, goodness me, don't let him get to you."

"Well, of course I have to," she argued. "I mean, he's right. We're not supposed to be walking on the grass. And I try hard to keep everybody in line, but, you know, they're animals."

"I'll have a talk with him later," Nan said, with a dismissive wave of her hand. "We won't let him ruin our day."

"No, that wouldn't be much fun," Doreen murmured. She looked back but saw no sign of him, relieved that he was gone. Realizing that it was close to dinnertime, he was probably gone for the day. "Have you seen him around here before?" she asked Nan.

"Nope, he's new," Nan stated cheerfully. "That just means we haven't had the chance to train him."

At that, Doreen snorted. "You say *trained* as if it's so easy."

"It is. We let him know what we'll tolerate and what we won't," she declared. And then she gave Doreen a big grin. "Just relax, dear."

She sighed and added, "I'm trying to."

"I think this case with Mack getting shot really did you in, didn't it?"

"It was a reminder that life doesn't always go the way we're hoping it goes." She smiled at her grandmother. "I don't ever want you or Mack to get hurt again."

"You're really starting to care for him, aren't you?"

Doreen shrugged, knowing that she couldn't hide that from her grandmother, and nodded. "Of course I care. I care about both of you. No, I'm not prepared to get into a discussion about my relationship with Mack," she muttered.

"Don't have to," her grandmother replied comfortably. "It's written all over your face."

At that, she glared at her. "Better not be."

"Well, it is. You've never been any good at subterfuge."

She stared at her grandmother. "You know that my ex would say that I was really good at it," she noted.

"Ah, but that's when he was there with his hand ready to whack you across the face if you did something wrong," she reminded her. "But the fact of the matter is, you don't have that abuse in your life anymore, and now you're almost a different person. I'm not upset about that at all."

"Am I really that different?" she asked curiously. "I know Mack mentioned it once too, and I kind of wondered, you know? It seems like an odd thing, but …"

"I don't know that it's an odd thing at all," Nan corrected. "The fact of the matter is, with all those chains no longer hanging on you and fear not being part of your psyche anymore," she explained, "it does feel like you're different, in a good way—freer, more open, happier. Definitely happier."

Doreen smiled. "Of course I'm happier," she muttered. "Without Mathew here to make my life miserable, it's been a lot easier."

"And that's the way it should stay too," Nan added, with a bright smile. "Now sit down. Let's eat," she murmured.

At that, Doreen pulled Mugs a little bit closer, he had been standing with his front paws up on the flower box, staring at where the gardener had been.

"It's okay, Mugs. He's gone now."

Mugs woofed and raced around and greeted Nan, having ignored her until now.

"Oh goodness me," Nan noted. "He was really focused on the gardener, wasn't he?"

"Yes," Doreen agreed. And, with that, she looked around for Goliath, but there was no sign of him. Worried, she stood up and poked her head around the corner, and, sure enough, there he was. The gardener was still gone, but Goliath stood watch. "It's okay, Goliath. Come over here."

He looked at her, his tail twitching, but he slowly meandered toward her.

"I do love that the animals come when called," Nan stated.

"I don't know about coming when they're called." Doreen laughed. "Sometimes they do. Sometimes they don't. I think very much it's a case of whether they approve of what I'm asking of them or not. They do what they want to do, when they want to do it."

Nan just nodded. But Goliath popped up and walked across the flower box, until he came close to her, and she stopped and immediately petted him. "It's such a joy to have these animals though," Nan murmured. "I know that we're not supposed to let them get away with stuff, but it's hard not to, when they're so special."

Privately Doreen agreed with her grandmother. They

were all one of the joys in her life, and, as long as it brought some smiles to her grandmother's face, she was happy to bring the animals every time. As she sat down, she took a look at what Nan had put in front of her. "Was this dinner tonight?" she asked.

"It was," Nan confirmed. "It's Greek something or other." She rolled her eyes at that. "They're trying new things in the kitchen."

"Trying new things isn't bad," Doreen replied. She looked at the little golden pastries that looked a bit oily. She asked, "What's in them?"

"Spinach and cheese and things." Nan gave a wave of her hand, as if trying to brush something away. "I call them *spanks*."

At that, Doreen almost sputtered. "As in the women's shapewear?" she asked.

Nan looked at her. "Good Lord, do women wear stuff like that? Are we talking about girdles?"

Doreen shrugged. "There's a whole line, and I think they're called that, just spelled differently. How did you mean it?"

"Can't remember the word. Starts with *spank* and then something in the middle, before adding *pita* at the end of it," she explained.

"Ah, spanakopita." Doreen nodded, and she looked down with interest. "I haven't had this in a long time." Plus she saw skewers of meat and a large Greek salad. She rubbed her hands together. "This is lovely, thank you." She served herself some salad and took one of the skewers, but first and foremost she picked up the spinach pie and took a bite. "Oh, my goodness," she murmured, as the flaky, golden pastry filled her mouth. "That's lovely."

Nan looked at her and asked, "Is it good?"

She immediately nodded. "Yes, it's really good."

At that, Nan picked up hers, took a bite, and smiled. "Yep, that's what I thought it was. And you're right. They are good."

After that, not a whole lot of talking happened while they ate. Even Mugs quietly sat here at attention, hoping for a piece to fall to him. Doreen caught Nan dropping little bits and pieces his way. She cast a glance her grandmother's way and frowned.

Nan just looked guilty and then beamed. "We have to share with those we love," she said, with that smile that was hard to argue with.

"Maybe," Doreen agreed. In a more serious tone, she murmured, "We also can't get him sick from eating such rich food."

Nan looked down at the spinach pie and nodded. "I guess." So she immediately took a chunk of meat off the skewer and dropped it on the patio floor.

"Nan," Doreen cried out.

Nan shrugged. "I get to feed them too. Adds some joy in my life."

Almost a pitiful tone overtook Nan's voice, and Doreen frowned. "That sounds like an excuse."

"Is it working?" Nan asked, looking at her under her lowered lashes.

Doreen sighed. "It's hard to argue with you at any time," she murmured.

Nan chuckled. "That's because you know you love me."

"I do, indeed," she stated. "However, if we want to keep the animals healthy, we do have to put some care into their diet too."

Nan frowned at that, but she didn't give any more chunks of anything to Mugs. Much to his disgust.

On the other hand, Thaddeus seemed to be quite happy to steal a cucumber out of the salad. Doreen watched in horror as he literally put his beak into the middle of the big bowl and stole a piece, walking off to the side. She moved the bowl off to the side and said, "That's enough of that out of you too."

He ignored her, and Nan laughed. "He does that a lot, doesn't he?"

"The trouble was, I didn't give him a piece of something, and you gave Mugs something." Doreen sighed. "So definitely he's out to help himself."

"At least it's a cucumber, so it can't hurt him," Nan noted.

Doreen couldn't argue against that because the cucumber really wouldn't hurt the bird. She didn't know about the Greek dressing though. When Thaddeus pecked away on his piece and seemed to be completely happy, she just smiled and turned her attention back to her meal.

When Nan asked, "Have you got a new case yet?" Doreen spluttered. Nan looked at her in astonishment. "Already?"

Doreen shrugged a little uncomfortably because she hadn't figured out what to tell anybody yet. "Maybe, … it's a really old cold case though."

"Well, you have a lot of really old cold cases already in those files from Solomon."

"I don't know how many of those files are still unsolved though, remember? Just because Solomon was investigating doesn't mean that they were criminal cases and doesn't mean that he had enough for anybody to go on."

"No, but, if you ever get around to those," Nan replied, with a waggle of her eyebrows, "I'm sure there'll be an awful lot to work on in there."

"Probably," she muttered. "It's almost a lifetime of Solomon's work. It's hardly something I can just finish in the next few months."

At that, Nan nodded. "Besides, you shouldn't have to work quite so hard."

"Maybe," Doreen muttered. "There's an awful lot still for me to do."

"So tell me about this new case."

She hesitated, then shrugged. "It was a drive-by shooting in Vernon about forty years ago."

At that, Nan's jaw dropped. "Goodness, that would have been unusual back then."

"Exactly," Doreen agreed. "So I'm not sure how much help I can be on it. There were no adult witnesses either."

"Well then, you can't do very much, can you?" Nan noted quietly. "I know you want to help everybody and to solve every case, but …"

"And that's part of the problem," she murmured. "In this case I really want to help the person, but it might not be that easy."

"Sounds like it won't be that easy at all. Who is it?" Nan asked.

Doreen looked up and frowned. "I don't know if I need to keep it secret yet or not," she explained. "I never thought to ask him."

"So you don't want to tell me until then?" A note of hurt was in Nan's voice but also some understanding.

"Yes," Doreen agreed. "He's kind of a bigwig in town, and, although he's had it looked into many times, nobody has been able to solve anything. So he knows it's a long shot, but, if I can do anything, of course I want to."

"Of course you do," Nan agreed warmly. "I'll wait another day or two, so you can ask him."

She laughed. "Thanks for that."

"Hey, I want to be told. You know what it's like when somebody holds out on you," she added. "Curiosity will get the best of all of us."

"Maybe. Let's hope not. I might need your help on an awful lot with it because it's back in your day."

At that, Nan stared. "Good Lord. You're right. Forty years ago is a long time. And I was around here back then, but I'm not sure that I would have known much about something like that. And Vernon was still just far enough away that, although I went there, I didn't *go there*, if you know what I mean."

"I do know what you mean," Doreen stated. "So maybe I'll track down people from that era who would have gone to Vernon more often than you did?"

"Talk to truckers, delivery people, tradesmen, others like that," Nan suggested, with a nod. "And, of course, you may have to go to Vernon and talk to some people there."

"I would if I could identify anyone, and they would have to be old-timers too."

"Now that is an idea." Nan looked up at Doreen, with added interest. "We do sometimes have bowling contests with other old folks' homes, and we have done some in Vernon too. I could probably track down a few names for you."

Doreen looked at Nan in delight. "That would be lovely."

Nan smiled. "It's nice to know that you do appreciate

that I have something to offer."

"Oh, believe me. I'm well aware of how much you have to offer, and I won't ever take that for granted."

Nan chuckled. "No, that would be a mistake. Am I supposed to look for people who might have seen this drive-by shooting or what?"

"No, not necessarily. According to what I have in the case file, there was only one witness, but he was also just a kid himself. So he doesn't remember very much either, and he didn't notice very much."

At that, Nan stared at Doreen and asked in a low, harsh whisper, "You're talking about Captain Hanson, aren't you?"

She stared at Nan. "What?"

"His friend was killed many years ago." She stopped and frowned, thinking about it. "Yeah, like forty years ago."

"But how do you know it was him?"

"Because, at one point"—she paused and stared off in the distance, over Doreen's head—"I mean, I could be wrong about the time frame, but maybe ten years ago, maybe fifteen years ago, the captain put out a plea for information on a cold case, and this was the one. And he mentioned that he had a personal connection to it, and he gave us a little bit of detail."

"Now that's interesting," Doreen replied. "Well, in that case, I don't need to try and keep it to myself then, do I?"

"It *is* him," Nan crowed in delight. "I always thought, at the time, that it was so sad to have a man who had all the resources available to him as captain and still not getting to the bottom of something like this."

"Unfortunately he didn't have the resources until he became captain, and look at all the years that have passed in the interim? The trouble is, he was the only witness," she told

Nan. "And, as a child, you know that they are proverbially unreliable in terms of details. Plus, he was also in shock. His cousin had just died, and he was in the hospital for a bullet wound himself," Doreen explained.

"Oh, right," Nan murmured. "That's terrible, isn't it?"

"It certainly wasn't much fun for anybody, I don't think. In his case, it would be just that much harder because, of course, he felt guilty for not saving his cousin."

"How was he expected to save his friend though?" Nan asked, with a headshake. "I mean, he was a child. Regardless, not a whole lot of logic is involved when it comes to emotional circumstances like that."

Doreen gave a sage nod. "And, as I've learned from you, survivor's guilt is quite a thing."

"It can be," Nan murmured. "It really can be." They talked about it for a few more moments, and then Nan frowned at Doreen. "I don't know how you're supposed to find any information on this from that many years ago when even the captain can't help you."

"I don't know either," Doreen admitted, looking up at her grandmother in worry. "And yet I really hate to let him down."

Nan slowly nodded. "In a way, it's not fair that he even asked you."

"I know, but, when desperate for answers," Doreen replied, "I think you have to consider all possibilities. And the captain isn't really expecting me to solve it, but, at the same time, if I can come up with anything that will shed light on this," she murmured, "I know he'd be grateful."

At that, Nan gave her a fat grin. "And that is worth a lot, to have the captain in your back pocket. Ooh, I like the sound of that." And, with that, she went off in a cackle of laughter.

# Chapter 6

***Monday Morning …***

WHEN DOREEN WOKE up the next morning, she rolled over and stretched, surprised to see it still so gray and dark-looking outside. She checked her watch, and it was not even 6:00 a.m. But on a summer morning it was normally bright and sunny out. She got up and wandered to the window to see a big storm threatening overhead. And that was also unusual. Storms in the afternoon, storms in the evening maybe, but first thing in the morning? Not so much.

Deciding she was too awake now to go back to sleep, she got up, had a shower, got dressed, and, with the animals in tow, she headed to the kitchen. There she put on coffee and fed them. She checked the cupboards and smiled. With the yellow diamond reward check cleared, she had enough money to pay the bills and to stock up on food. She'd done a couple shopping trips, with Mack giving her suggestions on easy-to-cook foods.

And she had done a little bit more cooking on her own. She made more than eggs now. She could do a frittata; she was comfortable cooking potatoes. It was just more of those dishes, like chilis and the like, that got her. And she wouldn't mind something hot and spicy like that, as she stared at the storm outside, and then she laughed. A bowl of chili was one thing; a pot of chili was something else.

But thinking of Mack, she sent him a text and asked how he was doing. He responded, writing, **Good, back at work.** She winced as she checked and realized, yep, he was back at work already. She sent him another text message, telling him to take it easy and to not hurt himself again. He sent her a heart emoji and wrote **Same to you.**

She laughed at that. Not a whole lot of trouble she could get into on a forty-year-old cold case. But then she winced because she'd been working on cold cases for a while, and still people had gotten hurt.

With the first cup of coffee, she opened the back door and stepped out onto the deck. Such an odd atmosphere to the air. Almost ominous, and yet not really. Made no sense. Still, she sat at the deck table and had her coffee, while she pondered her next move. She had a few questions for the captain, and, if he had a moment, she knew he'd get back to her. She just didn't want to bother him too much with stuff that she had no clue about yet, so she wanted to gather all her questions for now on one list and then would go from there.

Trouble was, she really didn't have any avenue to even head for. She needed to find and read all the related newspaper clippings, and, with that thought, she got up, wandered inside to Solomon's files, and checked her printed index. But, no, absolutely nothing at all on the victim or on the shooting itself.

"Well, that's no help," she muttered.

Her gaze did land on a Henderson file, but that wasn't who she was after. She needed *Hanson or Hephtner*. Still caught in that turmoil of what to do next, she pondered and realized that what she needed to search Solomon's files by the type of crime. She grabbed her laptop and brought it outside with her.

She brought up the Microsoft Word documents and the PDFs that she had scanned in regarding Solomon's files and started searching for drive-by shootings. Of course drive-by shootings could be mentioned in many ways. At the end of her search, she didn't find anything with a hit for *drive-by*. And then she brought up everything to do with guns, shootings, deaths, and then anything to do with children. With that data set to search for, she found very little search-word-related information at all in Solomon's files.

She sat back. "I don't know if I should be happy about that or sad," she muttered to herself.

When another voice spoke up, she looked around.

"For you to be unhappy is unusual," Richard noted. "Maybe we should write it on the calendar."

She looked over to see her neighbor poking his head over the top of his fence. She smiled at him. "Hey, Richard. How're you doing?"

He glared at her. "If you're staying out of trouble and not bringing more tourists around, then I'm good."

She smiled at him. "You know what? I think all that gruff exterior of yours is just that, a facade," she murmured.

He glared at her. "It is not."

She shrugged. "Is too."

"Is not."

She laughed out loud. "Okay, it's not. So how long have you lived in town?"

"I was born and raised here, so all of my life," he replied proudly.

"Do you ever go to Vernon?"

He stared at her. "Sure, it's the next town over. Lots of people go there."

"I know. Do you remember a drive-by shooting forty years ago that involved two kids?"

He nodded. "The captain was one of the victims."

"He was certainly one of the people shot during that time, yes," she confirmed. "I'm kind of looking into it."

His eyebrows shot up. "Why you?"

"Why not me?" she asked in a wry tone.

He thought about it and then didn't say anything, just nodded. "I guess you're nosy enough."

She glared at him, and he just smirked. She sighed. "I'll let you get by with that one, but do you know anything about it?"

"No, only what I heard on the radio on the news at the time," he told her. "Back then, there wasn't any internet. The print newspapers were sold on a daily basis, but old news was only kept alive by people digging into it," he explained. "Otherwise it became second-page news real quick. As much as we bought newspapers back then, and we pored over them, if nothing needed updating, those stories didn't last in the news for very long. Although I think because children were involved, that story probably got more coverage than most."

"I guess I'll go to the library and see if I can find those newspapers," she muttered.

"What good will that do?" he asked her.

"I'm not sure that it'll do any good, but any information right now is more than what I have."

He laughed. "So will this one stump you?" he asked almost gleefully.

She glared at him. "Do you really want me to fail on this one?" she asked him. "I mean, it'll happen at some point in time, and Lord knows I've got enough cases in my kitchen to keep me busy for a long time."

"Then why do this one?" he asked.

"Because I was asked to look into it," she said quietly, "as a favor."

He stared at her and then slowly nodded. "I can see this would eat away at him, especially being the captain and not able to get answers. But, if they can't find answers," Richard asked her, "what makes you think you can?"

"I'm not saying I can. All I can do is try."

He pondered that and then shrugged. "It's your loss."

"*Thanks.*" She gave him an eye roll. And, with that, he disappeared. "I guess that's a no for having been in Vernon around that time, *huh*?"

As he noisily clambered back up on the chair on the other side, he popped his head over. "I certainly didn't shoot those kids," he stated in astonishment. "You can't even possibly think I'd do that."

"Not at all," she agreed. "I just wondered if you might have been there at the time or might have known anybody who was there at the time. I mean, I need somebody to talk to. I have to look for anybody who might have been around at the time."

He looked at her and frowned. "You're really grasping at straws on this one, aren't you?"

She glared at him. "I'm trying to help the captain, so any help from you would be appreciated."

He shrugged. "I wasn't there and don't know anything about it."

"Fine," she muttered. And watched as his head quickly

disappeared on the other side. "What about your wife?" she called out again.

And this time he called back, "Nope, she wasn't there either."

A mystery surrounded his wife. Doreen wasn't sure what the deal was, whether the woman was even alive back there or not. Doreen really wanted to pop her head over once in a while and take a look for herself, but that wasn't exactly kosher. Then again, he did it to Doreen all the time. She pondered it for a moment and then realized she should pick a better time to do that. Still, she needed to find somebody.

With that, she thought about Mack's mother. Doreen quickly picked up her cell phone and called her. When the woman answered, she said, "Hey, it's Doreen."

"Oh, good, Doreen. I was wondering if you could come do some gardening today, instead of on Friday. I have ladies coming over for tea on Friday."

"Perfect. Are you alone now?"

"Yes, Mack's gone back to work, and Nick is gone back down to the coast."

"Ah, in that case, why don't I come now?" Doreen checked her watch. "It's pretty early, but I don't know whether that storm will break or not."

"Oh, if you would come now, that would be lovely. I wouldn't have to worry about it anymore then," she murmured.

"On my way," Doreen replied cheerfully.

And she quickly grabbed the leashes. Even though she hadn't eaten yet, now that she'd committed her time, she really didn't have time for breakfast. So, with the animals in tow, she headed over to Mack's mother's place. When Doreen arrived, the older woman sat on her porch, waiting for her. Doreen waved at Millicent and asked, "What in particular is bothering you?"

She pointed. "Those weeds all along the pathway," she fussed.

Doreen looked down to see there were, indeed, four—not many—but they were directly in the older lady's view.

Knowing Doreen's ex-husband would have been on the gardener's case for exactly the same thing, Doreen just nodded. "Let me go grab the wheelbarrow, and we'll do a quick pass through."

Doreen did that, and then she found a bunch of weeds hidden around the base of the roses and then a few more, and she smiled. "We'll have to take care of these too."

With Millicent pointing out various things that were really bothering her, Doreen ended up doing a full hour's work and then grabbed the edger and trimmed the pathway. With that done, she looked back at Millicent and asked, "How does that look?"

"It looks lovely," she replied in amazement. "Funny how just having that little bit cleaned up makes a difference."

"I'm sure it does," Doreen agreed. "And what we really want to do is make sure that you're not fussing over something that we don't need to add to your stress about."

The older woman laughed. "You are very good to me."

Doreen smiled. "Hey, we just want to make sure everything's good."

And, with that, as soon as Doreen was done, Millicent pointed at the table. "I made a fresh pot of tea. Will you join me?"

"I'd love to," she said, as she sat down at the table across from her. "I'm sure you must have thoroughly enjoyed your sons' visits."

"Oh, I did. I really did. It's hard to have one of your sons live a long way away."

"But at least you have Mack close by," Doreen noted.

"That's true." Millicent smiled. "And neither of them are married yet, and so neither of them have given me grandkids."

At that, Doreen chuckled. "I can't say I'm terribly surprised at that. They both seem immersed in their careers."

"No, me neither, and yet I look forward to having grandkids. Meanwhile, I enjoy my tea outside on the deck and my good friends."

"And that's good too," Doreen stated. "I'm glad to see that you're enjoying everything."

"I understand you went paddleboarding with both of them."

Doreen laughed. "Yes, well, they went paddleboarding. I went paddle*falling*."

At that, the woman looked at her in shock and then started to laugh. "On my, I do love that. You're so very good to be around."

Doreen chuckled. "They got a good laugh, but they were very good to me out there."

"Good." Millicent nodded. "And what about work?"

"Ah, I've applied for jobs all over the place," she shared. "However, I am not quite so badly in need now that I got the reward money for finding the real yellow diamond," she murmured.

"Isn't that amazing?" Millicent crowed. "That was a lot of money, I heard. That is lovely. And what will you do now then?"

"I do have another case I'm thinking about."

Millicent raised her eyebrows. "And?"

"You've been around Kelowna for forty years, haven't you?"

Millicent confirmed, "Absolutely I have. … In this house most of the time. Why? Is this a cold case?"

Doreen nodded. "And apparently one that was brought up about fifteen years ago, and the local authorities went public, trying to get any information. Interesting case," Doreen noted.

"In what way?"

"It was a drive-by shooting in Vernon," Doreen explained. "Two boys were shot. One died immediately with a bullet to the head. The other boy got a bullet in the arm."

"Captain Hanson," Millicent said immediately.

Doreen sat back, looked at her with a smile. "So you have heard of it."

"Oh, absolutely I have. Captain Hanson was only an eleven-year-old boy, and he's the only witness. He says it was a pale-blue truck, but that's all he can remember." At that, Millicent nodded slowly. "I do remember that." She stared off in the distance.

Then she continued. "I remember when it happened because we hadn't been here all that long, and I was looking to have a family and thought about how absolutely terrible it was, you know, for the child's mother. It was … It was just mind-boggling that something like that would happen. It's not like we have all these drive-by shootings now here either, but certainly we've heard about lots of them elsewhere."

"Exactly," Doreen agreed. "And there's always a problem trying to get any reliable answers from something so long ago."

"Yes, that would be terrible," Millicent murmured, considering it for a moment. "A couple neighbors were around, who had something to say about it," she noted, "but I don't remember who."

"When you say, *neighbors* have had something to say about it, … your neighbors here or some in Vernon?"

"Vernon. It wasn't the best neighborhood," she noted, looking at Doreen, "if you know what I mean."

At that, Doreen nodded slowly. "It's funny how you see the captain now and realize that he possibly lived in a very different situation back then."

"Oh my, yes," Millicent added. "His parents didn't have degrees and didn't have great jobs. I think his dad worked in the hardware store, and I think his mother worked in the grocery store." She paused for a moment. "Not jobs that would make enemies necessarily, but they weren't wealthy. So then the neighborhood they lived in—although they owned their own home—wasn't one of the high-end neighborhoods either."

"Right. So you're saying that this wasn't expected."

"No, not at all. Back then, anything like this was very unexpected. I think it's just, you know, if you want to start looking into this," Millicent suggested, "you must understand that, where they lived, if it were to happen, it would be in a place like that."

"Right." Doreen understood what Millicent was trying to say. "And did you know anybody who lived in the neighborhood?"

She nodded. "You know I did, but I'm struggling to remember the name of the couple. And I haven't seen them in forever, so, of course, I don't know that they'll be of any help—even if I did remember who they were," she noted in exasperation. "Losing your memory is definitely not fun."

"I fight forgetting things too," Doreen admitted. "There

are plenty of times when I'm looking for something in my brain, and it struggles to pop up, so I can then grab on to it."

"Exactly," Millicent agreed. "It's just right there." She sighed. "I'll have to phone you later, if it comes up."

"Okay, that's good enough," Doreen said, "and thanks for that. If I even had somebody who lived in the area at the time, who was still around and could at least talk to me, it would give me an idea if they knew more about Paul's family."

"And, maybe, after all this time, they would say something, right?"

"Well, a lot of people don't say anything at the time because they don't want to get involved, or they don't want to get in trouble, or they just want it all to go away."

"I understand that perfectly," Millicent noted, with a wry tone. And of course she did, having had her own problems way back when. "The thing is, at least at this point in time," she murmured, "enough years have gone by that there are probably no charges to be filed."

"Ah, that's not true though," Doreen corrected her quietly. "That little boy was murdered. And there's no time limit on charging people with murder."

Millicent looked at her and then nodded. "I'm really glad to hear that. I'd like to see justice done for that little boy and for his poor mother, who went through so much agony at the time." She stopped and thought about it. "You know what? I think that was her only child."

Doreen winced. "And that makes it so much worse."

"Right?" Millicent nodded, showing her palms.

The two women sat here in contemplative silence.

"Now that you've brought it up," Millicent said, "I can't seem to stop thinking about it."

"I'm so sorry," Doreen murmured. "I just wondered if you knew anybody I could talk to. I mean, at this point in time, with the older cases, I really do have to talk to the longtime residents because nobody else is familiar with the case."

With that thought, Millicent stared at Doreen and then nodded. "That's a very good point. If we don't solve it pretty soon, there may not be anybody around to remember it. I don't even know if the parents are still alive."

"And that's something I'll have to find out too," Doreen stated quietly. "And they may not appreciate my coming around and getting involved in that investigation, bringing up the hurt again. Yet, if that's the only option I have, I must speak with them."

"If it were my child," Millicent stated firmly, "I would want to know that somebody still cared enough to keep looking into it."

"Well, let's hope that Paul's mother feels the same way," Doreen said. "I have her name. I just want to check in with the captain to make sure I had the right parents, and then I will give them a call."

"You go home, and you do that. That mother has been through enough. She doesn't need to wait one more day for some news."

# Chapter 7

AS SOON AS Doreen got home, she composed an email to send to the captain, looking for information on Paul's parents, who were actually his aunt and uncle.

*I only see a mother listed. Do we know who your uncle is? There's no autopsy report or a link. It would be helpful to know what type of gun was used. I'm not seeing that information in here either. Also, did anybody talk to the neighbors? Doesn't appear to be very much in the way of statements collected by anybody in the original investigation. I have a couple names here. I'll follow up with them, as soon as I get some of these answers.*

She sent that off and got a response back not long afterward, as the captain informed her that his aunt was a single mom. The father wasn't in the picture, hadn't been in the picture, and Paul's mother had worked with her sister, the captain's mother, at the local grocery store. They were both checkers.

That confirmed what Mack's mother had mentioned too.

The captain confirmed the weapon used was a .22 handgun, but, because it'd hit Paul in the head and had gone through his eye, it had killed him instantly, whereas, in the captain's case, it hadn't caused that much damage. Mostly because of where the bullet hit him. He wrote more details.

It was considered at the time to be a random shooting and not targeted. Since then I have pondered that, wondering if there was any way and or any reason why anybody would target either of us. I keep coming up blank. There was no reason. We weren't bad kids. We weren't thugs. We weren't busting into things or breaking into things. We were just two ordinary young kids out playing. Need anything else, email back.

And, with that, she stared at his answers and reviewed them. If that were the case, then there wasn't a whole lot of reason to target the kids at all. Which meant that the parents needed a closer look. And, according to both the file and the captain, the original investigators had looked. But nobody had come up with anything.

The fact that the father was missing bothered Doreen. A father shouldn't be missing. They were part and parcel of the same family, so where was he, and what was he doing at this time, and had he been involved in a custody dispute or something along that line?

She flipped through her hard copy of the file, but she saw no mention of a custody issue or of the father even having anything to do with Paul. She really needed to talk to Paul's mother. These notes, after so long, didn't really have much bearing anymore. What she needed was to get a firsthand account of exactly what had gone on. And, with that, she picked up the phone and dialed the number from fifteen years ago, but the number was not in service anymore.

Doreen thought on that for a long moment, and then sent the captain an email back, saying that she needed current contact information for his aunt, since the phone number on file was not active anymore. It took a little bit longer, but she got an email back with another phone number. She quickly picked up her cell and dialed. When a woman answered, Doreen explained who she was. "And I don't want to upset you, but I'm once again looking into the shooting death of your son."

There was a gasp on the other end. "No, that won't upset me," she stated. "I keep hoping that somebody will reopen the case. However, the police have just never found anything to go on."

"I'm not sure there is anything now either," Doreen murmured. "And I'm … I'm not guaranteeing anything, but I do want to take another look."

"Well, I'm very pleased that you are," she said quietly, "but I don't know how I can help you though. Everything I know I have already shared with the police time and time again."

"No, I understand that," Doreen replied, "and I have a copy of the police file in front of me, but it's a little skimpy."

The woman gave a broken laugh. "There wasn't anything to add to make it thicker," she murmured. "It was just such a sad thing. I mean, from one minute to the next, the boys were out there playing, and then my son was dead."

"And were you inside at the time?"

She explained, "I was inside, making dinner. Henry was coming over, and he was staying for dinner, and then he would go home. They lived right next door."

"Right, so very convenient in terms of the kids being able to play together."

"Exactly. They went to the same school, and they were next-door neighbors, so, for us, it worked out well. We also often worked different hours at the store," she added, "and my sister Marilyn and I used to shift the kids back and forth as needed."

At that, Doreen added in her own notes that Marilyn was the captain's mother. "And what about your husband?"

"My husband," she began, "took off when my son was just a couple years old," she murmured. "He's not part of this at all."

"Could I have his name?"

The woman hesitated, and then replied, "Jon, J-O-N, Sawyer."

"You have a different last name though," Doreen pointed out.

"I reverted to my maiden name," she explained. "My name would have been Sarah Sawyer, and now it's Sarah Hephtner."

"So you changed your son's name too."

"Yes. With my husband out of the picture, it just seemed easier to move forward in life with his last name and mine being the same."

"Did your husband pay child support, anything like that?"

"No, he just wanted out, and, when he wanted out, he meant *out*-out."

At Sarah's note of such bitterness, Doreen winced. "I'm sure you could have used the help over the years."

"I sure could have, at least up until the point in time where there was absolutely no help for Paul." She sighed and added, "And then I needed help to bury poor Paul, but the community came together and helped me do that."

"I'm so sorry," Doreen murmured. "I don't have any children, but it's got to be the worst thing ever."

"It is, indeed," Sarah stated, her voice stronger. "And now the only thing that keeps me alive is hope that somebody will solve this before my time has come."

"And are you …" Doreen hesitated.

"No, I'm not sick. I'm nothing," Sarah replied, "outside of sick of life. It's hard to grow old, especially when your only child is dead and when you were hoping to have them with you for the rest of your life. … Paul never had a chance to get married, never had a chance to have a family of his own. It just breaks my heart every time I think of it."

"Of course it does," Doreen agreed quietly. "I honestly can't imagine."

"What else can I tell you about it?" Sarah asked, with almost a pathetic eagerness to her voice.

"I'm writing down notes, and I'm going through what I have," Doreen shared. "I'll hit the library and go to the newspapers back then and see what they might have popped up with."

"And, of course, they don't always print the truth," Sarah snapped.

"Did you have trouble with the media back then?"

"Sure, it was an instant story, and they kept looking for angles, something that would explain why my son was targeted. I didn't have any angles for them," she stated bitterly. "I didn't … my son didn't do anything. I didn't do anything. It wasn't connected to my husband. There was just nothing there."

"Did your husband know about your son's death? Or does he still think he has a son out there?"

"I honestly don't know," Sarah admitted. "If he followed the news at all, he would know, but he certainly didn't contact me."

And, once again, there was that note of bitterness. "I'm sorry," Doreen said. "That would have been tough too."

"No, by that point in time, it was just … it was better that he wasn't there. It's not as if he could do anything. It's not as if he'd been there in time or around to help out," she explained. "So I was just as happy that he was not part of it either."

And again Doreen could understand that, particularly in light of her own divorce problems. "And what about other classmates? Was there any kind of strife with any other kids? Did anybody have any beef with Paul or maybe with your nephew—Henry? Did you have any arguments with people who you worked with? Anything?"

"No." Sarah laughed. "Paul was one of those class clowns. He was always full of fun—bright and cheerful. I don't know why anybody would have wanted to kill him."

"And the problem is whether he was the target or whether the captain himself was."

"The authorities looked at all those possibilities," she noted, "but, without any real background or much history on the boys, other than from their school and from their parents, we … we never got any answers."

And such bewilderment filled Sarah's voice—even now, forty years later—that it made Doreen wince.

Sarah continued. "I … I expected the police to just snap their fingers and get answers. It was a real shock to realize that they didn't have anything to offer. They were looking at me to give them leads, and I was looking at them to get out there and to find leads, but there wasn't anything to find," she muttered. "And I know that it's really bothered my nephew. Ever since he made it into the police force, I've been cheering him on."

"I'm glad to hear that," Doreen said. "I know this is something that's really bothered him all these years."

"No, I know," Sarah confirmed. "And it's not his fault, but, of course, at the time, that made him question why he was alive and my son wasn't."

"I don't think anybody ever understands that at the time," Doreen suggested. "And I'm sure, over the years, he's come to realize that, even if you did happen to say something to him back then, it was the pain talking."

"Maybe, … but I did feel like I wasn't as kind to him as I should have been. I didn't want to hurt him. I just wanted my son back." And, with that, she sobbed. "I can't talk anymore. Call me again later, when I've had a chance to adjust to the fact that somebody is looking at this again."

"Sure," Doreen agreed. "I'll do that."

And, with that, Sarah hung up.

# Chapter 8

AFTER THE CALL, Doreen wondered about whether she should head down to the library or not. She quickly checked online and noted that it would be open for another couple hours. Determined to get something accomplished, she locked up the animals in the house and headed down to her favorite library. There were multiple branches in town, but this one was a little bit closer, had great access for the microfiche files, and, of course, then there were the librarians. Some better than others. Generally they were accustomed to Doreen at this point, although she still hid what she was doing. The last librarian though, had been quite helpful on Doreen's previous case.

As she wandered in the front door, the same helpful librarian looked up, frowned, and then her face cleared. "Hey, I haven't seen you in at least a few days." A note of humor filled her voice.

Doreen nodded. "I know, right? Some days, it seems like I'm rushed off my feet, and other days it just seems like absolutely nothing is going on."

"And why are you here now? Will you finally get a few books to read?"

"I was thinking about that too," she noted, "but I need to get into the old newspaper archives."

At that, the librarian raised her eyebrows. "Another case?"

Doreen nodded slowly. "Yeah, not much to go on either."

"Interesting." She stared at Doreen, then hopped up and said, "Let's get you set up then."

As Doreen followed the other woman's rapid clip to the back area, where the microfiche machines were, the librarian called back, "You do seem to have quite a bit of luck with your investigations."

"And I think that's what it is—luck. The trouble is, when people start counting on me to have answers or be able to find answers, then the pressure's on, and it becomes a big worry because I can't solve everything," she admitted.

The librarian turned toward Doreen and nodded. "And nobody should expect you to. You can only do your best."

Doreen appreciated the other woman's sentiment, but it was hard to explain that a part of the big pressure was what Doreen placed on herself. When she got up to one of the machines, she quickly sat down and started scrolling through.

"I don't suppose you can tell me what it's about. I might be able to help," the librarian offered hesitantly.

"In this case, you probably do know a little bit about the case," Doreen suggested, "if you've been around here for a while." Doreen deliberately withheld the forty-year mark. "Ten, fifteen, I think it was fifteen years ago that Captain Hanson brought up this cold case to the public, desperately seeking info and looking at it again for any leads to move forward on it."

"Cold cases are notorious for that, aren't they?" she agreed.

"They are, indeed. And, in this case, it had a personal angle for Captain Hanson."

At that, the woman looked startled. She stared off into space and then nodded. "I do think I remember something about that. Not any details though." She looked at Doreen expectantly.

With no reason not to say something, and Doreen sure could use any help the woman had to give, Doreen explained about the captain's invested interest.

"Oh my," the librarian said in horror. "That would have been terrifying."

"It certainly set a course for the path he is on now," Doreen admitted. "Nothing like watching your best friend and cousin get gunned down beside you and realize that nobody could do anything about it and that this gunman gets away with it. The captain's followed the case, looking for answers himself all these years."

"And now he's asked you?"

"It was more of a *Hey, if I'm bored and if I can come up with any ideas that they might have missed out on, he's all ears,*" she replied, misinforming the librarian about the real turn of events because somehow it seemed like maybe something the captain wouldn't want anybody to know about.

"No, but you can certainly understand," the librarian noted. "That's a terrible thing to happen to anybody but to boys at that age? So sad."

"And Paul was the only child of a single mom," Doreen added, "and she's still waiting for answers."

At that, the librarian shuddered. "I can't imagine anything worse."

Neither could Doreen. "Which is why I'll give it my best to try and come up with something."

"And, of course, then the police can take it from there," the librarian stated, with a wise nod. "Let's see what we can get you then." And she quickly disappeared.

Doreen wasn't sure just what the librarian was planning on doing. However, as Doreen turned around, she noted other people in the library, possibly needing attention. Maybe the librarian went to help them, which made sense.

As Doreen focused on her own problems, she finally found the newspaper articles on this drive-by murder from forty years ago, but not a whole lot was here. After sending those PDFs to her email address, she moved forward in time to when the captain had brought up the case publicly, searching for any help. And she quickly found those articles from fifteen years ago as well.

As she sat here, reading through the information, all of it correlated to what she'd already found out. So nothing was new, but at least it confirmed what others had told Doreen.

The thing was, somebody had to know something. It was quite possible it was a random shooting, and those were always the worst to try and track down. Checking her watch a little bit later, she only had another twenty minutes before the library closed. And that wasn't good news. She quickly went through as many of the sites as she could, downloading paperwork to look at later. By the time she was searching for the last little bits, the librarian came up behind her.

"Hey," she said, "hate to say it."

"Right, you're closing, aren't you?" Doreen said, twisting around. She stood up from the machine, and the woman nodded.

"Yeah," the librarian confirmed. "I did find a little bit—

maybe a duplicate of what you've already got." The librarian handed Doreen a stack of about ten pages. "This is it."

Surprised and touched, Doreen smiled at her. "Thanks."

"Hey, that case needs to be solved," the librarian declared. "Not only has Captain Hanson done a lot for us, but any little boy who's been gunned down like that needs somebody to care." And, with that, she hurried to the door and unlocked it for Doreen.

Once outside, Doreen headed toward her car, pondering the turnabout with this librarian—from being cold and disdainful and constantly watching over her shoulder, to becoming that warm, caring person who Doreen hadn't realized was inside, but should have.

It was just too easy to judge people from their actions. And yet one really never knew who and what they were on the inside or what were their motivations. Doreen had been just as guilty of that as anybody. She sighed at another of her failings and headed home. When she got in, she quickly locked up the house and headed to bed. Tomorrow was a new day, and then she'd sort out this paperwork. The days were going by, and she was making very little progress.

# Chapter 9

***Tuesday Morning ...***

WHEN DOREEN WOKE up the next morning, Mugs was bouncing all over her and woofing in her face. She groaned as she slowly sat up and checked the clock—8:30 a.m.

"Oh, I'm sorry." She yawned. "It was such a terrible night that I overslept now. You probably have to go out, don't you?"

He barked in her face. She took that as a sure sign of *Yes, get moving*. Because of the time, she just headed down to the kitchen, without even getting dressed for her day, and opened up the back door for Mugs. Still groggy, she put on coffee, then made her way back upstairs to find some clothes.

Feeling a little bit better and a little bit more awake and prepared to start the day, she headed back down to see all the animals were outside. She fed them quickly, and then, with her first cup of coffee, she grabbed the stack of papers that the librarian had given her and headed out to the deck. In the morning sun, she sat down on a deck chair and started to flip through them.

Some of it was a repeat from the pages that she had

saved, but she was grateful to have them printed off. A few were different, that she hadn't seen last night, at least ones that she didn't remember seeing. She'd gone through so many pages, it was hard to say at this point. She quickly speed-read them and noted a couple comments from neighbors—one was a Thurlow. She frowned at that and quickly wrote it down on her notepad. Thurlow couldn't be that common of a name.

She nodded, reread the passage again, and then contacted Nan. When her grandmother's bright and cheerful voice answered the phone, Doreen had to smile. "Well, I'm glad somebody got some sleep last night," she muttered.

"Oh, dear," Nan replied. "Did you not sleep?"

"No, it wasn't a good night." Doreen rubbed at her left temple. "Still feel kind of cruddy."

"Are you coming down with something?" her grandmother asked in alarm.

"No, I don't think so. Just a bad night that I can't quite shake off."

"Have some more coffee, dear," Nan suggested comfortably.

Doreen grinned at that. "I'm trying, while reading in relation to that case that I'm working on."

"You mean, the captain's?"

"Yes, and a name of a neighbor popped up, the Thurlows. Do you know anything about them?"

"Thurlows?" During a moment of silence, Doreen could almost hear Nan's brain ticking over, and then she replied, "No, I don't think so."

"Okay," she muttered. "It just came out in one of the articles from about fifteen years ago, but it was a Vernon family who apparently had lived in the same neighborhood at the time."

"Well, I haven't found anybody yet for you to talk to, so maybe they'd be a good one," Nan said.

"Yeah, I just have to find a way to reach them because I don't have any contact information. I haven't looked in the phone book yet though," she admitted. "You never know what I might find there. If nothing there, I'll search online."

"Give me a moment," Nan added. "I'm trying to think who here had connections to Vernon."

"Considering it's the next town over, it could be anybody," Doreen said. "I'll go grab a second cup of coffee. If you find or think of something, give me a ring back." And, with that, she hung up the phone and headed to the kitchen. When she returned to her deck, she was no longer alone. Mugs was busy showing Mack just how much he loved him. She sighed, as she sat down in the deck chair again. "I'm not sure I'd get the same greeting from him if I was gone for a while," she noted.

Mack looked over at her and then gave her a fat grin. "No, it's obvious he prefers me."

She glared at him. "That's not funny."

He burst out laughing. "Obviously I didn't mean it, and obviously this guy absolutely adores you," Mack stated. "And you don't get that kind of greeting because you never leave him alone that long."

"Maybe," she said.

He looked at the coffee in her cup. "Is that the last cup?"

"Nope." She eyed him carefully. "How's the shoulder?"

"Definitely in need of coffee." She frowned at him. He just laughed and stated, "I can get it myself. That's okay. Don't put yourself out."

"I wouldn't anyway," she called back, as he walked past

her and headed for the coffeepot in the kitchen. When he joined her a few minutes later, she asked, "So what do I owe this early morning visit to?"

"What's the matter?" he asked. "Don't I get to stop by and just say hi?"

"Sure you do," she replied. "Normally you have a reason though." He gave her an injured look, and she just gave him a sideways disgusted glance. "You know I'm right."

"Maybe I do have a reason," he admitted quietly.

"And what is that?"

He shrugged. "I want to know how you're getting on."

She frowned at him. "So are you checking up on *me* or on my progress?"

"Is there a difference?" he asked, his eyebrows raised.

"Maybe not," she stated, a little confused herself. "I guess the next question is whether you're hoping I have some progress or whether you're worried that I'm getting into trouble over my progress."

He burst out laughing. "I can almost guarantee that it is a case of you getting into trouble. What I would like to know is if there has been any progress."

She shook her head. "Not necessarily, no. I'm still trying to track down people who were in the neighborhood that long ago."

"And what will that tell you?"

She knew it wasn't a case of Mack checking up on her technique but more about what she thought she would find. "I need a general idea of what the neighborhood was like back then. What the two families were like. Whether there was a drug connection. Whether there was anything to do with that ex, the father, things like that."

Mack nodded slowly. "And you're counting on the

neighbors knowing something?"

"Neighbors often know more than we think, and neighbors often observe things that they don't realize how important they are, then or later."

"Very true, but, after all this time, it's hard to verify any witness statements."

"And again that's why I'm looking for a general impression of the area. Just because Sarah told me that her husband wasn't around doesn't mean he wasn't for a while or she didn't have many replacements. I did go to the library last night and got lost in the archives, trying to find any bits and pieces from the newspaper."

"Understood." Mack nodded. "Anything pop?"

"Not so much popped but confirmed. I did get one name, Thurlow, which I asked the captain about this morning—to see if that name meant anything to him. And I got a no back."

"And, of course, as a kid himself at the time of the shooting, he wouldn't necessarily have known the players."

"Right. I'll phone Paul's mother, Sarah Hephtner, again—only I wanted to have a few more questions, so I don't bother her too often."

"That's a good idea. How did she take the fact that somebody is looking back into the case?"

"She was excited," Doreen replied quietly. "Had given up hope, I think, and just really wanted to get answers before she dies."

"Of course," Mack agreed. "I can't imagine losing a child like that."

"I can't imagine losing a child, but to know from one day to the next that it happened and to not get answers, resolution, nothing?" She shook her head at that. "The librarian also helped me last night and got a bunch of articles for me."

He looked at her, an eyebrow raised.

She nodded. "I don't know if I told you, but she hasn't been exactly the easiest person to get along with."

He chuckled. "But then, over time, as you have proven your value, I'm sure that has changed too."

"Well, also," Doreen noted, "to give credit where it's due, the fact that this is a case your captain was personally involved in makes a difference to how people view helping me. If I can help him, then they're all for it."

At that, Mack smiled. "It's one of the reasons I'm here. I know there's nothing I can really do to help, but I'm here, if you want my help."

She chuckled. "Well, if I thought you could do something to help, I would certainly ask you—or I would go to your boss."

At that, he gave her a wry look. "Yeah, and this time you would have the right to do so."

"I know." She rubbed her hands together. "It's kind of a rush."

He gave her an eye roll. "Don't let it go to your head."

"Nope, I won't, but I really do want to help him."

Mack smiled. "And that's because of who you are," he noted quietly. "And that's, I think, why so many people talk to you, since you come from heart. Well, if you come up with anything …"

"Yeah, I'll keep you informed. Not only that, I'm pretty sure you'll want me to tell you ahead of time anyway."

He chuckled. "Several of us know what you are currently working on, so we're all interested to see if you come up with anything."

"Have you had anything to do with this cold case?"

"No, I haven't," he admitted. "I've looked at a few cold cases but not that one, not until yesterday. Cold cases do get examined every so often, especially if there's any new lead or any new technology, anything that we can figure out how to move forward with. Then we'll reopen it. But, in this case, I guess the last time it was looked at, there was nothing. And now that fifteen more years have passed from the last check, I think the captain just decided to ask you to take a look."

"Hey, I'm honored that he asked. At the same time it's a little disconcerting because there's a good chance I won't find anything." So she suggested cautiously, "If you come up with any avenues to pursue, it would be helpful if you pass them along my way."

"Will do," he told her cheerfully.

She smiled. "You really did just come to check up on me, didn't you? Did the captain ask you?"

He laughed. "He did mention it, and I told him that I hadn't talked to you this morning."

"So it was his suggestion." She nodded. "That's a problem. That hope, that … that expectation."

"It doesn't have to be that way," he reminded her. "You do the best you can, and, if this happens to be the one that you can't solve, then it's the one you can't solve."

She glared at him. "I didn't say that I couldn't solve it."

"Neither did I say that you couldn't solve it," he argued gently. "It's just a reminder that sometimes things can get a little more complicated than we thought."

She snorted at that. "Complicated, yes. But they don't have to be. I'm just not sure what to do," she muttered. She motioned at her notes. "It's a pretty thin file."

At that, Mack nodded. "I took a look at it while I was at

work yesterday. And you're right. It is thin," he admitted. "Did you get anything helpful from the mother the first time you spoke with her?"

"Not much. I'm still trying to track down the father, but Sarah says she hasn't had any contact with him."

He pulled out a notepad. "Do you have a name?"

She gave him that info and added, "The mother changed her name after he walked, told me that he hasn't been in the picture for so many years that she wasn't even sure if he knew that their son had died." At that, Mack frowned at her. She shrugged. "When he walked, I guess he decided to really walk. And then of course—" She stopped and stared at Mack. "Maybe he's been gone so long because he didn't have a choice."

"Meaning?" Mack asked, writing down notes.

She frowned, as she thought more about it and muttered, "No, that's a little too bizarre."

"Hey, you know bizarre often works in our cases," Mack noted. "What are you talking about?"

She shrugged. "I mean, I get that, a lot of times, men do walk off, and that means that they're never seen again because they make sure that they're never seen again."

"Yes, and?"

"I'm just wondering whether he did walk off forever or whether he didn't have a choice. Maybe he was killed."

Mack sat back and stared at her.

She shrugged. "I know. It's a little bit odd."

"No, but … it's one explanation of what could have happened," he clarified. "It doesn't mean that it did happen through."

"And it would be very nice to know where he is so that we can at least check his alibi. According to the file, he was never located back then, so his alibi couldn't be checked."

Mack nodded about that. "I wondered when I saw that too, but tracking down an individual from forty years ago?"

"Make it more like forty-eight," she corrected.

He stared at her.

"He walked off when Paul was just a couple years old," she explained. "And the mother had no contact with him since, and she really could have used the help. Raising Paul on her own wasn't easy. She was just a grocery clerk, like the captain's mom."

"Right." Mack nodded. "I remember his dad worked at a hardware store, and one of the things that they always drilled into the captain was, it was an honest day's work, even if it didn't make a whole lot of money. At the end of the day, they were a happy family."

"Exactly." Then she grimaced. "If we had DNA, we might see if he's in a database."

"Yeah, what database?" he asked, with a humorous smile. "Collecting DNA wasn't done back then. And no need to collect Paul's DNA, as we knew who he was."

She nodded slowly. "Did anybody do a ballistics check on the bullets? I didn't see anything in the file. I presume the two bullets came from the same gun."

He wrote that down. "I agree, but I will check on that too."

"I mean, it would be helpful if we knew if that gun had been used in another killing."

"It would, indeed." Mack tapped his notepad. "I'll look when I go back to the office, but, if they were smart, they'd just hold onto the gun."

"And, if it hasn't been done already, surely with the captain in his position, we can get the ballistics checked?"

"I'll make a request for that too, if it hasn't been done. … It's likely to all still be a dead end."

"It's a dead end if this was a completely random killing or if this person just decided from one day to the next to kill somebody and then to never do it again. But what if he did kill again? What if he threw away the gun, and someone else found it and used it?"

"Good points. I'll check." Mack took a sip of his coffee. "What else have you got rattling around in your mind?"

"Well, the father is a big issue. Yet I get it. He probably just took off, but it's one of those avenues I can't just let go of. I also need to find out where he worked, what kind of work he did. Was his work something where he could head down to the US and get a job easily enough? Or did he stay in Canada?"

"So you really want to focus on the father?" he asked, looking at her.

"I can't write him off if I don't have any information to write him off with, and I would like to be able to."

"Do you really think a father would shoot his own son?"

"Well, there's the other question. Maybe it wasn't his son he was trying to shoot. Maybe it was the neighbor's son."

"You mean, the captain?" Mack asked, his eyebrows raised.

"The two of them were there, and two shots were fired. So either both boys were intended to die or the shooter didn't care who died, who didn't die, or whether either died. Maybe the gunman wanted both of them dead and only managed one. I mean, because we don't have the shooter, it's hard to know. However, there has to be some reason why the shooter chose these two boys, even if it was literally that they were just in the wrong place at the wrong time."

"And, as you know," Mack pointed out, "those stranger killings end up being the hardest to solve."

"Right, because nothing links the killer to the victim." She nodded. "I still have to try."

He smiled, a beautiful warm smile, and replied, "I know you do, sweetheart. And believe me. Regarding this case, everybody at the station is rooting for you."

She looked at him in surprise, and then her heart warmed. "That is really nice to hear. … And I'll remind you of it when I start pissing you off again."

He burst out laughing. "Maybe … and, then again, maybe you won't."

"Oh, I will." She grinned.

"At least you're okay for money now, right?"

She nodded. "I am for a little bit, hopefully until the antiques get sorted. … And I did hear back from the book specialist via email. Apparently he has a deal in the works and mentioned it could be quite profitable for me."

He raised both eyebrows. "You could end up being a very wealthy woman."

She laughed. "I don't know about that," she corrected. "But, as long as I'm not starving from week to week and month to month, I'd be happy."

He grinned. "So, now that my brother's gone back to Victoria, do you want another cooking lesson for dinner this weekend?"

"Sure." Then she hesitated. "Can you teach me to cook something new?"

He slowly raised his head and nodded. "Yeah, sure can. What do you want to learn?"

She pondered it for a few minutes. "Any chance we can do something fancy?"

"Sure. Like what?" he asked. "I mean, what you call fancy and what I call fancy might be out of my wheelhouse."

She didn't have an answer right now. "I'll get back to you on that."

"Think about it. We have time."

He left about twenty minutes later on his way to work.

# Chapter 10

DOREEN SAT BACK and smiled. For the first time she felt like she and Mack, even the captain, were working together. It might have taken the captain to make this happen, but she was grateful to him nonetheless. It was great having Mack's help. She had no doubt that, if things turned official on this cold case, she'd be the one who got cut out real fast. But, if she even got this case that far, she'd be happy because it would mean she'd managed to do something that nobody else has been able to get done.

This wasn't about ego. This was about justice for that poor little boy and to help the captain move past such a terrible event. She couldn't imagine how he even managed to handle gunfire at the age of eleven. PTSD was a real thing; surely it would have affected him. But then training and time was probably a great healer, and getting a sense of control over his life and over people like that would have helped too.

She grabbed her phone, and, after apologizing once again to Sarah, Doreen explained that she was looking for a family named Thurlow.

"Thurlow, Thurlow," Sarah repeated calmly. "Oh, they were the neighbors." And then she stopped. "They weren't right next door. They were two houses down."

"So they were your neighbors back then?"

"Yes, they were. Why? Did they have something to do with this?"

"No, I'm not at all sure about that. Their name was just mentioned in one of the articles I found, and I wanted to go over their story."

"I doubt anybody even remembers at this point," Sarah replied sadly. "Everybody else got a chance to move on. And I understand that. I envy them."

"And a chance to move on is great for them, but you need that same chance." Doreen wondered how much she could push the questioning. "I don't suppose you know if they're still there, do you?"

"Well, I'm not still there, so I don't really know. It's possible though."

"Okay, so can you confirm the address where this happened? And then I will go talk to some of the people in the neighborhood."

Sarah quickly gave Doreen the old address, confirming what was in the file. With that, she asked a couple more questions that had been bothering her. "Was your son involved in any school teams or in any local community club programs?"

"No," Sarah said. "Paul was gifted at softball, and we had him try out for the team one year. But that year, I didn't have anybody to get him back and forth to all the practices and the games. It would have been a different story if my nephew had played too." And then she laughed. "I've been calling him the captain for so long that it seems weird when I consider he's the nephew who went to softball tryouts with my son."

"And did the captain make it?"

She pondered that for a moment. "I think he did, but then I seem to remember that he never did get to play for some reason."

"So were any other kids jealous?" Doreen asked Sarah. "Was there any other nightmare scenario that you can possibly think of where somebody didn't like your son?"

"No," she stated quietly. "And believe me. I've thought about it over and over again. You wonder if even just that little bit of a slight that maybe he did to somebody in class or maybe teasing somebody too much or … You hear all these horrific stories, but, because I don't know what went on that day, I just can't imagine."

"And he appeared to be normal that day, when he got home from school?"

"Yes," she replied. "Then again, I had had a bad day at work, so maybe I missed the cues," she added. "I've trashed myself over and over again, about every little detail over the years."

"And that's not helpful," Doreen stated firmly. "Obviously we're looking at absolutely everything, yet it's important that we don't blame ourselves for something we didn't realize would happen. … And I get it. I mean, I can't imagine having a scenario like that happen where you *don't* blame yourself, but, in this case, let's try to stay positive and to be constructive. So much time has gone by that we'll have to jog people's memories."

"But if it didn't work fifteen years ago," she cried out fretfully, "I highly doubt it'll work now."

"I'm not so sure about that," Doreen disagreed firmly. "I've had a hand in all kinds of cases that were solved, even though many, many years had gone by."

"As many as forty?" Sarah asked bitterly.

"Yes," Doreen declared in a firm voice. "Absolutely."

A startling silence came on the other end, and then Sarah gasped. "You're that crazy lady." And then she gasped a second time. "Oh dear, I didn't mean that in a bad way."

"No, maybe you didn't," Doreen agreed, trying to keep the wince out of her voice, but it was hard when everybody kept referring to her that way. "And, yes, if you're talking about the crazy lady who keeps solving all these cases, that is me."

"Oh my," Sarah said in awe. "In that case, I'm even more hopeful that the captain contacted you."

"That's because I've helped him on several local cases," Doreen replied gently. "And, as this one is very close to his heart, and he knows that time is running out to find witnesses, he asked me to take a look."

"That makes total sense." And once again Sarah's voice was positively glowing. "And you have no idea how happy I am that … you're doing this."

"Yet," Doreen warned, "I still need lots of details. I need to know his teachers' names. I'll check the people at the school he went to, because I need to know about what other kids he might have played with and what his social interactions were like. I need to know everything you can possibly think about from that day, that week, that month before."

Sarah paused. "Are you thinking it's connected to his schooling?"

"What I do know," Doreen stated, "is it's connected to something, and his days were mostly at school, weren't they?"

"Yes, absolutely," she confirmed, her voice getting stronger. "I never even thought of it like that," she murmured. "I was thinking school absolutely was a nonissue because he was a kid."

"Sure, but he was killed as a kid, so we have to look at his day, which was a typical day of a kid."

"Look. I have some … old journals that I used to keep. I was into that, supposedly to make my life healthy and all that good stuff that you should do, along with positive affirmations and the like. I started journaling just before he was killed, but I do have a few notes written down after the shooting."

"Notes would be helpful," Doreen said. "Do you want me to drive up there and grab them?"

"Oh, will you make a trip up here?"

"I planned to come up on Saturday," she shared. "I wanted to talk to any of the neighbors who might still be around—or maybe I should drive there tomorrow." She considered that. "I'll have to check what's going on around here, and then maybe I'll make the drive tomorrow. It's not that long."

"No, goodness no, Vernon is maybe forty minutes from Kelowna."

"You know what?" Making a sudden decision, Doreen stated, "I'm up for it tomorrow. I'll stop in, if that's all right with you?"

"Absolutely. That'll give me time to find the journals," she replied excitedly.

And, with that meeting set, the two women rang off. Doreen sat here for a long moment and then decided that she wouldn't tell Mack because he might understand, but, at the same time, he was back at work, and he couldn't go with her, so he'd just worry. She would do it alone regardless.

As she pondered it though, she thought it would be nice

to have somebody to go with her, and that *somebody* really was only one person available. With that, Doreen picked up her phone and called her grandma. When Nan answered the phone, Doreen asked, "Hey, feel like going for a drive tomorrow?"

"Sure," Nan agreed immediately. "Where are we going?"

"I thought maybe we'd go to Vernon."

Nan gasped in delight. "Oh, yes. Are we going sleuthing?"

Doreen chuckled. "Well, in a way, yes. … I need to get a feel for the area, for the crime scene. I need to talk to some of the neighbors, see if anybody's still around who was there back then, that kind of a thing. Plus, we'll stop and see the victim's mother. She's got journals from that time."

"Ooh," Nan replied, with a wealth of feeling. "You're getting somewhere."

"I'm getting a whole lot of nowhere," Doreen declared, "which is why I can't delay going up there to the actual scene. I have the address where the shooting happened, and I need to go on from there," she shared.

"Absolutely. I understand. What time do you want to leave?"

Doreen contemplated that. "We don't want to hit rush hour, so maybe I'll pick you up at nine a.m.?"

"Perfect," Nan replied. "And, if we'll be in Vernon, there's an absolutely awesome Indian restaurant up there."

"Perfect," Doreen said, already feeling her stomach growling in anticipation. "That sounds like a great deal."

Nan chuckled. "Anything that involves food, you consider a great deal."

Doreen smiled. "You could be right. But since when was that a bad thing?"

"It isn't at all," Nan confirmed, laughing. "And, in your case, you still need fattening up. Mack likes his girlfriends with a little bit of meat on them." And, with that, Nan hung up.

Doreen stared at her phone in horror. "You did not just say that," she cried out. But, of course, Nan wasn't there to listen anymore.

Still glaring, she got up and walked outside to the garden, feeling a bit of temper sparking inside her at the comment. She looked down at herself. "You're not skinny," she snapped.

A snigger came from around the corner.

She turned and looked slowly at Richard's side yard. She called out, "Do you think I'm fat or skinny?"

Slowly Richard's head popped over the top of the fence. "You're neither," he replied. "Who said you were?"

"Nan," she stated in disgust.

At that, he started to laugh. "And why do you care what she says?" he asked, smirking.

"She's my grandmother. It was just the way she said it that made me think that something is wrong with the way I look."

"Nothing is wrong with the way you look," he stated, giving her an odd. "And since when do you care what anybody thinks?"

"What do you mean?" she asked him.

"Well, I've asked you how many times to stop bringing in all this ugly attention, and you don't seem to care how people see you."

She frowned at that. "It's not so much that I don't care how people see me," she explained, "but I was just trying to help people. So I didn't want what people thought of me to matter. I've already been called crazy so many times in the last few days that it's quite irritating."

He looked at her in astonishment, but she caught the very moment when a smirk filtered across his face.

"What do you expect?" Richard asked. "You wander around town, completely uncaring about the fact that you have the animals in tow all the time. You go into buildings with them. You've got a bird that talks on your shoulder, and he even insults people."

"He hasn't done anything like that in quite a while." Doreen glared at Richard. "Besides, all I'm trying to do is help people."

He nodded slowly. "And that may be, but that doesn't mean you won't be seen as a unique person in town."

"*Unique.*" She rolled that word around. "Does that mean crazy?"

He burst out laughing. "In some cases, yes."

As he went to disappear again, she asked, "Do you know the Thurlows?"

He looked over the fence again. "*Thurlows, Thurlows.*"

"They were a family who lived in the same area as the shooting."

He thought about it and shook his head. "I don't think so, although the name does sound a bit familiar. Have you looked in the phone book?"

"I have spent a lot of time looking in the phone book since moving here," she stated, "but, no, I haven't looked at that name in particular."

"That's where you should start," Richard stated, as if giving her an important piece of guidance. And, with that, he disappeared over the fence again.

She groaned and muttered to herself, "Everybody's a

critic, even when they've got no reason to be."

He must have heard her because he called out, "That's enough of that."

She glared at the fence. "Yeah? Why's that?"

"Because somebody might call you skinny again." And then he went off in gales of laughter.

She sighed. "See, Nan? Look at what you did."

But, of course, Doreen could hardly blame her grandmother for that. And, if Doreen were too skinny, she'd been working on it. She had certainly been eating these days, now that she had her half of the reward money to spend. Couldn't fault her for that.

And, with that thought, she remembered that her conversation with Mack had gotten off-kilter over food. And she sent him back a meal suggestion. **Beef stroganoff.** She got a question mark in response. **Can you teach me how to make beef stroganoff?** And she got a thumbs-up in reply.

She grinned at that and rubbed her hands together. "Now," she stated out loud, "what we need is to find some answers, so we can really enjoy having that dinner celebration because, in the meantime—man, oh, man—this case has proved to be a little bit frustrating."

But taking Richard's suggestion to heart because, well, it was on her list to do anyway, she grabbed the phone book and sat down, searching for Thurlows. And, sure enough, she found three. She phoned the first number and got an older-sounding lady, and the woman confirmed that part of her family lived in Vernon, her brother in fact. But she didn't think it was the same Thurlows who had lived in that area of the shooting.

"And why not?" Doreen asked curiously.

"Because I don't remember anything about a murder like

that," she stated.

"And are you close with the family?"

The woman hesitated and then added, "Well, maybe not, but everybody would talk about a shooting, particularly if it was in their neighbors' yard."

"*Hmm.*" Doreen wasn't so sure about that. Sometimes people went out of their way to avoid letting people know of a drive-by shooting just two doors down because there would have been criticism about where they lived. "Are they still in Vernon, do you know?"

"Sure," she replied, "but they don't live in that area."

"Maybe not," Doreen noted, "but I … Would it be possible to get in contact with them? And I can just write it off my list."

The woman hesitated and then said, "Whatever. Just don't tell them that I gave you their phone number." And she passed off the number to Doreen.

With that in hand, Doreen quickly called them. This time she got a younger woman on the other end of the phone. When Doreen explained who she was and what she was looking into, the other woman was so surprised.

"After all this time," she asked, "why would you call here?"

"Because I understand," Doreen shared, "that maybe someone in your family, probably not you, lived in the area at the time of the shooting.

"My, that was a long time ago, but you're right. … I'm not exactly sure how that worked. I'm the next generation down, and my grandfather, Graham Thurlow, is in a home here," she noted. "I don't know if he could help you out with any information because it was so long ago."

"That's true," Doreen agreed, "but, in a lot of these cases, memories can be spotty, but they can also be right on for some of the oddest things."

The other woman laughed. "My name is Paige, by the way, and you're so right. Grandpa never remembers anything in the last few months, but, boy, things from a long time ago? He's got them nailed down—names, dates, places. Yet he can't remember what TV show he watched last week."

"Exactly," Doreen confirmed. "Any chance that I could go see him and ask a few questions?"

The woman hesitated. "I wouldn't want him upset though," she added.

"No, I wouldn't want him upset either," Doreen agreed. "However, time is running out to get answers here from any possible witnesses, and Paul's family still doesn't have any closure."

"Oh dear," Paige said. "Well, I could meet you there at the seniors' home. Maybe that would be okay. Are you okay if I'm with him?"

"That's fine," Doreen replied. "I'll have my grandmother with me too."

"Oh, good, that might make Grandpa feel a bit better as well."

"Sure. I just want to clarify some of the details that we have, and I don't really know anything about the victim's family themselves. Of course getting information from the family is always a little bit dodgy because they never quite see themselves as everybody else sees them."

"No, that's true," Paige agreed. "We'd like to think that we are honest about who we are, but I see it happen time and time again. We have a perception that is not the same perception others have."

"And, if you happen to know anybody else from that

area or that era who may have some insight," Doreen suggested hopefully, "I'd really appreciate any names of other people you know I could contact."

"You should probably contact my great uncle," she said.

"What's his name?" Doreen asked immediately.

"Well, it's another Thurlow," she stated. "Grandpa and he are brothers, but they didn't live on the same street as Paul, yet were close by."

"Perfect," Doreen exclaimed. "Maybe he's the one I'm looking for, anyone close enough to have heard something that day."

"Maybe. Uncle Sterling's not as far gone as my grandfather," she added, with a laugh. "And he'd probably be angry at me for even saying anything about that day, but I know he's talked about that shooting multiple times."

"In what way?"

"Just that he wished it was solved because it still bothered him," she relayed. "That's one of the reasons why I'd help you is because I know he's still upset about it."

"I think something like this is hard on everyone, until it's solved," Doreen said. "And there's just not ever a rhyme or a reason sometimes for what people do and for what they have to put up with."

"No, that's quite true," Paige murmured. "Anyway, this is his number, and I will meet you at the home tomorrow morning."

"How about eleven o'clock?" Doreen suggested.

"Oh, eleven o'clock sounds good," Paige agreed.

With that, Doreen hung up. And then she called Nan right back. "Do you know a Graham Thurlow or a Sterling Thurlow?"

"I thought we decided that I didn't know any Thurlows," she replied crossly.

"Maybe, but this Graham guy lives in an old folks' home. Something like Windmill Manor?"

"Oh, we've had lawn bowling competitions with them. All in good fun of course."

"Of course," Doreen said, with an eye roll. "You probably made a mint off them with your betting."

"Maybe. I don't remember."

At that, Doreen laughed. "Well he—and his brother, Sterling—are guys from the neighborhood at the time of the shooting. So, if you're with me tomorrow as we visit the seniors' home, that might make it easier for him to talk. Apparently some of his memories aren't all that clear."

"None of ours are all that clear," Nan noted in a tone that didn't surprise either of them. "The fact of the matter is, nothing's quite the same as you get older."

"I'm sorry, Nan," Doreen said gently.

"Well, you'll find out. Your time will come too," she noted cheerfully. "And I'll be in heaven, watching you."

At that, Doreen chuckled. "And you know something? I'd be quite happy to know you are there, still looking out for me."

"Ah, you do say the nicest things," she replied, with a happy tone. "But sounds like we have a busy morning tomorrow."

"It does, doesn't it? I'm just a little worried it might be too much for you."

"Oh, don't you even start with that," Nan argued. "I'm looking forward to it. I've already told Richie, and he's quite upset that he can't come."

Doreen's eyebrows raised in alarm. "He definitely can't come. No way I can handle two of you up there," she admitted, with feeling.

At that, Nan burst out laughing. "Yeah, I told him something like that. He understands. I mean, when the two of us get together, we can be quite a force."

"You sure can," Doreen agreed, with feeling. "And the only issue is the fact that we need to keep this focused on getting answers. Otherwise we'll run out of time."

"Got it," Nan said. "I'll see you tomorrow at nine a.m." And, with that, Nan hung up again.

That was the second time she'd done it too, in just a matter of minutes, making Doreen wonder what her grandmother was up to. It could be anything. She lived such a busy, full life at Rosemoor that even Doreen couldn't have guessed how happy her grandmother was there. But it certainly went a long way to making Doreen feel like she hadn't put her nan out of her house. And she knew that her grandmother would be quite peeved to think Doreen even worried about such a thing.

Still, knowing Nan was happy and healthy was the bottom line. Doreen didn't want to lose her anytime soon.

# Chapter 11

***Wednesday Morning …***

THE NEXT MORNING the sun dawned bright and clear. Doreen got up, had a shower, ate a good breakfast—because she wasn't sure how long she would be out and about—packed a granola bar from her last grocery shopping trip, where she'd managed to buy a couple boxes on sale and put them away for her reserve. And then, with the animals loaded up, she headed to Rosemoor. The animals were barking and howling and squawking by the time she pulled up to the front, eager to get out, but instead Nan was already there, waiting to get in.

When she hopped into the car, she looked over at her granddaughter and grinned. "Road trip." She almost cackled with glee.

"It is at that," Doreen agreed, looking at her. "I gather you like those."

"Oh, I do," Nan stated. "I used to do a lot of day trips around here. Not exactly like this, obviously," she added, with an eye roll. "But still, it was really good to have these kinds of trips. We tried to get the home to put on more day trips like this, but it's harder for them to get everybody into a vehicle and out in any kind of normal time frame," she complained, with a wave of her hand. "It wouldn't be so bad if they did something just for the younger group, but the older people want to go too."

The way Nan made it sound like she was one of the younger group and like the older group were even older than Nan kind of concerned Doreen.

As they drove off and headed toward Vernon, Nan asked, "Did you tell Mack? I'm surprised he didn't go with you."

"I haven't told Mack." Doreen glanced over at her grandmother. "He's back at work now."

Nan looked at her and nodded slowly. "Oh dear, do you really think he'll be happy that you're going without him?"

Doreen shook her head. "I was planning on telling him afterward."

At that, Nan started to laugh and laugh. "I hope I'm around for the fireworks."

She glared at her grandmother. "That's not fair. I can't be hampered by staying home per Mack's orders all the time or just following Mack's instructions. In order to work this case properly and efficiently, I have to be free to do what I need to do."

"*Absolutely*," her grandmother said, with a big smirk.

Doreen sighed. "How much trouble do you think I'll be in?"

"A lot," Nan declared, with a complaisant nod. "Absolutely *a lot*."

Trying to dismiss Nan's comments, Doreen drove carefully but with quiet confidence, loving the beautiful landscape all around her.

"Look at these lakes." Nan sighed happily. "We do live

in God's country, dear."

"We do indeed." It was hard to argue when Doreen saw just how beautiful the countryside was, and the drive from Kelowna to Vernon was absolutely stunning. When they made it to the town's limits, she was surprised at how quickly the trip had gone by. "It really isn't very far, is it?" Doreen asked.

"No, absolutely not. That's why I told you to consider the tradespeople because they would come up here for work without even a thought." Nan grinned.

"Of course they would," Doreen agreed quietly. "And there'd be too much money lost to ignore a whole town." She understood what her grandmother meant, and she was quite right. Back then, like now, there were just enough days where things went wrong that you had to cover for other people, especially during unforeseen circumstances.

"Well, the good news is," Doreen stated, "that we're here now. So we have some time before we meet with Sarah and then off to the seniors' home." And, with that, she headed to the address where the shooting had occurred all those years ago.

As soon as they got there, Doreen slowed and drove past the crime scene address, turned around, came back, parked on the opposite side of the street, and just stared at her surroundings. "I wonder if it even looks the same," she asked. "Unfortunately I don't have any images from back then."

"Time does have a habit of freezing things, but, as Vernon's grown, I imagine people have dropped their homes and moved on."

"And yet look at the residences here," Doreen pointed out. "It doesn't look like this area has had much development."

They both studied the other houses, and Nan nodded. "You're right. These all look like they're still from way back when, like the 1960s easily."

"Which also means then that property prices around here aren't worth a whole lot."

"And did Paul's mother own the house?" Nan asked. "That would be a different story too."

"I'm not sure she did," Doreen said. "That's one more question to ask her, but I know she was pretty broke, so I don't think so."

"Well, it depends on her husband though, right? And when he disappeared?"

"Exactly. More questions to ferret out." Doreen made a mental note to add it to her list. "We'll meet her today. She's our second stop."

"So she's not still in the same house?" Nan asked, then shook her head. "I would struggle to leave a home where my child had died."

"I don't think I would," Doreen stated. "I wouldn't want the bad memories."

"And yet that's where all the memories of the good times would be though too," Nan stated, looking at her.

"I guess." Doreen considered that. "I guess it's back to the fact that people have to deal with grief in their own way."

"Of course," Nan agreed.

Doreen got out and said, "I'll take the animals up and down the block."

Nan looked at her and nodded. "Okay, I'll just sit here and wait."

With a smile in her grandmother's direction, Doreen quickly buckled up Goliath and Mugs—Thaddeus already atop her shoulder—and wandered the street, just getting a sense of the area. She went down the block in both directions. By the time she returned to her vehicle, Nan stood on the corner, talking to somebody. As Doreen walked up closer, Nan waved at her.

"I just saw an old friend of mine," she told Doreen, laughing. "This is Lizzie." Nan pointed to the older white-haired lady, this one using a walking cane.

Doreen walked over and smiled at her. "Hi, Lizzie."

The woman looked at Doreen and asked, "Is it true?"

"Is what true?" Doreen asked, looking at her grandmother.

Lizzie replied, "Your grandmother here says that you're looking into that poor boy's shooting."

"Yes, that's quite true," Doreen confirmed. "And I know it was a very long time ago, so it's not as if we have very much to go on."

"No, of course not," Lizzie stated. "It was such a sad time. Everybody was so scared that all the kids were kept inside for weeks after that. Then slowly, over time, you forget, and the kids were let back out. It's just like life moved on for everybody but that family. For them, everything just froze."

"And it was just the mother and her son, correct?" Doreen asked Lizzie.

She took a moment, frowning. "I feel like a man was there, but I'm not sure he survived the shooting incident."

At that, Doreen realized she hadn't asked Paul's mother if she had had a partner at the time. "I know the father left after little Paul was just a couple years old. I'm meeting the mother in a little bit. I'll ask her if there was a partner. I hadn't considered that yet."

"Oh, you need to," Lizzie stated. "This was a pretty rough neighborhood."

"Was it?"

"It was a poor neighborhood, but decent folk were here, and they were just trying to raise a family," she explained quietly. "You know that one of them ended up being a police captain in downtown Kelowna."

Doreen smiled. "Yes, I know. I talked to him about this case already."

The woman nodded, as if that were old news. "Well, I don't know that I can help you any more than that," she said, "but you can always give me a call with any further questions. I haven't lost any of my brainpower," she stated, with a grin at Nan. "Good thing, huh?"

Nan nodded. "It's tough to watch all our friends go, isn't it?"

"Oh, it so is," she agreed. And that sent the two of them off on reminiscing.

Doreen was desperate to get the conversation back onto what she needed but was at a loss as to what questions to ask Lizzie. "I guess you never saw that vehicle used in the drive-by shooting, did you?" Doreen asked.

"I'm not sure I ever knew what vehicle it was. They told me it was a truck. A light-blue truck," she added. "But anybody with a light-blue truck almost automatically turned them over to the police to get checked over, so they were not suspects. Still, even the innocent people might not have done that."

"Exactly, and it could have been a stolen vehicle too," Doreen noted.

"And there was a rash of thefts at the time," Lizzie stated, looking at Doreen in admiration. "So you know that would have made more sense too."

A lot of things made sense; it's just picking on the right thread that would take her somewhere. Doreen nodded. "Well, if you do think of anything ..." And she quickly handed over her card.

Nan looked at the business card and remarked, "Oh my, I didn't realize you had cards made up."

Doreen shrugged. "I just printed them off at home," she noted. "I should go to the printer and get a few done, but I don't want people to think this is super official or anything."

At that, Nan looked at her and winked. "You mean, outside of the fact that it *is* super official?"

Doreen sighed. "Well, maybe." She smiled at her grandmother, then looked back at Lizzie. "If you can think of anything helpful, I'd really appreciate it if you called me."

"Well, I'm delighted that somebody's looking into this still," she stated. "That was such a terrible time, so traumatic for everybody."

"You mentioned you didn't think that a boyfriend survived the shooting," Doreen began. "I guess you don't know anything about who that boyfriend might have been?"

"Well, if you're going there, you can ask Sarah," Lizzie suggested.

"Oh, I will. But you also know that not everybody either remembers or chooses to remember."

The other woman's eyes widened. "Oh my, isn't that the truth," she said immediately. She looked back over at Nan and murmured, "She's really good."

Nan beamed, and Doreen just sighed. "Still, if there's anything else that you can help with, I'd appreciate it."

"Of course. And the boyfriend also had a son," she shared.

At that, Doreen turned and looked at Lizzie. "Pardon?"

"Her boyfriend. I think another boy was hanging around all the time, and I remember her saying that he was her stepson."

Doreen stared at her and nodded slowly. "About the same age?"

She frowned. "Maybe a little older. I'm not exactly sure."

"Okay, good enough. I'll keep that in mind."

As Doreen walked back to the driver's side of her car, she pulled out her notepad and made a few notes. It almost made the two women stand up straighter, as if they'd had something helpful to add. And they had, no doubt about it. It was just one of those things where Doreen wasn't even sure what they had. But it was important—she knew that. And she was glad she'd found it out well before the meeting with Sarah and Paige.

"If you have anything else …" Doreen reminded Lizzie.

"Will do."

And, with that, Doreen urged Nan back into the car, as it neared the time for the meeting at the old folks' home, and Doreen still had to swing by Sarah's for the journals and a few questions. As they drove away, Doreen asked Nan, "How did you run into her?"

"I saw her walking down the street. Honestly I really struggled to remember her name, and so I had to ask her," she admitted. "It's kind of embarrassing when you can't remember things like that. But then it hit me—we used to tease her about her name. We called her *lizard* all the time."

"Oh, Nan, you didn't," Doreen said, looking over at her grandmother.

Her grandmother shrugged. "She gave as good as she got. That's the thing about people. Generally people get over stuff like that."

"Maybe," Doreen murmured.

But she just wasn't sure how much something like that could have had an effect on these two boys. Because if this shooting revolved around the boys—and wasn't some random shots fired—then the shooting also revolved around things that would have happened to the boys. Doreen focused her attention on the next address. "Now let's go meet Sarah."

And, with that, she headed to the next address. By the time they pulled in, an older woman stood on the porch, seemingly impatiently waiting for them. Doreen hopped out and brought the animals with her, with Nan following along.

Sarah's face lit up. "Wow, I didn't realize you traveled with the crew."

"Yeah, they're my team." Doreen grinned. "And this is my grandmother, who wanted to get out for a ride."

At that introduction, Sarah nodded at Nan too. "Come in. Come in. I put on the teapot. I hope that's okay."

"That would be absolutely lovely," Doreen said gently. As she walked inside, she asked Sarah, "When did you move out of that house, by the way?"

Sarah didn't even pretend to misunderstand; she answered almost immediately. "I stayed for quite a while, thinking that it would help me stay closer to my son. Yet there wasn't any resolution to his death, and I was poisoning myself over and over again with the what-ifs. I would stare at the sunflowers and hate everything in my world because—well, of course—they represented a reminder of what I couldn't change."

"I'm so sorry," Doreen murmured. "You're right. That would have been pretty rough."

The women all sat down to enjoy a cup of tea, and, as soon as Sarah had a cup of tea in her hand, she looked over at Doreen expectantly and asked, "So what have you found out?"

Realizing Sarah would not let them go without revealing something, Doreen shrugged and said, "I was just over at the house. I'm still doing all that lovely time-consuming research to establish just what went on. … I know it's frustrating to wait for all of us, but there are more questions to be asked."

"There are always questions to be asked," Sarah stated painfully. "Even questions that don't make any sense to us."

"Of course." Doreen nodded. "Did you have a partner at the time?"

She nodded. "Kind of. We were off-again, on-again. In a way it should have just been permanently off-again. But you know when you're lonely and when it doesn't look as if your life will ever get any better, you kind of grasp at straws to have something to smile about. And sometimes you're just so afraid of being alone that you stay with anybody, even if you shouldn't be with them."

"So tell me about him," Doreen said, pulling up her notepad. Mugs lay at her feet, his head dropped down between his paws. Goliath was on Nan's lap, and Thaddeus was once again perched on her shoulder, eyeing what looked like cookies on the tea tray. Worried that he might help himself, Doreen asked, "May I have a cookie?"

Sarah immediately became the good host. "Yes, yes, of course."

Then Doreen winced and asked Sarah, "Would it be terrible if I offered Thaddeus here a little piece?"

Sarah appeared to be charmed at the idea. "Here. Let me get him one." She reached for one on the plate, grabbed another plate, and quickly crumbled up the cookie into a few pieces for him.

Doreen chuckled. "It's almost as if you know birds."

"Well, I've certainly fed more than my fair share outside." Sarah smiled. "I've always been a bit of a bird lover." As she held up the plate closer to him, Thaddeus reached down delicately and took a piece off the plate, let it roll around a little bit in his mouth, and then proclaimed, "Thaddeus is here. Thaddeus is here."

Sarah was delighted. "Oh, and he talks," she exclaimed in joy.

"Yes, sometimes too much," Doreen admitted, chuckling.

Sarah nodded. "I can so imagine."

Giving Sarah a chance to relax, Doreen ate part of a cookie, fed Thaddeus some of her cookie, then gently prodded by asking, "Now, you were saying?"

"Ah, yes." Sarah frowned. "I shouldn't have been with him anyway. It was just one of those things."

"Okay, but we do need to know what *one of those things* means."

Sarah grimaced. "His name was Cleve. I don't… Cleve …" She paused and frowned. "Now that was a long time ago." She thought about it for another moment and then smiled. "Cleve Massey."

"Okay, and what was the relationship like before this all happened?"

"It was good. It was easy. It was just so I wasn't alone."

"Right," she murmured. "And after the shooting?"

"After the shooting I wasn't fit to be around honestly," she admitted. "I pretty well kicked him out of the house. He said something sideways that hurt me one day, and I couldn't handle it. I ended up opening the door and telling him to go, and honestly it was the best thing I could have done."

Nan was automatically nodding her head in agreement. And, in one way, she probably did agree because Nan certainly spent more than a few years alone on that same kind of path.

By the time Doreen got all the details out, it was the same old story. He was a bit of a drinker; she wasn't at all. He had lost his job; she was working. He wasn't contributing, and she was going crazy, trying to pay the bills. And, after the shooting, losing her only son, she just fell apart, and he wasn't there for her.

"And do you know where he's gone on to?" Doreen asked.

"No, he's still in town, though," Sarah stated. "I saw him maybe about a year ago. I didn't say anything to him. I just walked on by. I was pretty sure he didn't even recognize me." She smiled. "And that was the best scenario."

"Right," Doreen murmured. "Would it upset you if we talk to him?"

She looked at her, sighed, and then nodded. "If you're going to turn over rocks, you might as well turn over every rock."

"Good. Do you have a phone number?"

Sarah shook her head. "This was all before cell phones anyway. When I kicked him out, we didn't stay in touch."

"Okay, I'll see if I can get that run down too," she murmured.

By the time Doreen finished asking all her questions. Sarah sat back, looking more than a little tired. "I didn't expect this to be so exhausting," she admitted quietly.

"Dredging up anything so emotional like this is terrible. And I wish I didn't have to do it."

"No." Sarah shook her head. "You need to do it. It's the only way we'll get to the bottom of this, and it would be really nice to have closure at some point in time."

Doreen smiled at Sarah. "We're working on it." Then Doreen looked down at her watch and said, "And now we have to go to the next appointment."

Sarah immediately hopped up and walked her to the door. "Thank you for coming."

And such a pathetic gratefulness filled Sarah's voice that Doreen felt bad. "Hey, we're doing what we can," she replied gently. "Don't lose hope."

"I know. I know," Sarah stated. "And I know it'll … it'll come out in the wash. It's just, you know, that whole *waiting for things to happen* is so hard." Sarah smiled, and, as they turned to walk outside, Sarah handed Doreen a cookie and added, "This is for the bird, for later." She reached up gently and stroked him.

Thaddeus cluck-clucked and moved back and forth, his head bobbing with interest as he eyed the cookie.

Nan took the cookie and put it in her purse. "She said, *for later*," she told Thaddeus in that *don't argue with me* tone of voice.

Thaddeus just glared at her. And, with a smile, Doreen ushered her crazy menagerie out to the car. Once everyone was settled, she headed in the direction of the seniors' home. She looked over at Nan. "You're awfully quiet."

"Well, it's humbling to see you in operation, my dear. You're very gentle with these people."

Doreen shrugged. "They've all been through a lot of trauma. How can anybody be anything but gentle?"

And Nan smiled. "You see? That's just part of what makes you so special."

Doreen chuckled. "Yeah, I don't know about that." She shook her head. "But, hey, thank you for the compliment." She pulled into Windmill Manor and said, "Now we're here to see the Thurlows."

"Good," Nan replied. "And, by the way, I still haven't heard from Mack."

Doreen stared at her grandmother, as she turned off the engine. "You contacted Mack?"

"Sure did," Nan snapped. "If you won't tell him where you've gone, I have to."

Doreen rolled her eyes at that. "He does have his job to do, you know?"

"He does, and he does have a job, and part of that job is looking after you," she declared in a tone of voice that brooked no argument.

"Nan, I don't need a keeper."

She laughed. "Sometimes you need way more than that," she stated, in that scolding tone of hers.

Doreen added, "We can talk to Mack afterward. First, let's go talk to these people."

# Chapter 12

DOREEN PULLED UP in front of the seniors' home, looked at Nan, and asked, "Are you ready for this?"

Nan immediately nodded. "This should be fun. I always like to see other homes and compare them to the one I'm in."

"Oh, that's interesting," Doreen noted. She looked at the animals and shook her head. "Sorry, guys. You have to sit this one out."

She carefully locked up the vehicle, leaving the windows open slightly for them. She had to especially watch out for Thaddeus when doing this. Mugs couldn't fit through even a half-open window, but Goliath and Thaddeus were two different stories. "I hope we won't be too long here."

Nan noted, "If we are, you or I can leave long enough to check on the animals, to walk them even."

Doreen felt better with that thought and led the way to the front reception area. As soon as she got inside, she looked around and saw a woman, standing off to the side, talking on her phone. Not sure whether that's who she was looking for or not, she headed to the front reception desk and asked for Thurlow.

The receptionist smiled at her and then pointed to the woman on the phone. "She's been waiting for you."

"Ah, good enough." Doreen walked toward the woman, who immediately got off the phone.

She asked, "Are you Doreen?"

"I am, indeed. You're Paige?" At the woman's nod, Doreen added, "Thank you for meeting me here."

She shrugged. "I don't know why we're even here. It's not like he'll remember anything." She looked at Nan curiously.

Doreen quickly introduced her. "I brought my grandmother along for the ride."

Paige nodded. "It's always nice to get out on a day trip, isn't it?"

Nan smiled at her. "It absolutely is. I wasn't sure whether I knew your grandfather or not," she noted, "just because we have done a lot of lawn-bowling tournaments back and forth."

Paige stared at Nan in surprise. "Do they even do that?"

"Yes, sure they do," Nan stated. "It's amazing how many people enjoy lawn bowling, and we do it among ourselves at Rosemoor, but, every once in a while, it's nice to bring a bus back and forth to include another home."

"Vernon is a little far for traveling, isn't it, don't you think?"

"I didn't think it was very far at all," Doreen disagreed calmly. "The drive went really fast. I hardly even noticed that we'd arrived because we were suddenly here already."

Nan nodded. "It's only about forty minutes away."

"Then of course"—Doreen laughed—"I'm used to Vancouver, and we'll spend forty minutes just getting to a doctor's appointment, without ever leaving the city."

Paige shuddered. "I can't imagine. That's not the lifestyle I want."

"No, I much prefer the lifestyle here," Doreen stated, with a bright smile. "So may we talk to your grandfather?"

"Sure. I did tell him that you were coming this morning. He looked kind of excited, but I'm not sure he really understood."

Doreen nodded. "I had a bunch of other things to do in Vernon, so it's not as if it'll be a wasted trip."

Paige looked relieved at that. "Okay, but don't say I didn't warn you." And she led the way to an open area. "We have to meet all visitors out in the common area."

Nan sniffed at that, and Doreen glanced at Nan and frowned. But then she also enjoyed a different and more independent role at Rosemoor, and she had a ground floor with a patio, which gave her indoor-outdoor access, whether she was allowed it or not.

Nan just gave her a beautiful smile and whispered, "I'll be good."

Doreen chuckled at that.

Paige glanced back, a confused look on her face, as if wondering what was to even laugh about here.

And Doreen appropriately noted, "It's a beautiful place."

Paige shrugged. "All these assisted-living homes look the same to me. And they're so depressing," she whispered. "I just … I don't want to end up here myself."

Nan looked at her and added, "You know that some of them are really nice."

"Maybe," Paige replied, "but they have that same, you know, *this is your final stop before death's door* look to them. Who would want that?"

Doreen couldn't believe Paige was saying all this in front

of Nan. Thankfully her grandmother was built of sturdy stuff.

As Paige walked into another room, she stopped and looked around. "Grandfather's over there." She pointed and led the way to the back corner, where a man sat, staring out the window.

Doreen approached cautiously. She'd seen a lot of older residents sit by windows and then get badly startled when people talked to them. But Nan had absolutely no such hesitation; she walked right up to the man and patted him on the shoulder.

He turned and looked at her and frowned. "And who are you?" he asked in a querulous voice.

She introduced herself and added, "I'm from Rosemoor in Kelowna."

He looked at her in confusion for a moment. "Lawn bowling," he declared. "Dang, we beat you fair and square," he said, showing her a fist.

"That's true," she admitted, with a grin. "I'm just hoping one day we can have a rematch."

He burst out laughing. "And we'll still beat you." Then he looked over at his granddaughter and frowned. "I wasn't expecting you today."

"I told you that I was coming," she said quietly, "and we talked about it this morning."

He just shrugged and looked over at Nan. "I don't know how they think we're supposed to remember all this stuff." Then he added hesitantly, "Was it you I was expecting?"

"Me and my granddaughter." Nan motioned to Doreen.

He looked over at Doreen and frowned.

She smiled at him. "Hi, I'm here to ask you a few questions about that drive-by shooting all those years ago."

He stared at her. "Paul Hephtner."

His answer came out so fast. She nodded slowly. "You do remember."

"How can I forget?" he said. "It was a terrible day, an absolutely terrible day for that poor mother."

"And yet you know her by her new name. Not the name she used to be known as."

"She changed her name while she was there. All of us were quite perturbed by that because it seemed like she was permanently getting rid of the father, so there was quite a heckling contest over her decision." He shrugged. "But it died down soon enough. She was a good woman. She didn't have any money, but she worked hard to keep a roof over her boy's head."

"I forgot to ask her if she owned that house though," Doreen mentioned out loud. "Dang."

"She didn't," Graham Thurlow replied quietly. "One of my neighbors owned it and rented it to her then sold it off but she stayed there still."

"Ah, well, there you go. Interesting that you have that kind of information," Doreen stated.

He shrugged. "I've kept in touch with a bunch of the people from the old neighborhood over the years," he explained. "It always bothered us that nobody was ever caught for that murder."

"And that's why I'm taking another look at it," Doreen replied. "Anybody from the neighborhood back then might forget something useful the longer we push this off."

"Shouldn't have been pushed off at all," he snapped, glaring at her.

"And you're right," she agreed. "We shouldn't use that phrase. At the same time, there has to be something new in order to push the investigation forward."

"I guess," he muttered, as he stared off in the distance.

"What do you remember about it?" she asked curiously.

He looked over at her. "Are you testing my memory?"

"No, I'm not," she replied honestly. "I'm hoping you do remember something because a lot of people have forgotten."

"Maybe," he noted. "My son used to play with that boy. Believe me. At that time, we were all holding our kids close and were all thankful it wasn't ours who got shot. And I know the captain." He snorted at that. "We all call him the captain. We've always called him the captain since we found out where he was and what he was doing when we heard from him fifteen years ago," Graham explained. "He's been trying really hard to get this reopened and to solve it. Doesn't seem like it's working though."

"Well, he did ask me to look into this now," she noted gently.

At that, Paige frowned at Doreen. "He did?"

Doreen nodded. "Yes, he did."

"Oh." And that almost seemed to give Paige more confidence in Doreen, as if now her visit had some validity. Paige looked at her granddad. "So what can you tell us about what happened?"

He frowned. "Not a whole lot to say. The kids were out playing, and a truck drove up and shot them. The killer was never found."

"And nobody recognized the truck?" Doreen asked. "I find that hard to believe in a close-knit small-town environment."

He nodded. "So did a lot of us, honestly," Graham agreed. "But it had a pretty bad paint job, and we figured that maybe it was just a paint that would wash off afterward."

"Which would make this killing premeditated," Doreen noted calmly. "So somebody deliberately went and hunted that boy down?"

Graham stared at her. "Well, that's pretty obvious, isn't it?"

"Well, it is and it isn't," Doreen replied. "When you think about it, it's also quite possible that whoever did this was looking to maybe shoot the other boy—the captain, as you say."

He frowned at that. "We did consider that at the time, but I don't think that's quite the way it worked."

"No, and why not?" she asked curiously.

He gathered his thoughts before speaking. "It was just so targeted. It was almost like the second shot, for the captain, was deliberately nonfatal, as if they just wanted to wound him instead of kill him. Like a message sent. And honestly the captain was the more popular of the two. The other one was a bit of a—" Graham stopped, winced, and added, "I shouldn't say anything bad about the dead."

"No, we don't like to say bad things about the dead," Doreen admitted, "but, if it's something important, I need to know."

"Well, Paul was a bit of a tattletale. You know the kind of kid you didn't want to hear your secrets because pretty soon everybody in town would know them?"

"He was only ten though," Doreen reminded him.

"I know. I know, and that was part of the problem. As soon as he was killed, no one wanted to say anything bad because it just makes you look bad, right?"

She nodded slowly. "Very true. I guess that's how a lot of people would look at it. When you say something against somebody, it makes it sound like you're the one in the wrong."

"Exactly," Graham agreed. "And so a lot of us didn't really say anything back then."

"And what about since then?" she asked.

He shrugged. "Not a whole lot to say, honestly. At that point in time, with just so much wrong with everything going on, there wasn't a whole lot to say without defaming the dead."

"Maybe," Doreen said, "but, if you didn't say it then, what was it that you would have liked to have said?"

"I'd like to have said that he was a sneak and a cheat and that he was the kind of boy who you just didn't want on your team."

"And do you think somebody would have killed him over that?"

He shook his head. "It's kind of hard to think anybody would care that much about what a mere boy said, but he was also the kind of kid who would look into windows and see things he shouldn't."

Doreen stated, "His mom told me that he was a bit of a class clown."

Graham nodded. "I'd agree with that too," he replied quietly. "He was definitely the kind who always had to make fun of people."

"But maybe not in a nice way?" Doreen asked.

He looked at her steadily and nodded. "Not in a nice way."

"Interesting. So, anybody else have a truck close to that kind used in the shooting, regardless of paint color?"

"Yeah, we found a lot of trucks close to that type. A bunch of us got together and tried to solve the mystery way back when, and one swore it was a neighbor's truck, but the truck had disappeared, and, of course, we never could prove it then."

"And was it that similar?"

"Well, it was similar," Graham said, "but lots of things are similar. That doesn't mean that they're the right vehicle."

"Of course not." Doreen wondered where to go with the next question.

It was Nan who asked, "What are the chances that this kid saw something he shouldn't have?"

He looked at her and nodded. "That's certainly something we wondered, but we didn't have any way to prove it. We didn't have a way to even question it."

"Did you bring it up with the adults at the time?"

"We brought it up with law enforcement. We brought it up with everybody in the neighborhood, and, of course, it was all taken into consideration, but the cops couldn't find anything."

"No, of course not, too little details," Doreen murmured, thinking about that.

He looked at her and remarked, "You got a look in your eye."

She nodded. "I do, but I'm a long way away from having anything concrete."

"Well, I would sure like to find out some answers before I die," he stated. "A lot of us were affected. It's like the loss of innocence, you know? The kids never got to play out in the front yards anymore. They had to go play in backyards, where people couldn't shoot them." He looked at her steadily and then slowly nodded. "Between you, me, and the lamppost, I'm pretty sure it was very targeted, and Paul was it."

"But, of course, you know as much as I know. There are drive-by shootings for no reason at all," she added, "and that part is something I struggle with."

At that, somebody walked up and stated, "Time for his medication."

He glared at the woman. "Can't you see I'm having a talk?"

She sighed. "Then take your medicine, without giving me any trouble," she stated, "and then you can continue having your talk."

He grumped, but he took his medication and tossed it back without a whimper.

The woman looked over at Nan and Doreen and stated, "You guys should be here more often. He at least behaves himself."

Doreen hid her grin, but Nan didn't.

As soon as Nan turned back to Graham, she said, "Good for you. Fight it all the way."

He nodded and brightened. "Right? I have to stay alive long enough for your granddaughter here to solve this case." And then he shook a fist. "And so I can get back down and whup your butt in lawn bowling again."

She burst out laughing. "Yeah, that's not happening. We're too good."

He gave a snort at that. "So good that I won, huh?"

"And we've improved since then," Nan noted cheerfully. "We worked hard at it."

"It won't be enough," he smirked, with that smug awareness of a winner.

Doreen just chuckled at him and added, "If you think of anything else …"

"Yeah, I know. I'll call you. But I need a number to

reach you."

She held out one of the cards that she had printed off.

He looked at it and tucked it in his pocket. He said, "That truck is the key."

"Yeah, it's also who was with him and where Paul might have been during the previous days," Doreen added. "Did you ever hear anything about what he was doing on those last few days?"

Graham stopped, looked at her, and then shook his head. "No, but I know who would."

She nodded slowly, as she looked at him with a knowing gleam. "Yep, somebody I'll have to sit down and interview."

Nan looked at her and asked, "Who?"

And together, Doreen and Thurlow said, "The captain."

Almost immediately it seemed like Mr. Thurlow started to get tired, as if the medication had worn him right out. He started yawning and mumbling to himself.

At that, his granddaughter sighed and said, "That was the end of anything lucid you'll get out of him now for quite a while." As she nodded to her grandfather, she bent over to kiss him and said, "We'll head back, okay?" And he just stared off into the distance.

Nan looked at that and shuddered. "Did anybody double-check his medications?" she asked. "That doesn't seem terribly natural."

Doreen privately agreed with her grandmother, but, since she didn't know anything about Graham's health, she had no idea if that was something that needed to be looked at or not. But, if it were her grandfather, she certainly would. She looked over at the granddaughter, as Paige led them farther out back to the other area. "Does anybody approve his medications?" she asked Paige. "It does seem like that reaction happened very soon after he took it."

"I don't know," Paige replied, clearly frustrated. "I'm not his legal caregiver. I'm just family.'

"Who is the caregiver?" Doreen asked quietly.

"His daughter, my aunt, and she's the one who handles all that."

"Maybe you need to mention to her that the medication needs to be reassessed," Nan mentioned delicately. "Nobody should be that drugged in the middle the day—or even at night. … Not sure what your relationship is with the rest of the family or how often the aunt comes and sees Graham, but I certainly think something is off."

Paige laughed nervously. "Nobody comes and sees him. Just me."

"And that's sad too," Doreen whispered.

Paige turned to Doreen. "It might be sad, but it happens all over the place." And, with that, she added, "And I've got to head back myself now. If you want to give me your card, if anything else pops up, I'll let you know."

Doreen quickly handed over her card and said, "Thank you. And, by the way, how would we get a hold of your aunt?"

Paige stared at Doreen, frowning. "Why would you want to?"

Doreen shrugged. "For the same reason that we talked to your grandfather and will speak to your great-uncle. I just need to confirm a few details."

Paige shrugged, and, as soon as Nan pulled out her phone, Paige gave her a phone number to call.

"I can call her right now if you'd like," she said, dialing the number.

"And where does she live?" Doreen asked as she waited

to see if the aunt would answer.

"She's in Kamloops," Paige replied. As soon as her aunt answered, Doreen awkwardly introduced herself and asked the couple questions confirming the details she had. The call was short and not very sweet. But nothing suspicious popped up so that was good.

"So why is the one person who is to look after your grandfather not even living in town? That's like what, a two-hour drive away?" she didn't understand that but hadn't wanted to bring it up on the phone.

Paige nodded. "Most of the time it's fine. Then, every once in a while, it's not fine, and my aunt calls on me." And, with that, she waved goodbye. "Now if you'll excuse me." And she walked to her car and disappeared.

Doreen and Nan shared glances. Doreen spoke first. "Well, that was an interesting visit."

"It was, but now we need food."

Doreen asked her, "Are you hungry?"

"I am, and now I'm thinking, because of the animals, maybe we should just pick up some food and go to a nice park. Then we can figure out if we're done for the day."

"Sounds good to me," Doreen agreed.

And that's what they did.

# Chapter 13

ON THE WAY home, Doreen looked over at Nan and frowned.

Nan, almost instinctively knowing what Doreen would say, waved her hand and said, "I'm fine. Just a little tired."

"Well, it was a busy day," she murmured.

Nan chuckled. "It was a lovely day. And we should do it again sometime."

"And we can," Doreen agreed, looking at her grandmother. "It's not that long a drive to Vernon."

"No, it absolutely isn't."

"Lots of other small towns are around here too," Doreen noted. "I think we should make a point of going out and exploring all of them. Particularly if it has nothing to do with business, right?"

At that, Nan chuckled. "You know something? I'm pretty sure there'll be a cold-case excuse to go to every one of these places before long."

"And here you're the one who told me to come to Kelowna because it's such a lovely place to live," Doreen recalled, with a snicker. "Who knew there were so many cold-case killers out there?"

"Not me," Nan admitted. "You've certainly opened my eyes to the crime element in town."

"And I'm not sure that's a good thing either," Doreen replied, "or that it's fair. I mean, an awful lot of people are here who are beautiful and generous and loving and giving, and crime was not part of their world. And then there's a whole other element of people, where they're in exactly the same place, but life hit them sideways, and they did something that—once you go down that pathway—it's pretty hard to claw back from."

At that, Nan nodded slowly. "You're right. Now I'm sitting down, I am just that little bit tired," she admitted. "Are you okay if I have a nap?"

"Absolutely," Doreen stated, looking at her grandmother. "Close your eyes and rest. We'll be back in town in no time."

And, with that, Nan shifted slightly to get a little more comfortable and closed her eyes. With a gentle smile in her direction, Doreen returned her gaze to the road. It had been a good day. Lunch had been fantastic. She hadn't had an Indian meal like that in a very long time, and she had thoroughly enjoyed it. Of course she hadn't been to a lot of places in a long time because of her memories of her ex or her lack of money or a million other things.

She'd tried to pay for lunch, and Nan wouldn't have anything to do with it. Even though Doreen now had money to have paid for lunch, Nan kept telling Doreen that she would need it, so hold on to it. And, of course, that was always the scary thing. It seemed like you always needed more money than you had.

Even with her doing her best to stay on a budget, it seemed like the money just didn't go very far. That was probably one of the biggest lessons of being on her own. Plan for the expense to be X amount of dollars and just automatically double it. Good lesson for the future. And to always be grateful to have the money that she did have.

She glanced at what appeared to be a turnoff to a spa. She thought about the days when spas were a regular part of her life and shook her head. Even the whole reward check wouldn't buy her a spa trip, not to a place like that, she was sure. And yet she wasn't certain she even wanted to go back to that lifestyle. Maybe a special spa day as a stress relief or to share with a girlfriend. But along with her lack of friends in town was her lack of funds.

Doreen knew Nan would probably go, but then Doreen would have to fight with Nan to pay for it. Doreen smiled at that and looked back behind her at the traffic, but everything seemed to be moving along at a steady pace with her. She wasn't into speeding, but she was happy to be a regular motorist on this trip, not some racing fanatic. She stayed in the slow lane, knowing that a group of people always had to be the first and the fastest, and she was okay with that, as long as they left her alone.

Traffic whipped past her at a pretty steady rate. She was enjoying her drive in the slow lane, and she had no pressure to move faster because she had a lot of space in her lane. So she was good to go. She drove along quite happily, and, as she reached one of the towns closer to Kelowna, she saw the marinas and the other lakes opening up in her view, and she sighed happily. "It truly is beautiful here," she murmured.

Nan snored gently beside her and didn't answer.

Doreen glanced over at her grandmother with a gentle smile. Then she looked into the rearview mirror and frowned.

That one truck had been behind her for quite a while now. It seemed like a truck was always behind her but this one, kind of a flat-black color, had stayed on her tail and was starting to get antsy that she was in the slow lane. Which made no sense because, if he wanted to pass her, he could have. Not only could have, should have. That's what the passing lanes were here for.

And regardless of how she felt about anybody else's driving, she didn't want to be pressured into going faster than she was comfortable with. That was a recipe for disaster.

Keeping half an eye on him, she kept trucking along, inching up the speed a little bit, but she was right on the speed limit now. Of course most people drove just over the speed limit, so maybe she was pissing him off by not going a tad faster. But the fast lane was empty, and he could have passed her at any time.

She thought about that and then tried to slow down a little bit, so that she could read his license plate. And realized there wasn't one on the front. Of course immediately her mind went to a dozen things, none of them good. Why would somebody not have a license plate upfront? It was illegal. Of course maybe it was sitting up in the windshield because he was getting work done or the hanger broke.

She let her mind stew on it a little bit, until the vehicle drove closer and then closer still, until it was riding right on her tail. Now she was starting to get angry. And as it got closer yet again, she also started to get a little bit afraid. She frowned and drove a little bit slower yet again, wishing he would just pass her. Other vehicles tore past them at a merry rate, so why wasn't he?

And, of course, the only answer she could think of is that he could, if he wanted to, and yet he wasn't. Therefore, he didn't want to. And that just meant that he was up to no good. She frowned at that, kept a good eye on the surrounding area, wondering where she could pull off the road and let him go past. And right up ahead was a long wide shoulder. She kept going along at the same speed, and then, at the last minute, she whipped off onto the shoulder. The truck raced on past her, and, for that, she was grateful. She waited for an opportunity to get back into the traffic, and, as she slowly pulled over into the main road, she realized that she was shaking.

She frowned, looked down at her hands, and whispered, "I don't know what that was, but I hope he's gone."

There were all kinds of possibilities with some jerk on the road like that. None of them were good. And she knew that Mack would likely just toss it off as being a driver out to scare her a little bit. And she didn't understand that mentality. Like, why would you want to try and scare somebody? And she had a little old lady as a passenger, so how fair was that? But most people didn't give a care, unless it had something to do with themselves.

Still, nothing major had happened, and he was long gone. She drove ahead, only to realize that truck had pulled off the road up ahead too. She didn't even have a chance to register that until she had already passed him. As she watched carefully behind her, sure enough, he appeared behind her again. She sucked in her breath, and just then Nan woke up.

"What's the matter, dear?" she asked.

"I've got a driver who's not a very nice person, and he's got no license plate."

Nan looked at her inquisitively, twisted in her seat to look behind them, and asked, "That truck?"

"Yeah, that truck." And she explained what had happened earlier.

Nan's eyes widened. "Oh my." She stopped, thought about it, and asked, "Now who could we have pissed off today?"

Doreen winced. "I was hoping you wouldn't make that connection."

Nan snorted. "It's pretty hard not to. You've never been on this road. We go to Vernon and start asking questions about a murder from a very long time ago, and now you get somebody like this on your tail."

"Exactly. And I pulled off the road once, and he stayed just far enough behind that, if I do it again, he'll pull off behind me next time."

"Well, we can always stop and talk to him face-to-face."

She looked over at Nan.

Nan shrugged. "It saves time, you know?"

"Well, it does save time, unless he's really not a nice person," Doreen noted quietly.

At that, Nan stared at her, and then Doreen's meaning filtered in, and Nan's eyes widened. "Oh my." She gripped her purse a little tighter. "I never thought of that."

"I didn't really want you to either, but I can't imagine there's any good reason for him to be doing what he's doing."

Nan brought out her phone, and, without even asking Doreen, she phoned Mack.

Doreen groaned. "Nan, you don't have to call Mack. It's fine."

But Mack was already on the other end. "Nan, what's the problem?" he asked briskly.

"We have a tail on the road," she announced. "And it's

threatening to push us off the road."

There was a moment of shocked silence, and then Mack yelled out, "What?"

Nan had embellished it a little bit, but, being fairly circumspect with her description, she relayed what just happened to Mack.

"Now I slept through most of it, and, darn it, I wish I hadn't," Nan said. "All the good stuff happens when you're sleeping—you know that," she scolded Mack.

He groaned. "Give me a license plate if you can."

"We already tried that," Doreen called out. "There isn't one on the front. And I passed him too quickly when he was parked on the shoulder to see if he had one on the back."

"Can you give me a description of the truck?"

"Not easily, it's just a dusky black. It's kind of a weird paint job," Doreen explained, "like, … like flat, not shiny."

"Ha," Mack replied, "so custom."

"Or a kid," she replied immediately. "I don't know what to say. I wasn't even going to call you."

At that came an ominous groan on the other end of the line. "So it takes Nan being with you to make you sensible?"

"Don't even start with me," Doreen snapped. "I took Nan so we could talk to some people in Vernon. We had a great day, and now we're heading home, and this guy appears."

"Isn't that just perfect timing," Nan told Mack. "I mean, obviously it's somebody after us. And, therefore, it's somebody who didn't like our line of questioning."

"And what was your line of questioning?" he asked curiously.

At that, Nan looked over at Doreen. "Do you have an answer for him?"

"Nope, I sure don't. You know what I'm working on," Doreen told Mack, her voice louder than normal, so that he could hear her. "We talked to the Thurlows—the granddaughter, the grandfather, and the aunt—and we talked to Paul's mother. I still need to speak with Sterling Thurlow and Paige's aunt again. But, other than that, we picked up our lunch at an Indian restaurant and went to a park."

"And it was so good." Nan gave a happy sigh. "You really should take Doreen out more often," she scolded Mack. "A woman should have a few good and fun things to look forward to in life."

Even Doreen heard Mack's sigh on the other end. She grinned. "Yeah," she joined in, her voice smug. "You probably should."

At that, Mack replied, "Well, in that case, I'm coming over Friday night for your next cooking lesson, so how about we go out Saturday?" And then he immediately switched the conversation back to Nan. "Nan, can you get any description of the driver? I don't want Doreen looking because she needs to keep her eyes on the road."

She glared at the phone, not sure how she was supposed to get out of this dinner date. And between the two of them, she felt like she'd just been set up. But Nan had already twisted in her seat, trying to look at the driver of the truck.

"I could see his head over the top of the steering wheel," she noted. "Whoever he is, he's likely six foot."

"Okay, so smaller, and tell me something else," Mack said. "You're a good judge of character, Nan. Is this a male or a female?"

Nan studied the driver again. "I would love to tell you definitely it's one or the other," she stated, "but I really can't. He's wearing a baseball cap."

"Ah, the nefarious baseball cap," Mack replied, with a sigh. "Whoever invented it also invented a lot of ways for bad guys to hide."

Nan agreed. "Maybe we can get it outlawed."

He burst out laughing. "Yeah. No, that won't work."

"If it lets criminals get away with crimes," Nan stated in a reasonable tone of voice, "you'd think it would not be hard to ask our MLAs to make changes like that. They represent us, after all."

He chuckled again.

Nan frowned into the phone. "You really don't have to laugh at my ideas, young man."

Doreen snickered. "Yeah, Mack, you really don't."

But Nan wasn't done with telling her off either. "Besides, the two of you need help getting together, and, if it takes somebody like me to do that," she declared, with a hard sniff, "you really should listen to other ideas I have too."

"Sorry, Nan," Mack said immediately.

Yet Doreen could almost see him rolling his eyes at the same time. However, she grinned because he was getting told off, and she wasn't. At least she hoped she wasn't. Nan would get to her eventually. As they drove along, Doreen added, "He's just staying right there, behind me."

"So how do you even know that that this guy's after you?" Mack asked.

"Well, I told you what happened earlier," Nan replied. "He came up so close, and he was almost touching her bumper, and she just pulled off the road to the shoulder, not even hitting the brakes because she wanted to get out of his way."

"And, yes, I'm in the slow lane," she told Mack. "And

there's not very much traffic beside me. Absolutely everybody is moving along, and he could have moved over at any time. He's choosing not to."

"Right," Mack noted. "How far out of the city are you?" She gave him landmarks of where she currently was, and Mack replied, "I'm in my vehicle, heading toward you."

"What good will that do?" she asked.

He sighed. "Possibly none, but maybe I can get an idea about this vehicle and who is driving it, and maybe I can get on his tail and track him."

"Oh, I like that." Nan rubbed her hands together. "This is lovely, dear."

"We're just coming up to the big Esso station, as you're about to enter into town," Doreen stated. "And, yeah, he's still right behind me. But, if he sees you, you know he'll take off."

"He'll see me first," Mack noted cheerfully. "Now stay on the phone with me. And I want you to stay in the slow lane and keep giving me signs of where you are."

And, with that, they drove a few more miles, while Mack headed toward them on the highway. By measuring off landmarks, Doreen told Mack, "I think you should be coming up on us right now."

"I can see you," Mack confirmed. "And, yeah, I can see him too."

"Well, that's great," Doreen noted, "but you're going the wrong way."

"No, I'm not," Mack corrected her. "I went past you ever-so-slightly and waited on a crossroad. And now I'm on the freeway right behind him."

"Oh, lovely," Doreen said gleefully. And then she stopped. "Where am I supposed to go? I'm not driving home. And no way I'll let this guy follow me back to Rosemoor, and I need to take Nan home."

Mack suggested, "Why don't you go to the mall? If nothing else, you can get lost in there for a few hours."

"Well, Nan can," Doreen noted humorously. "I'm not so sure about me."

"Absolutely we can," Nan agreed, "and that's a good idea. It's a big parking lot, and he'll never find us.'

"Oh, he'll find us easily enough," Doreen argued sadly. "He's been looking at our vehicle for the last half hour. Anyway, he knows right where we are because he's still behind me, riding my bumper."

But, with the mall coming up quickly, she put on her signal and sighed. "Okay, I'm heading into the mall," she told Mack. And, sure enough, behind them was the truck, also flipping on his turn signal. "He's coming in behind me."

"Yeah, and I'm right behind both of you," Mack replied calmly. "I don't want you to get out of your vehicle. Find a parking spot somewhere close by, so I can keep track of what he's doing, and I want you to just stay in the car."

"Well, we're probably better off if we go into the mall," Doreen suggested. "I really don't want Nan to get involved in any of this."

Nan immediately spoke up. "I'm fine. I'm fine. This is the most excitement I've had all week."

Doreen groaned at that. "You know you're not supposed to have lots of excitement, right?"

"Ah, posh, don't you worry about me." But then she added, "Still, it'd probably be a much better idea if we got Doreen out of here and into the mall, don't you think?" she asked Mack.

"Unfortunately you could be right," Mack noted. "I'm

not sure what this person's after."

Doreen slowly drove through the mall, looking for a parking spot close to a mall entrance. "I'm right across from the bookstore," she told Mack. "A parking spot just opened up, so I'll pull in, and then we'll dash inside." She looked over at Nan and said, "Let's go. And fast." They both unbuckled, and she turned to look at all the animals and told Nan, "I can't leave them."

Nan looked at the animals too and frowned. "Are we allowed to take the dog inside? But I don't like leaving the animals alone either."

"No, we aren't. Mack?"

"Stay where you are in the vehicle," he ordered, and something odd filled his voice.

"Did you see him?" Doreen asked excitedly.

"Not yet, I'm following the vehicle right now, and it's doing a couple loops through the parking lot."

"Ah, what are the chances he saw you join the parade?" Doreen asked.

"Maybe, but I've also called in for backup to pull the truck to the side of the road, once we can pin it down somewhere. However, if he takes off again, we'll never find it."

"Oh, I hear you," Doreen agreed.

Just then the truck whipped past her and parked nearby. And before she could even say anything, Mack was there right behind it, but the driver was already out and dashing through the mall itself, leaving his vehicle behind.

Doreen looked over at Nan. "Well, this was an exciting turn of events."

Nan nodded at her. "Wow, I didn't realize your life was quite this exciting."

Doreen chuckled. "It isn't. At least not always," she muttered. She looked back at the animals. "I'm kind of tempted to just go home and to leave this in Mack's hands. Because, if this guy comes back out again, there's a good chance he'll follow us."

Mack must have heard her because he said, "That's a good idea. Go, go, go."

And, with that, she peeled out of the mall, took the first exit onto the highway, and quickly found her way back to Nan's place. As she pulled into the parking lot, she deliberately parked between two larger vehicles. And she turned off the engine. With a sigh, she stared at her grandmother. "Are you okay?"

"Never better," she chortled. "Wait till I tell Richie about this. He'll be so upset that he couldn't come with us."

Doreen shook her head at her grandmother. "It wasn't supposed to be like that, you know?"

"Sure, sure." Nan gave a wave of her hand. "But I think everything with you ends up like this. Come in and have a cup of tea. Let's get your nerves settled."

"My nerves are fine," she muttered.

"Well, mine aren't. Besides, the animals need to get out. They haven't had an easy day either."

"I know," Doreen said, with a backward glance at her crew. She got out, and, with the animals, she walked up to Nan's place, where they sat on the patio. Goliath rolled on the grass several times. Doreen just hoped the new gardener wasn't around to get angry at him. And right beside Goliath, Mugs rubbed and rolled and scrubbed his back on the grass too. As if he was all hot and sweaty and just needed to unwind a bit.

Doreen sighed. "I should have driven home and then

walked everybody down to the creek for a bit," she muttered. "They need to get out and exercise a bit."

Almost immediately Goliath walked to a bit of sand and immediately used it as a sandbox.

"*Uh-oh*. Nan, do you have any poop bags here?" she asked. "I left mine in the car."

Nan immediately shook her head. "Nope, I don't, dear."

"Okay, you keep an eye on them, and I'll go get one." And she dashed back to her car and pulled out the poop bags that she always kept there. And, with that, she headed back to where Goliath was utilizing the Rosemoor garden. Just as she thought that she might have gotten away with it, a roar came from behind her. She turned to see the gardener racing toward her. She looked over at Nan. "I tried."

Nan just rolled her eyes. "It's okay, dear. Don't you worry about it. I'll take care of this."

Doreen walked the bag to the garbage in the front and dropped it into one of the big cans. As she turned around, the new gardener was berating Nan. And Nan looked positively cowed. Getting angry at that, Doreen racing back over and yelled at the gardener, "You don't have a right to talk to her like that. How dare you? That's called elder abuse."

The gardener frowned at Doreen. "You." He stuck out a finger. "How dare you let your cat go to the bathroom here."

"Yeah," she huffed, with a wry look. "Have you ever tried to stop a cat, particularly one that needs to go to the bathroom? It doesn't work so well."

He just stared at her, as if he couldn't believe what she just said.

She sighed and said, "Look. I cleaned it up already."

"No," he argued, "you didn't clean it up. That smell will

be here forever."

"*Forever*?" she asked, looking at him, with a raised eyebrow.

"*Forever*." And he went to poke her in the chest with his finger.

At that, she stared at him and declared, "I really wouldn't poke that thing at me, if I were you."

"And why is that?" he asked in disgust.

"Because I don't take kindly to people poking me," she snapped. "Especially overprotective guys regarding a little bit of grass. I'm quite happy to clean up the messes that my animals make. Nobody's ever had a problem with them being here before."

"*Before*," he repeated. "Well, now this is my domain, and I look after these gardens." And he fisted his hands on his hips and added, "And what will you do about it?"

And then all manner of madness broke loose.

# Chapter 14

BACK HOME, DOREEN quickly unloaded the animals, put on a pot of coffee, and poured herself a large cup. With the animals in tow, she walked down to the creek and collapsed on the bank. What a day, what an afternoon, what an ending. She'd managed to escape Nan's place pretty quickly, especially once things had blown up, starting with Richie coming and berating the gardener, and Nan going at the gardener, poking him in the chest for daring to touch Doreen.

Then it just got uglier from there.

Management had been brought in, and Doreen had taken that opportunity to disappear. Now lying on the grass in the late-afternoon sun, she was tired, worn out, and still worried about Mack. She pulled out her phone and sent him a text message, asking if he was okay. When no answer came right away, she fumed and fussed and worried some more. Mugs came over and sat down beside her, his head rubbing up and down her thigh. She scratched him gently, and even Thaddeus hopped up on her belly and just sat there, perched.

"I don't know, guys. It started off as a good day, and it

was still a good day by noon, but the way home and after that? Yeah, that was just not much fun."

She still didn't understand what the truck driver would have wanted, but the good news was, somebody was bothered by the questions she'd asked, and that was huge. It wasn't huge in a good way because, as soon as anybody started to get upset about things like that, Doreen had to wonder how far they were willing to go to keep the general public from finding out whatever they were afraid she'd find out.

Were they willing to kill her? That was the big question because, if they were, she was in trouble again. And she wasn't sure how she kept getting into that kind of trouble, but she knew, if Mack thought it was that serious, then he would put a stop to her investigation completely. The captain would back him up too.

But then again, if she could get enough details on this cold case for them to carry on with their own investigation, they wouldn't need her, and they could go after whoever this culprit was on their own. But trying to find somebody who was now lost in the mall was a whole different story.

Plus, if the driver didn't need that truck, they could just leave it behind, forgetting about it. Maybe it was stolen in the first place, in which case they only had to steal another one to get away. The mall offered an awful lot of opportunity for that to happen. Groaning, she lay here, just trying to empty her mind and to let everything that happened float freely about.

She still had a bunch of phone calls to make in order to get to the bottom of some of these answers. And one of those phone calls was to the captain. That needed to happen sooner or later, preferably sooner, before Mack got a hold of him and told him what craziness had gone down today.

With that in mind she hopped up, headed back inside to her notes and called the captain. When he answered, his voice was distracted. "Hey, Captain. It's me."

"Oh, Doreen. What's up?"

"I have a couple questions I need to talk to you about," she began. "As you're the only one I know of who was there in the days prior to all this happening, I really have to talk to you."

"Shoot," he said.

She heard a pen hitting the desk, as if he were leaning back in his chair, trying to disengage his brain from whatever had been occupying his mind.

"I was in Vernon, talking to various people connected to that time," she relayed, "all morning, in fact."

"Interesting, but I highly doubt there was anything to find."

"I definitely heard a few things, and not everybody had the same opinion of your cousin that you did."

After a moment's hesitation, he sighed. "He had another side to him that wasn't all that great, But let's not forget that he was still a kid. And kids make all kinds of mistakes."

"Absolutely. And they certainly shouldn't get killed for them."

"No, absolutely not," the captain agreed.

"So, when you say *another side* to him, the words that I heard in reference to him were *sneaky, cheater, somebody who skulked around, laughed at others, and quite probably was looking into windows that he shouldn't have been looking into*."

The captain sucked in his breath. "Oh, wow. You really were talking to people who didn't like him."

"And that's one of the things that happens when we do

this," she noted. "Everybody has a different viewpoint, and it's important that I get a rounded idea. To you, he was a cousin, a best friend, someone you saw day in and day out. So you were used to these parts of his personality. To his mother, he was perfect. She told me that Paul was the class clown, that he was good at school, that he was just one of those great all-round kids."

"Yes, and I would agree with that," the captain stated.

"And what about the other side that some of your neighbors saw that wasn't as nice?" she asked curiously. "Would you agree that Paul was sneaky and that he was somebody who cheated? Was Paul the kind of kid who would go peeking through windows that he wasn't supposed to?"

"You have to understand," the captain explained in a wry tone, "we were kids. I did that too. Not that I'm happy about it, but I would do it a little bit, and, yeah, he would do it a little bit more."

"So he would do things like this even when you weren't around, is that it?"

"Sometimes, yes. And, yes, he did like to spy on people. He thought of himself as a James Bond character," the captain shared. "And, when I look back, I realized it was all fun and games. There wasn't any animosity or evilness in him. Paul was just one of those kids to get into the role and to play it to the hilt. And, of course, let's not forget when we're talking about all that how Paul was only a ten-year-old."

"Exactly," she replied. "However, we also know that ten-year-olds who have secrets and who don't like to keep secrets or who like to torment people about secrets can also get themselves into a lot of trouble."

"Did he do that?" the captain asked in a harder tone. "I don't remember hearing anything about that at the time."

"And that's part of the problem," she noted. "At the time of the initial investigation, everybody was afraid to get in trouble by speaking ill of the dead."

He groaned. "Of course they didn't then, but what about fifteen years ago?" he asked in a waspish tone. "Did they really think that that would still be a problem?"

"In a way, yes," she agreed. "I'm still not exactly sure that I know what was going on here."

"But you seem to have brought up some issues that I didn't get anybody to talk about freely before."

"Maybe, but also remember. You're Paul's cousin. You got shot that same day. I don't think anyone would have opened up to you about Paul's *other side*," she suggested. "And I can tell you that, after today, we definitely upset some people."

"Well, you're talking about a dead child," the captain stated. "That goes with the territory."

"No, you're right there." She hesitated, wondering if she should say anything to him about the drive back to town with the truck following her and then decided not to. Mack would probably have enough to say about it as it was. "The thing is, what I need to know is, what were Paul's activities in the days and the weeks leading up to his death?"

"Activities?"

"Yes, what did you do after school every day? What would he have done if you weren't there? Would he have told you about what he did? Things like that."

"So what you're trying to figure out is, did he go to anybody's place and get into trouble, and then thought that maybe it was nothing, but somebody thought it was something."

"It's usually *something* if somebody is willing to kill over it," she noted gently.

"No, I hear you," the captain replied. "So let me think about that. You'd think that some of this stuff would be emblazoned in my brain, but somehow it seems such a long time ago and yet, at the same time, only yesterday."

"I hear you there," she murmured.

"And where are you?" he asked.

"I was sitting down at the creek behind my house," she murmured, "having a cup of coffee, but I came back in the house because I thought of all these questions in my head that really needed to be answered."

"Okay, here's one memory," the captain said. "One week we had a science project due, and he wasn't terribly impressed with the idea of doing it."

"And so this is probably where you'll talk about cheating. What did he do?"

"He decided that he had a previous year's science project that he could just modify."

"And would you say that's cheating?"

"Some people would. Some people wouldn't. In his case, Paul said it was being smart." The captain chuckled. "And, I mean, from his point of view, it was. We were kids. We wanted to play. We didn't want to spend too many hours doing homework. Why reinvent the wheel if you've already got something you can use?"

"And did the teacher find out?"

"No, the teacher didn't find out, but a bunch of the kids knew."

"Of course they did," she said. "Okay, and the sneaky part?"

"Well see, that is one of the things that he wasn't very nice about," the captain admitted, with a sigh. "I'd forgotten some of this. But somebody else had done a similar thing, and Paul tattled."

She stared down at the phone. "He tattled on somebody else for doing the same thing he did?"

"Yeah." The captain groaned. "As I said, I forgot about that part."

"Of course you did because you saw him in the best light. And so what part of all this did you have anything to do with?"

"Nothing. I did my science project. A totally new one. And I felt like I had been treated unfairly at the time too, I tell you."

She laughed out loud. "Right? Isn't it always the worst to be the one who does everything properly and to not get the credit?"

"And Paul did get the credit. That's the thing too," the captain added. "Paul was really good at making everybody believe him. And, in this situation, he did such a great job on his project, which he'd already done the previous year and just tweaked it a bit, that he ended up getting an award for it."

"Oh, ouch, I bet that pissed off some people.'

"Of course it did. It pissed off other kids."

"What about parents of other kids?" she asked.

He hesitated. "There was one father who did not take it kindly."

"Well, that's understandable though. I mean, particularly if you watched your son put in a lot of effort to find out somebody else didn't."

"I know, and, when I did talk to Paul about it and told

him how unfair it all was, he told me to grow up, and this was life, and one just needed to make the best out of things."

"Interesting," she murmured.

"I'm not feeling very good about either of our attitudes toward science projects right now, but it certainly is something that comes with age. And back then, neither of us were very old."

"No, and everything is forgivable when you're a child—or should be," she noted. "Interesting that he'd learned that kind of thing already though. And where did he learn something like that from? Was his mom like that?"

"No, she was a straight shooter, but the boyfriend was a loose cannon."

She frowned at that. "Mom's boyfriend?" she hazarded a guess.

"Although I don't remember all the details, I do remember him drinking a lot."

"Yes, I think that was part of the problem," she agreed. "Too much booze, not enough support, didn't have a job. Things like that are why your aunt Sarah booted him."

"He had a job," the captain stated. "I'm not exactly sure what it was though."

"I'll contact him as soon as I can," she stated, "but I haven't got a number for him."

"The police did talk to him back then although I don't think anything came of it."

"Sure, but the phone numbers are no longer current—unless you contacted him fifteen years ago, and maybe he still has the same cell phone number."

"Hang on a minute," he said. Then came a bunch of clicks on his end, and the captain said, "I do have a number. I don't know if it's still active though." And he rattled it off for her.

She wrote it down and replied, "Good enough. Now, what about other people, other neighbors, things like that?"

"I don't remember much, but I don't think any of the neighbors would know much about Paul or even me from back then," the captain replied.

"What about peeking in where he shouldn't be? Anything like that happen the weekend before or the weeks before Paul was killed? Did you guys ever go into, I don't know, say, deserted houses? Did you ever listen in on conversations? Did he ever, I hate to say it, spy on his mother?"

Dead silence ensued on the other end. "I don't know about spying on his mother, but he was upset for a while though."

"Upset, why?"

"Something about his mom and her boyfriend splitting. Paul was close to him."

"So Sarah told me that she and the boyfriend had already had problems prior to Paul's death, so that kind of makes sense too that she'd dump him after losing Paul."

"But did she mention that Paul was upset about the breakup?" the captain asked her.

"No, she didn't, but she did say that she should have done it a long time ago. So I mean, short of asking her specifically if they'd had problems, I'm not sure what that would do to help the investigation. I also have her journals here, but I haven't had a chance to go through them."

"She kept a journal?"

"Yes. I don't know whether or not it was offered to you guys fifteen years ago or not, but she found them here a few years ago, boxed them up, and would have just thrown them in the garbage, but hung on to them because, of course, her son's murder is not resolved yet."

"No, of course not. That would be interesting to see too."

"I'll scan them in, so that we have digital copies."

"Good idea. And I'd like a copy."

"Yeah, I can do that too," Doreen noted, "just need a little bit of time to get to that. So phone calls and then scanning. I'm pretty tired after being at Nan's and up in Vernon today," she stated quietly.

"Anything else?"

"No, I don't … I don't think so."

"And, yes, you're right. Paul could be a little bit of a brat. He was my friend, so I didn't think of it that way. Yet now, as I look back, well, yeah, it's pretty easy to see that he wouldn't have always left great impressions because of the way he acted sometimes."

"I don't think that that's all bad either," she murmured. "Sometimes life is just like that."

"It's more than *just like that*," the captain noted. "And, even myself, as I look back, I can distance from it all, get a better view. And I still feel the guilt."

"And why is that?" she asked.

"Because I haven't been able to solve Paul's murder," he replied. "What else?"

"That's what I'm just checking," she said quietly. "Was there anything that you were involved in as a child that might have been part of this?"

"No. And my parents kept me on a much shorter leash."

"Did you go out in the evenings with Paul?"

"Only if we were right at the front of the house or in the backyard—but only until eight p.m. I had to be in the house by eight o'clock every night."

"And what about Paul?"

"Nope, not at all. And, with Aunt Sarah working, sometimes she had to do night shifts. So Paul would be out a lot of times quite late."

"And did he like that?"

"I think he did and he didn't. It was both fun and a pain because he had to be alone all the time."

"What about the boyfriend?"

The captain pondered that. "Sometimes he was there, and sometimes he wasn't, but I don't remember where he might have been at the time. My parents were an absolute law, and Paul's mom and boyfriend weren't."

"Right," she murmured, wondering how a child like Paul could get a very different look at life. "Okay, that's probably it for the moment," she said, looking down at her notes. "If I come up with more questions, I'll contact you."

"Well, you've certainly given me lots to think about," he noted quietly. "And thanks for that."

"I think sometimes we become a little too sure that we know what's going on, and then—when you talk to other people and hear other viewpoints—you wonder if you even knew the same person at all," she suggested. "So I'm not trying to ruin your day by any means, but it's definitely something that we need to keep an open mind about."

"No, I hear you. I just hadn't realized how much I had protected him in my head, as being my cousin but also that good friend of mine, and, therefore, because he was dead, he could do no wrong."

Doreen added, "And in my head, somebody went after a child, and the only reason to go after a child is because that child knows something, has done something, or will do something. So, if Paul would've told anybody, talked to anybody, mention something to anybody, get big money from somewhere, or get a free pass to something," she suggested, "you need to let that roll around in your brain for a while."

"None of that sounds familiar at all," he muttered, "but you're right. I'll let it roll around in my brain and see what comes up."

"Good, and I'll talk to you in a little bit." And, with that, she hung up.

Almost immediately she reached for her phone again, and, as she was about to make a phone call, she heard a sound behind her. Mugs hopped to his feet and started barking. Slowly, very slowly, she turned, but nobody was there. Mugs raced to the kitchen, and she followed, wondering if she had even thought—when she was so exhausted—to lock up the front door.

Mack would have a heyday with her if she hadn't. But she walked to the front picture window and saw no sign of anybody, yet Mugs continued to bark terribly at the front door. Hating to, she peered through the windows again and couldn't see anything, but there was no doubt that Mugs was bothered by something. She opened the door and let him out and peered outside but found no one there. Mugs immediately raced to the front porch steps, sniffing heavily, and then down the steps to the driveway and on to the end of the driveway. There, he milled around in a circle.

"Was somebody here?" she whispered.

She quickly called him back to her, but he took a minute before he was calm enough to make his way back to her, and his back was still bristled.

"Well, whoever it was, you didn't like them being here

at all. Not only did you *not* like them being here but you didn't like anything about them."

Sighing, she turned and brought him back inside, and this time she locked up and set the alarm. But now she didn't want to go back down to the creek. She poured herself a second cup of coffee and headed to her laptop. As she looked outside, she saw somebody walking along the creek past her property, studiously not looking in her direction.

For some reason, that made her suspicious. Of course now she was worried that whoever had followed them in town from Vernon had also followed her here to her home. How could that be? Then she realized that she had left her vehicle parked in the garage but had yet to close the door. And that was not good.

She immediately got up to rectify that problem.

However, that meant that somebody, if they were looking for her, could have easily recognized her vehicle and now knew where she lived.

# Chapter 15

LATER THAT EVENING, at almost 7:30 p.m., Mugs bounded to his feet and started barking like crazy. Doreen stared at him and slowly got up from her chair and walked to the living room window, where she peered out. Something was odd about his bark, but, at the same time, it was a calmer, happier bark. And, with relief, she saw Mack pull up. She opened the front door and stepped out. "Hey," she asked, "is everything okay?"

He nodded. "Yes, it is, and yet, at the same time, it isn't."

"Ah," she muttered. "Meaning, you didn't catch him."

He shook his head. "He disappeared into the mall, and, we tried hard, but we found no sign of him."

"Right. Did you get the vehicle at least?"

He nodded. "It was stolen but from so long ago," he noted, looking at her carefully, as if she would understand, "that we don't have any leads to go on."

"What about the people it was stolen from?"

He grimaced. "Both deceased."

"Ouch." She crossed her arms, her fingers tapping her arm. She studied his face, as he slowly walked toward her.

"What are you not telling me?"

He looked up at her. "The vehicle was stolen forty years ago."

Her eyebrows shot up. "And, under that flat-black paint, I suppose it's a pale blue-gray?"

He winced. "We didn't even have to look too hard or to take any paint off because they hadn't done a great paint job, and the undercoating was still visible in spots."

"So I really did piss somebody off today, didn't I?" she asked, and then she grinned at him. "And that's the good news."

He glared at her. "Says you. I'll talk to the captain and have him stop this."

"I wouldn't do that if I were you," she suggested, glaring right back at him. "We need this solved. Come on board maybe. But take me off? No."

He put his hands on his hips, shaking his head.

She shrugged. "You can get as upset as you want. The captain asked me to look into it, and obviously something that I've done is helping."

"How can you say this is helping?" he asked in an ominous tone.

"Because you and I both know that somebody is running scared."

He stared off in the distance. "I'll talk to the captain in the morning."

"You can do that," she said. "I've already talked to him today. I asked him a bunch of questions, things that I needed answers for. I know he's mulling over his relationship with that childhood friend of his."

At that, Mack's gaze swung back to her. "What do you mean?"

"Let's just say that some people had a different view of that boy and what he was like than others did."

"Meaning that he deserved to get killed?"

"No, of course not," she stated, with a frown. "And you're here now, so you might as well come in."

At that, he asked, "Is there a reason you don't want to stand out here?"

She nodded. "Yeah, because it's been an odd day."

Taking that at face value, he stepped in and sat down at a kitchen chair. "Now tell me what you found out."

When she hesitated, he narrowed his gaze at her. "This is no longer something you get to just go off and be a wild cowboy on," he declared. "Somebody followed you home."

"And they may have followed me *all* the way home," she added quietly. "It is definitely something I'm considering."

"What do you mean?"

She told him about the scenario earlier. "Yet I will be the first to admit that it could have been just nerves. It's been a rough day."

He pondered that. "But you didn't close your garage, so if somebody did see your vehicle—"

She nodded. "If somebody did see, they would have recognized my car. However, it would take a lot for them to get over here and to find me."

He frowned. "There isn't any direct correlation, so it is pretty unusual for somebody to come up to this cul-de-sac and find out who you are or where you live."

"Exactly. So I don't feel like that is a worry."

"And yet you're worried."

"No, I'm tired. It's been a long day, and I was worried at the mall because you went tearing off inside, and I had no idea what happened."

"And I'm not sure we have any answers for you either at this point."

"And what are we doing about the truck, if anything?" she asked quietly.

"It'll be towed, and forensics will go over it, but they're not expecting much."

"Of course not. Just because it was stolen forty years ago doesn't mean that it's necessarily involved."

"And yet how do we *not* assume that?" he asked, with a wry look.

She nodded. "Believe me. I understand. I mean, I talked to a lot of people today, have a bunch to still talk to."

"And who's on your list yet?"

She explained about Sarah's boyfriend. And she had a few more questions for the grandfather, and she wanted to check with Thurlow's daughter, who had the power of attorney.

"Interesting that you hooked up with them."

"It's just a name I found in a newspaper article. They had spoken to the reporter way back then, and that put them on my radar."

He nodded slowly.

She got up, brought out the sheets of paperwork that the librarian had printed out for her, and showed them to Mack. "Honest."

He smiled. "I believe you. What did the captain say about the stuff you found?"

"I think he was shaken up, as he was forced to confront the fact that this cousin, his good childhood friend, may not have been the perfect citizen that the captain remembered him to be."

"Friends are like that though," Mack pointed out. "You

may think you know everything about them, until something happens, and their lives get torn apart."

"And, in this case, Paul may not have been all that nice of a kid," she added. "Did he have lots of room to grow and to change? If he had lived, yes. I certainly don't blame him in any way, and he was alone a lot, while his mother was at work, and obviously under the influence of other adults."

"Meaning, the boyfriend and possibly his son."

"Well, the boyfriend's definitely a part of this," she noted in a contemplative tone. "I just don't know how much of a part."

He stared at her for a long moment. "Do you really think he is?"

She frowned. "Let's just say, I need to talk to him before I figure out which role he plays in this. I don't know. Was he just a babysitter? What are the chances that he was involved in drugs and did drug deals out of the house? Sarah was gone all the time, and, if this boyfriend was trying to make a little bit of money—and I don't know that he was because, according to her, he didn't work and didn't do anything—but how does a grown man do that? He had a vehicle. How'd he pay for insurance on it?" She shook her head. "I mean, when it comes to all that stuff, I haven't had much experience, but I highly doubt that Sarah had money to pay for his car insurance too."

"Those are very good questions," Mack noted. "I think at the time he had a job though."

"Maybe, yet she told me that he didn't work. So did he work? Didn't he work? Or was it just one of those kinds of jobs where he worked when something needed to be done?"

"And there was lots of that back in the day too," he agreed. "And when people say, *They don't work*, it could just mean, from Sarah's point of view, that he didn't work *enough.*"

Doreen smiled. "See? That's the thing. I mean, until I talk to the boyfriend, I don't know what he's got to say. The police did check in with him fifteen years ago, when it was all brought back up again."

Mack looked at her. "And nothing triggered for the captain back then?"

She shook her head. "No, nothing triggered then. And I'm not saying that any of this would have triggered anybody. What we have is a dead child. Now whether that boy was in the wrong place at the wrong time—and the captain was as well—or whether it was a warning or a lesson, I don't know." She raised both hands in frustration. "We don't have enough information yet."

"And yet," Mack added, "you've managed to stir up more trouble in the short time you've had this in your hands than anybody managed to get done years ago."

"And I think part of that is decided by the people you talk to—and who's asking the questions—so you get a whole different perspective on what's going on. So then you have to ask different questions." She shrugged. "At the time of the original investigation, everybody said Paul was the best of kids."

"And yet this Thurlow guy didn't seem to think so."

"And when I talked to the captain about it, he could see that maybe other people had a different perspective on Paul. In the captain's own mind, Paul was the best guy ever, and he died and should be almost immortalized for being who he was. But, for people now, with time and distance from the murder, where they don't feel like they're doing something wrong by giving a different version of the truth," she suggested, "Paul's not quite seen in the same light."

He sighed. "And we see that a lot, don't we?"

"Always on the cold cases," she noted. "It makes you wonder at the mind-set of these people, when this stuff goes down. They do everything they can to preserve the memory of the victim, and yet a killer goes free."

Mack stayed for a little bit longer, and then he slowly stood, stretched, and said, "I've got to get home. I've got a couple early morning meetings."

She nodded. "And I need to get some sleep. My brain is on overdrive."

"Will you make those calls tonight?"

She frowned. "I'll probably wait until the morning," she replied cautiously. "I just don't want to trigger anything else tonight."

"What a good idea," he quipped, with a wry look.

She glared at him. "I'm not trying to cause trouble, you know?"

He reached out and tugged her into his arms and gave her a hug. "I know you're not. You just have that special knack."

She groaned. "And yet we have to expect a certain amount of this fighting back."

"And we do." Mack nodded. "And the fact that you're stirring up something is, as you and I know, both good and bad. And to get to the bottom of this, we have to make sure that whatever we stir up gets to the surface and gets purged. This case can't be allowed to go back under for another fifteen or forty years."

"Exactly," she agreed, as she wandered out to the front porch with him and watched as he left.

He called out just before he got into the vehicle, "Friday

night we'll cook beef stroganoff. Saturday we're going out, right?"

He got into his truck, without looking at her, but she knew he was waiting for her response. She shook her head. "Right."

He looked over, beamed her a smile, lifted a hand in a wave, and, with that, he was gone.

# Chapter 16

***Thursday Morning …***

DOREEN WOKE UP the next morning groggy, tired, as if she had been running all night. And she probably had, at least in her mind, she admitted to herself. Everything was floating around in her brain, making it seem like she was running double-time and not getting anywhere. And yet she knew *not getting anywhere* was not the truth because somebody was getting somewhere; she just didn't know if it was the place they wanted to be. And that left her feeling odd too.

Just something so weird was going on right now, and yet what she knew was that secrets were being uncovered, and things that had been covered up wouldn't be covered up anymore, and that was making somebody very nervous. Especially when there was absolutely no walking away from a murder charge just because it had been forty years ago.

That was the good thing. The bad thing was that she knew the most dangerous time of all was yet to come. She quickly made coffee, opened up the back door, and headed out to the deck. With the animals in tow, she still yawned—and her crew was not quite awake themselves—as the four of them sat outside and just tried to get a grip on the fact that it was already morning.

She looked down at Mugs. "I don't know where the night went, but it sure feels like I didn't get any sleep."

He woofed, almost in commiseration.

She smiled. "You're a good boy." She reached down to pet him gently.

He yawned, stretched out on the deck, king of all he surveyed. And she wished that sometimes he could tell her what it was he was thinking because he was very perceptive. It was foolish to think that the dog could solve these crimes, but sometimes she thought that, if only he and she could effectively communicate, he could solve a lot of this stuff. Dogs knew things, and sometimes they knew more than the people did.

Finally, with a second cup of coffee, her brain was turning on. She pulled out her phone, grabbed her notes, and quickly dialed the boyfriend, Cleve Massey. When a cranky voice answered on the other end, she winced. "I'm sorry. Did I wake you?"

"Of course you woke me," Cleve snapped. "Nobody's up at this hour."

She sighed. "Well, some of us are."

"Who are you, and what do you want?" he snapped at her again.

She winced. "I was in Vernon yesterday. And I have reopened the case of Paul Hephtner's murder."

A long moment of silence followed at the other end. "Jesus, not this nonsense again," Cleve muttered.

She bristled at that. "Well, considering a young boy died, it was a long time ago, and anybody who might still know something won't likely be around for much longer," she declared, "yeah, that *nonsense* is here again."

"Look. I'm not trying to be insensitive, but I didn't have anything to do with it. And, as much as I wanted all that solved a long time ago, I don't have any help to offer."

"No, and I get that," she replied. "I'm just trying to cross my *T*s and dot my *I*s."

"Sure you are," Cleve growled, "and that's why you called me."

"The same as I have called everybody else I knew to call," she stated. "So don't think you're special."

He burst out with a wry laugh. "I sure wish I wasn't special in this kind of a scenario. The cops looked at me pretty hard last time."

"But they let you walk, so I presume they didn't find anything," she stated immediately.

"Yeah, that's because there wasn't anything to find," Cleve replied. "Paul was a good kid."

"Well, I'm certainly getting a mixed view of that," she noted.

"What do you mean?" Cleve asked, his tone sharp. "Who would say something wrong against him?"

"It's not so much that people would say anything wrong, but now, as time has gone by, people are a little bit more open to talking about how maybe Paul wasn't quite the perfect kid as everybody was led to believe in the beginning."

"Yet he was just a kid. That's all that anybody needs to know. He's not responsible for any of his actions. He was just a kid, trying to figure out how life worked."

"And I'm totally in agreement with you," she affirmed quietly. "I certainly wouldn't blame a kid, no matter what."

Cleve seemed somewhat mollified by that. "Well then, don't go saying that he was to blame for this."

"I didn't and I won't," she stated, "not at all. But I do wonder what he was involved in, considering he was known to be secretive and sneaking around, cheating on various things, and bugging people about secrets that he'd gone to lengths to get from people."

Cleve started to bluster.

"And, yes, that's been corroborated by several people," she murmured. "I have to wonder who might have been pissed off or made wary by his behavior, thinking that Paul might have tattled or seen something he shouldn't have."

At that came an odd silence. "I always wondered about that," Cleve said.

"Always wondered about what?" Doreen asked, her curiosity piqued.

"I wondered whether he'd seen something. He was good at sneaking around. Matter of fact, I'd used him a couple times for a few deals."

"What kind of deals?"

"I didn't do drugs, if that's what you're thinking," he stated. "However, I had some jobs where I would get paid for information, and sometimes I would have Paul listen in on conversations when I wasn't there, so I could hear what they were saying about me. Maybe it wasn't the best thing for me to include Paul because maybe it got him into trouble. I've often worried about that." And he added, "There's nothing like time going by to make you realize that you should have done other things instead."

"Would anybody in your group of friends, acquaintances, coworkers, or employers have noticed what Paul was doing?"

"I don't know," Cleve said.

"And why didn't you say something about it back then?"

"What was I supposed to say?" he asked. "I didn't know if it had anything to do with nothing. I still don't."

"No, but we are now getting a very different view of this boy and what he might have been doing in the days leading up to that drive-by shooting. Would you have had anybody in your acquaintances back then who may have owned a gun and might have been involved in something like that?"

"I don't know about anybody owning a gun," he replied, "but lots of people hunted. So lots of people had guns."

"Exactly what kind of work were you doing back then?"

Cleve hesitated.

"If there's any chance of solving Paul's murder," Doreen added, "now is the time. We're out of options, out of people to talk to, and the ones who are left as potential witnesses are dying rapidly."

He groaned. "I wasn't doing anything bad."

"No? That's fine. However, if it was in any way connected to this murder, we need to know about it."

"I already told the police about it back then."

Her eyebrows shot up. "Okay, that's good. That's great. I would hope so."

"But I don't think they understood."

"What do you mean?"

"I worked for a construction company, and I did a lot of work for them," he explained, "but I wasn't full-time. So I worked when there was work, and I didn't work when there wasn't work."

"And when there wasn't work, what did you do?"

He hesitated. "I kept my ears open for information," he shared reluctantly.

"Interesting," she said slowly. "What kind of information? And were you paid for it?"

"Yes," he replied, "when the information was decent."

"What kind of information?"

"Just, you know, stuff."

"Okay, *stuff*," she repeated. "Where did you hang out and hear this stuff?"

"The pool halls."

"Interesting," she murmured. "What kind of information could you possibly find out down there?"

"That was the thing. Like, I spent a lot of time there, and, when I didn't get any information that the boss wanted, he would pay me a little bit to keep trying. Every once in a while I found information that was good, and the payoff was decent."

"And did you find this information, or did Paul find it?"

Cleve hesitated, then reluctantly admitted, "Paul did."

"Right. So Paul found out something, told you about it. Then you went to this guy, your boss, told him, and he paid you. Correct?"

"Yeah, but it really had nothing to do with anything."

"And what was it about?"

"Just some guy having an affair."

"Okay, and why was that of interest to anybody?"

"Because he was high up in a company that was giving my boss some trouble."

"Ah, so blackmail."

"I don't know," he snapped. "That wasn't my deal. The boss wanted to know a little bit about it. I got a little bit of information, and that was it."

"Fine, I get that, but what did Paul have to do to get it?"

"This guy's girlfriend was a teacher at his school."

Doreen winced. "And what was her name?"

"Shelley, Shelley Brewster."

"Okay, and that then gives Paul an opportunity to what? To listen in on a conversation that she had?"

"No, that wasn't it. The kid followed her home one day. And I picked him up from there."

"*Great.*" Doreen grimaced. "And what did that do?"

"Oh, just confirmed that she was having an affair with this guy, and my boss was thrilled because this guy had been all kinds of trouble and wouldn't let him approve some development permits. So my boss was looking for information to apply some pressure—but nobody would kill over that," he stated. "It's not as if we did anything illegal."

She frowned at that. "I don't know about illegal. It certainly was not ethical."

"Not a whole lot of ethics in this situation," he admitted. "And I knew the kid was just having fun, pretending to be James Bond, who was his idol back then."

"Right. So he wanted to be a spy, and you gave him somebody to spy on, but he ended up dead."

"I didn't have nothing to do with that."

"No, no, I hear you, but this seems to be a likely connection."

"But you don't know that. You don't know anything about it."

"No, and for that," she stated, "you'll have to talk to me some more. Did his mother know?"

"No, of course not," he replied hurriedly. "She'd have cleaned my clock if she did. As far as she was concerned, Paul was going places. He would be, like, a cop or something."

"Right," she murmured. "And what did he want to do?"

"He wanted to work for the Secret Service."

She raised her eyebrows at that. "Okay, not exactly something that most kids say at the age of ten."

"I don't think he would have ended up there either," Cleve noted, "but Paul certainly had a lot of fun, when we were out doing our stuff."

"And what about you? You had a son too, right?"

"Yeah, sure did, but we didn't have him with us all the time. He was with his mom much of the time."

"And who was his mom?"

"Lilly Madison. What difference does it make?"

"I'm just trying to know all the players. How often did you see your son?"

"Every weekend. And Paul's mom worked most weekends, so then my son would spend the weekend with me and Paul."

"So did you get your son involved in this side business of yours too?"

First came silence, and then he groaned. "Yes."

"Okay, and what's your son's name?"

"Jack Madison. Lilly gave him her surname on account we weren't married."

"And what was Jack like?"

"A good kid," he stated immediately.

"Sure, he might have been a good kid, but you also got him mixed up in this mess."

A hard gasp came from Cleve on the other end. "That's not fair."

"No, maybe not," she murmured. "But, at the moment, you and I both know that this could have easily played into Paul's death. Who was this guy you were trying to get the information on?"

"His name was Peter Hall, and he was married. His wife was pretty big with one of the local mills, and he wouldn't want to mess things up with his marriage. So keeping the affair quiet was paramount."

"What was the end result from the information you gave the boss?"

"The boss was really happy, and we got a bonus. I took the kids out for treats."

"Right, and how many days before the shooting did all this info-sharing go down?"

He sighed. "Two days. … Two days later Paul was dead."

"And where was Jack at that point?"

"He was back with his mom. Told my boss that Saturday. Jack went home late Sunday. Paul was shot Monday."

Doreen nodded, even though Cleve couldn't see her. "And tell me more about Jack back then. His age at this time? Any physical features that would make Jack stand out?"

"He was a couple years older than Paul, but Jack was small for his age."

"So they were about the same size?" Doreen asked.

"What?" Cleve asked. "Do you think they mistook Paul for Jack?"

"No, I'm not saying that," Doreen stated, but she was pretty sure that what she was *not* saying *yet* could be a good assumption. However, it was too early for that. "Look. I'll pass this information on to the police department here. So I need you to stay close to a phone. And tell me something. Did either of these men, your boss or Peter Hall, drive a light-blue truck?"

"No, they didn't. That doesn't mean they didn't know someone who drove a light-blue truck."

"And you've thought about this a lot over the last few years, haven't you?"

"Maybe," he admitted, his voice heavy. "Paul was a good kid. I wouldn't want anything I did to have brought this down on him."

"Yeah, well, might be a little too late for that."

"But it makes no sense, or Jack should have been killed too back then."

"And you have talked to Jack since, right?"

He frowned. "Yeah." But a hesitation filled his tone.

"Okay, that didn't sound very positive."

"Jack was killed in a car accident. About …" He hesitated. "I don't know, maybe thirty years ago."

"Oh my. I'm so sorry," she murmured. "Do you think there's any connection?"

"No, I don't think so. I don't know why there would be."

"Did Jack get along with Paul?"

"Absolutely. And, if you had said Jack was a bit of a loudmouth and a talker," Cleve added, "I might have agreed with you there. His mom, Lilly, was like that too. She gossiped about everything."

At that, Doreen winced. "Any chance that Jack might have said something to his mom?"

Cleve sucked in his breath. "I don't know. You're thinking that it's … that it goes back to this information that we got?"

"I won't say yes, but I won't say no either right now," she replied. "Do you know anybody who has a truck with a flat paint job—the ones that don't glow, that don't have a shine to them. Like some kid took a can of spray paint to them."

"No, I don't think so," he replied, surprised. "Why?"

"Just wondering," she murmured. "Something happened

here in the last few days."

"Ha. I know lots of these guys had trucks, and some of them had old trucks. But you know what? That's not exactly the kind of truck anybody wants to be hanging around in. The guys were all pretty *truck proud*."

"Right. Like I said, stay close to your phone. I'm pretty sure some people will want to talk to you." And, with that, she hung up.

She pondered that information, while she finished her second cup of coffee, and then decided that it would probably be easier to talk to the captain and Mack both at the office. She sent Mack a text message. **Can I come in and see you and the captain?**

She got a surprised **Yes** back.

And then he asked, **Are you all right?**

She was, but, at the same time, she wasn't. She sent back a thumbs-up sign. **Can you arrange the meeting so I can talk to the two of you at the same time? It'll save trouble.**

**Did you find out something?**

She sent back a **Maybe.**

**Fine, come on then. The captain and I will be here for the next hour, and then I have to go out.**

She looked longingly at her kitchen and realized that she would have to go now because, if Mack had to leave soon, then she wouldn't have a chance to get through the whole story, if she didn't get it done now.

So, with that, she looked at the animals, frowned, and then said, "Forget that. Come on, guys."

# Chapter 17

DOREEN GRABBED THE leashes, loaded everybody up into her car, and drove down to the police station.

Mack was outside, waiting for her. He rushed over. "Are you okay?"

She smiled up at him. "I'm fine."

"No more strange occurrences overnight?"

She shrugged. "I don't think so. I haven't noticed it anyway. I just loaded everybody up and came down."

"Okay, good." He stopped, looked at her, and asked, "Did you close the garage door?"

She frowned and then nodded. "I think so, but I can't be sure. I was so concerned about coming here and talking to you guys that it didn't occur to me."

Mack shrugged. He led her into a small meeting room and said, "The captain will be here in a minute."

When the captain walked in, he asked, "Doreen, do you have information on Paul's murder?"

She nodded.

"In that case, let's get the team in here."

She winced. "But it needs to be confirmed. I'm just thinking that you guys probably want a hand in this."

"I definitely do," the captain stated, "but let's go over here." And he led her to a larger conference room and let out a shout and told everybody to pile in.

She was surprised at the way he'd acted in such a cavalier manner, accepting her word without any details. "What if I'm wrong?" she asked Mack.

"Are you?" he asked.

She glared at him. "You know it'll happen one day," she muttered.

He chuckled. "Let's hope not on this one."

"Yeah, I know." She shook her head. As she turned around, there was Arnold, Chester, Jim, and a few others she knew.

They all looked at her and said, "Hey, Doreen."

"Hey, guys." At that greeting, she dropped the leashes.

Mugs immediately visited with everybody. She smiled at him. "You'd think the dog never got any attention. Although, after yesterday, it was kind of a rough day."

"And speaking of which," the captain added, with a glare in her direction, "you could have told me about that."

"I figured Mack would make an official report, as soon as he got back to the office. And I didn't want to get off-topic in our phone conversation."

He swung his arm wide. "Well, the floor is yours. What have you got for us?"

She took a deep breath and began, "Outside of the fact that we had a lovely drive home from Vernon yesterday, I had some phone calls still to make. One to the captain, and then I phoned Sarah's ex-boyfriend."

"Right, and what did the boyfriend have to say?" the captain asked, eyeing her curiously. "You know we grilled him several times."

She nodded. "At the time that you were grilling him though, you were grilling him thinking that this childhood friend of yours was the best guy on earth, right?"

He looked at her and slowly nodded. "But I'm not even now prepared to say that he wasn't."

"No, of course not." Doreen gave him a misty smile. "And I am fully prepared to believe that any ten-year-old, no matter what kind of trouble he gets into, didn't fully understand the risks."

"Okay, now you really need to back up and to give us all the details," Mack stated, looking over at the captain. "Maybe you should start with yesterday afternoon."

She groaned. "Okay, I need coffee then." He rolled his eyes but got up and poured her a cup. She took a hesitant sip, realizing it wasn't as bad as she had expected. Then she started with her activities from yesterday—the view of the crime scene, her meeting with Sarah and getting her journals, the meeting later that morning with the Thurlows, and then the drive home, so that everybody was on the same page. Of course she couldn't forget about Lizzie where she'd found out about Cleve's son.

At this point in time Chester looked at her worriedly. "Sounds like you're in danger again. This has to stop."

"Oh, I agree," she said. "Of course the good thing is, as you know, we're upsetting somebody."

He subsided at that and muttered, "Yeah, but you upset a lot of people.'

She glared at him, and he just grinned at her impudently. She raised her palms and sighed. "Fine. Anyway, to get back to my story, I did clarify with the captain some things about Paul's character, and then I phoned the mother's ex-boyfriend. He worked in construction, when they needed an extra laborer, but he was not really on the payroll full-time. So when there was construction work, he worked, and, when there wasn't work, he didn't get work. That was part of the strife between him and his girlfriend, Paul's mother.

"Seeing how the roof over his head was his girlfriend's house, he did a little bit of other work on the side. However, when you would have checked his construction job and found out if he worked there, you would have got the first story, but you would not have gotten the second story."

At that, the captain straightened and glared at her.

She held up a hand and explained, "He was a snitch, got paid for information."

Silence settled in the room.

"And sometimes to find that information, he got both his son, Jack, and Sarah's son, Paul, to help."

"Oh, good Lord." The captain stared at her in shock.

"And the information he got regarded a Shelley Brewster, who was a teacher at your elementary school," she shared, looking over the captain.

He nodded. "Sure, I remember her. She was beautiful. We were all young kids, but still, we were all half in love with her."

"Apparently she was having an affair with a married man, and that married man was fairly prominent in town and was married to somebody who had very big connections to one of the mills in town."

He stared at her. "Peter Hall?"

She laughed. "Bull's-eye."

The other constables and officers turned to look at the captain.

"And how did you know that?" Doreen asked the captain.

He slumped against the table, half hitched on it, and replied, "Because Paul used to talk about them all the time. He would laugh and say that he knew a secret. I didn't even think of it, not even after you mentioned that aspect of his personality, and I still would have sworn that he knew absolutely nothing," he stated. "But the minute you mentioned that teacher's name, Paul and I saw her and sometimes Hall at school every once in a while, but we didn't see them *together*."

The captain paced. "Just that, you know, Hall would be there, since his son went to that school as well. But they weren't our friends. We were the poor kids on the wrong side of town, and they were the wealthy kids, the kids who had an *in* in life and were on the fast track to be successful. I, at least, had two parents who were stable and who gave me a decent childhood, whereas Paul didn't have even that much. Not only did Paul not have these advantages, but this boyfriend – a man Paul really looked up to – and his son Jack were also part of all this.

"And yet we can't talk to Jack," Doreen noted.

"Why is that?" Arnold asked.

"He died in a car accident, quite a few years ago. What I'd like to know is whether that vehicle that you guys impounded yesterday"—she turned and looked at Mack—"if there's any way to know if that truck would have been in a car accident, from like thirty years ago, or if underneath all that flat-black paint is the light-blue paint of the vehicle used by Paul's shooter?"

"But that still doesn't explain why I was shot," the captain added.

"It does though," she said sadly. "I don't suppose you and Paul were about the same height, were you?"

"I was a little bit bigger. Why?"

"Because Jack and Paul were living together in the same house, mostly on the weekends, and you were in front of Paul's house. And Jack and Paul were known to be involved in this snitch business," she explained. "So I think whoever it was who shot at you two decided that he had found the right place with the right boys. He took his shots, and he took off, and one was the right boy and one the wrong boy. You were in the wrong place at the wrong time because Cleve's son had already gone home to his mom for the week. He was there for weekends only. Paul and you were shot on Monday."

The captain slowly nodded his head. "That's true. Jack did spend a lot of time there. And the original investigators did talk to him at the time, and I'm sure he was just as traumatized."

Doreen nodded. "And also another consideration as to how somebody found out about the kids. Paul and Jack were known to talk about secrets, and Jack was known to spread a lot of gossip. Even more so did Jack's mom. So it's quite possible that Jack told his mom what was going on, and she might have ripped into her son, or he may have given her a truncated version of what happened, and it leaked to somebody else. At that point in time the shooter knew who the culprits were spreading secrets, and went after the two boys."

The captain just stared at her in shock. He looked over at Mack, back at her, and then got up and walked out of the room.

She opened her mouth, closed it quietly, turned to Mack. "I'm sorry."

He walked over, put an arm around her shoulders, and

gave her a brief hug. "It's not your fault."

She slumped in place. "It's not my fault, but it is. It always is. You know that."

He smiled. "But just think? We might get to the bottom of this now." He looked over at the rest of the officers, who were still writing down notes.

"And that's why you wanted to come in this morning, isn't it?" Chester asked. "Here I figured you would give us all grief because we didn't know who owned that vehicle left at the mall yet."

"It was stolen," Doreen noted, "which makes sense. But it's also been held by somebody for all these years. So it'll be somebody who's got space to store it for that long. Somebody who wields a mean spray can of ugly paint. … And I don't know whether this person was some third party hired to shoot Paul or one or more of the players in this mess. Was it the schoolteacher girlfriend rich man Peter Hall was having an affair with, or perhaps Peter himself? Or—hate to say it, guys—a very disgruntled wife who decided to shoot the messenger? And the rest of her rich family might not want anything like that secret to go public either."

"Right," Chester replied, while the men gathered here continued to write down notes. Chester grinned at her and added, "At least you left us a little bit to do."

She smiled. "I left you a lot to do. Plus I'm pretty sure that I had somebody at my house last night, twice, either looking to see if I lived there, looking to see if I was a danger to my visitor or something," she guessed. "So the sooner you guys find this jerk, the better."

At that, they looked at her in alarm.

She shrugged. "Never any good news comes out of stuff like this," she noted quietly. "The other thing that we have to keep in mind is that somebody who has killed once may very well have done it twice or more. We do have another suspicious death—Jack Madison. And I don't even know if any of these other people involved are still on this planet today."

She looked at Mack. "For all I know, the couple with the cheating husband have since divorced, and who cares now? Yet somebody is trying to hide their tracks from long ago. And that somebody is the one I want to go down for this." She looked from one cop to the other in this room and added, "You know perfectly well that the captain needs something in order to find closure himself."

They all nodded slowly.

And she got up, handed the coffee cup back to Mack, and said, "That's not a terrible cup of coffee. However, I'll go visit Nan and do something that makes my heart feel good right now."

And, with that, she waved at the others. "If you've got any other questions, write them down and give me a shout."

And she walked out of the station.

# Chapter 18

IT WAS HARD to admit, but Doreen's heart felt pretty heavy at the thought of somebody killing a child because of something they may have overheard and then passed on to somebody else. And Doreen wasn't even sure whether it was just about the affair or that anything else was involved in Paul's murder. …What she really needed right now was something to make her heart feel better. With the animals uncharacteristically quiet beside her, she dropped her car off home then walked to Rosemoor.

Mugs immediately ran across the lawn and jumped over the little barrier into Nan's patio and started barking at the door. Goliath, not to be outdone, raced in the opposite direction, turned around and then came racing back, as if to tell Mugs that he was going in the wrong direction.

As it was, Goliath's antics got worse, as he raced across the lawn, did a funny pivot, and then raced back again. Doreen could only hope that the gardener wasn't here. With Thaddeus on her shoulder, she walked on the stepping stones, careful to ensure that she stayed on the stones, all the way over to Nan's little patio.

Nan had the patio door open now and was welcoming

Mugs with a great deal of affection, as she always did. She looked up at Doreen and asked, "To what do I owe this unexpected visit?"

Doreen shrugged. "Let's just say I need a cup of tea."

Nan, always perceptive, looked at her and frowned. "Ouch. Not a good day, huh?"

"It's a fine day," Doreen replied, "but sometimes humanity sucks."

Nan stared at her for a long moment and then waved her granddaughter over. "Come. Sit down. I'll put on the teakettle." And she disappeared from view, with Mugs following her inside.

It wasn't a sunny day, but it wasn't a gray day either. It was lovely enough that sitting outside was a pleasure. Doreen sat down on the patio chair and automatically pulled a couple weeds from Nan's flower boxes.

As Nan came out, she chuckled. "Do you ever do anything but work?"

"I know. Right? Which is kind of bizarre," Doreen noted, "because I didn't even get a chance to work for all those years I was married."

"A lot of women would have preferred that."

Doreen looked over at Nan, and her lips quirked. "At the time I didn't even know what I was missing." Then she spied another little weed and plucked it. She handed the weeds to Nan and asked, "Can you throw those into the garbage?"

"Sure can." Nan glanced around, saw the gardener on the far side, and, while he watched her, Nan threw the weeds out onto the lawn.

"Oh, Nan," Doreen muttered, with a heavy sigh.

"You could have done it yourself at the same time," Nan

suggested, with a fat grin.

"Are we trying to piss him off?" Doreen asked her.

As the gardener raised a fist at her, Nan looked over at Doreen.

Doreen grimaced. "You know he'll blame me for this."

Nan sniffed. "He'd better not. He's on tough times right now anyway."

"Oh, Nan, what have you done?" Doreen asked.

"None of us want you tormented while you're here, and everybody loves to see the animals, and you've done so much for the place that it's hardly an issue to have the dog and the cat roll around in the grass." Nan rolled her eyes. "Who would have thought that something like that would be considered a problem?"

"For a non-animal lover, it would be an issue," Doreen stated quietly. "And I'm trying not to antagonize people in town."

Nan looked at her, with a big smirk. "Too late."

Doreen sighed. "How come it's always too late?" she muttered.

At that, Nan sat down, immediately picked up Doreen's hand, and said, "I don't like the sound of this. What's the matter?"

Doreen shrugged. "Just this case."

"Ah," Nan replied.

In the distance Doreen heard the teakettle whistle. Nan hopped up, disappeared inside, and quickly came out with a pot of tea and cups on a tray. And beside them were cookies.

Doreen chuckled. "And where did you get cookies from?"

"I have my sources," Nan smirked. "Besides, cookies are nectar from the gods. They should be a standard food for everybody. I just don't understand why everybody thinks they're bad for us." Nan gave another shake of her head.

"Because people gain weight on them," she muttered.

"Well, that's not your problem, so eat up."

She laughed. "If I keep eating cookies, it will be my problem."

"You're too skinny anyway," Nan reminded her.

At that, there really wasn't a whole lot of point in talking to her grandmother when she got on that kick. Besides, Thaddeus was already on the table, eyeing the cookies.

"These are not your cookies," Doreen told him in a serious tone of voice.

He just looked at her, as if to say, *Yeah? Says who?* And he reached out with his beak, and, faster than she could even say anything to him, he'd snatched up a whole cookie. He now strutted across the table, turning around, strutting back, as if he were in a military troop line with other soldiers. And he couldn't squawk very much because his mouth was full of cookie.

She glared at him. "That's just being greedy," she snapped.

He put the cookie down, and immediately his *he-he-he-he* carried around the patio. And his head bobbed with joy.

She smiled. "I really shouldn't let you get away with that," she murmured to Thaddeus, "but anything that puts a smile on my face today is a good thing."

"Exactly," Nan agreed. "Sometimes we need to do what we need to do."

Doreen looked over at her grandmother and nodded. "Very true, it's not the easiest though."

"Is it because it's a child?"

"It's because it's a child. It's because I read the mother's journal. So did the captain, and he came to the same conclusion. It's about parents who are worthless parents and adults who are worthless adults." Doreen shrugged. "There's really no rhyme or reason. It just all came down on me today."

Nan looked at her, worried, and pushed the cookies closer.

Doreen chuckled. "What is this? Food therapy?" she joked.

"Absolutely," Nan stated. "And, if cookies do the job, it's cheap therapy at that."

"No, you're right about that, and I am loving being here with you. I just needed to come someplace where I knew I was welcome and where I knew there would be laughter and joy," she added.

"And that's a lovely thing to say." Nan smiled. "I'm so grateful that you live close by me."

"Me too," Doreen agreed. "It seems like sometimes things just don't go the way we expect them to."

"Oh dear, you're really down in the dumps, aren't you?"

She shrugged. "It's okay. I mean, I'll get over it."

"Of course you will," Nan stated in that bracing tone. "But sometimes we need a little bit of help, so cookies are a perfect way to get a pick-me-up."

Doreen laughed, reached for a cookie, and, as soon as her fingers touched it, Thaddeus crowed, "Don't touch that. Don't touch that."

She turned and glared at him. And he went back to his *he-he-he-he*.

Nan laughed in delight. "I don't know where he keeps getting all this stuff from, but it's so much fun to have him around."

"Well, it is, unless it's your fingers being virtually smacked." And Doreen snatched up a cookie, glared at the bird, and took a big bite.

As soon as she took a bite, he snapped off a piece of his own cookie and worked away at it too.

"Surely he won't eat the whole cookie," Doreen said worriedly to Nan. "That can't be healthy."

"No, I don't imagine it is all that healthy," Nan agreed. "And the fact that they're oatmeal may not help much either."

"No, not at all," Doreen replied, with a heavy sigh. "But you know what? I guess, at the moment, I'm not prepared to do a whole lot about it."

At that, Nan chuckled. "Not if you want to keep a finger."

She looked over at her. "Has he ever bitten you?"

"Nope, but he wouldn't have talked back to me like that either."

And that just made Doreen feel worse. She sat here in a glum mood and ate her cookies and had her tea.

"Now can you tell me what this is all about?" Nan asked, when she had finished her cookie.

"Just this case. I had a meeting with the captain and everybody at the police station this morning," she said, as if it were commonplace.

But, for Nan, who didn't realize how Doreen's morning had gone, opened her mouth and said, "Seriously?"

Doreen nodded at Nan. "Yeah, I had some information that I needed to discuss with Mack and the captain, so he brought everybody in, so I only had to say it all once."

"That makes sense," Nan replied slowly, "but I hadn't imagined that you had meetings with everybody."

"I don't think it was a *meeting*-meeting, just that's how it worked out," Doreen said. "Besides, all I did was update them on the information I had. It's not as if they updated me on any information they had," she stated, with an eye roll.

"Of course not," Nan said. "That would be police business."

"Right?" Doreen said, staring at her grandmother. "How's that fair?"

"Did you ask?"

She thought about it and then shook her head. "No, I didn't. I really didn't. I was thinking of something completely different." She looked over at her grandmother. "And how are you feeling after yesterday's trip?"

"Lovely." She then rubbed her hands together. "When do you want to go again?"

Doreen stared at her grandmother, who seemed genuinely interested in another outing.

Nan shrugged. "It was lovely. Lovely to get out a bit and, of course, it gave me talking points with everybody here."

Doreen frowned. "Talking points?" she asked cautiously.

"You know—something to tell them, something to make everybody stand up and listen," Nan explained. "You get quite a lot of points for having the best story around here. And then everybody wants to be close to you and get to know you."

"So your popularity rubs off on them?" Doreen asked in a dry tone.

Nan laughed joyously. "Absolutely."

"Nan, I hardly think you need any talking points."

"Nope, I sure don't, but it's always nice to get a few. And being your grandmother has given me an awful lot of kudos in this place." She chuckled. "Everybody wants to know what you're up to, how far you've gotten on various cases. They also want updates on previous cases," she shared in a thoughtful tone, as she looked at Doreen. "I'm really stuck sometimes for answers to give them."

"And I don't have a lot of answers either," Doreen noted, with a nod. "You know how these things wend their way through the court system very slowly."

"*Very* slowly," Nan agreed, with a nod. "Too slowly if you ask me. How come the criminals get to go be a criminal and get away with all that so fast, but then it seems to take justice so long to catch up with them?"

"And yet I think the police are doing everything they can though," Doreen replied, "and it hasn't exactly been fair that I have dumped so much more on them with my leads in these cold cases."

Nan chuckled. "Fair, *shmair*," she said, with an airy wave of her hand. As if to say, *All's fair in love and war.*

And Doreen wasn't exactly sure that Nan was wrong there either. Finally, with her tea gone and the animals getting a little bit bored, Doreen said, "I guess I should go home."

"Not unless you want to," Nan stated firmly.

She smiled at her grandmother. "That's lovely of you to say, and I'm fine now. I just needed a pick-me-up."

"I'm not sure how much of a pick-me-up I gave you," Nan replied, frowning at her granddaughter. "You still seem kind of down."

"And that's why I'll go home, and I'll grab a book, and I'll lie outside in the garden and forget about everybody." She bounced to her feet, the animals immediately hopping up and jumping to her side.

Thaddeus flapped his wings and cried out, "Thaddeus is here. Thaddeus is here."

She smiled at him, picked him up, popped him on her shoulder, and said, "Let's go back and play in the creek." Immediately Thaddeus crowed with delight.

She smiled, leaned over, gave her grandmother a hug, then a kiss on the cheek, and added, "I'll talk to you in a bit." And, with that, she headed out.

As soon as she hit the creek leading back to her house, she felt some of the peace starting to flow within her again, along with the flow of the current. Just something about the water seemed to bring her a certain amount of satisfaction and to take away a lot of the stress in her world. And it wasn't even so much about stress today; it was sadness. Sadness about people just being … people. Why did they have to be, well, people?

She shook her head, knowing she wasn't even making any sense in her own brain, but some of this was just a little too hard to sort out sometimes. By the time she made it back home again, she was uncharacteristically tired. And yet determined to follow through on what she'd said told her grandmother. So she grabbed a book that she had struggled to find time to get into lately. With that in hand and a big bottle of water, she headed down to the section of creek at the end of her backyard, and, instead of sitting on her bench, found herself lying on the grass.

With nobody on a leash, the animals paddled gently in the creek beside her. Mugs thoroughly enjoyed this chance to get wet and to roll around. It was perfectly safe for them today, with the low water levels. And, with that, she could relax too. She sat up, smiled at the world around her, and picked up her book. And proceeded to bury herself for the next little bit. When her phone rang, she checked the screen and saw it was Mack. "Hey, Mack. Did you find anything?"

"Finding lots of things," he replied, "but not much is specific."

"Of course not," she murmured. "That would be too easy. Nothing you can really fill me in on, I presume," she said, with half a laugh.

"It's not even that," he replied. "We just don't have much that is definitive."

"Any idea who this guy could be?"

"We're assuming that it's related to Peter Hall," Mack noted quietly. "But there's one problem with that."

"And what's that?" she asked. And then she sucked in a breath because she knew. "Oh no, that would not be good."

"What?" he asked, with a note of humor. "You won't even let me get out the answers yet."

She sighed. "Not if you'll say what I think you'll say."

In exasperation, he added, "Well, you could let me say it, and then we could go on from there."

"Fine. What about Peter Hall?"

"He's dead," Mack confirmed quietly.

"Yeah, that's what I was afraid you would say."

# Chapter 19

IT WAS STILL a bit of a shock for Doreen to hear those words from Mack. Mack had rung off not long afterward, saying that he would stop in later. She hoped he did, just because it was such an odd day for her that anything would be a good distraction. However, if he only brought more news like that? Well, that's not what she wanted.

She sat down at her laptop in the kitchen and brought up the name Peter Hall. And there was an article about his death, which had happened, she counted the years back, thirty-five years ago. Paul was the first related death, some forty years ago. Then Jack's death was thirty years ago. She shook her head at that. So was somebody killing every five years or were these really "accidents"?

As she read this newspaper account, Peter Hall's death had also been by a car accident. She sighed at that. That detail wouldn't make her any happier. And she didn't believe in coincidences. She sent Mack a text. **Too similar to Jack's death.**

**I know. We're on it.**

And she took that as a brush-off, Mack's way of saying, *Hey, you tossed it to our plate, and we're now running with this, so stay out.* But she wouldn't stay out. It didn't take long for her to search out who Peter Hall's wife was—a Toko. Henrietta Toko. Of the multimillion-dollar mills' industry. Just as Cleve had mentioned in his tale of the adulterer married to some super rich woman. At that, Doreen frowned.

"So Toko, Henrietta," she murmured, "did you have anything to do with this death?"

That would be a whole lot harder to find out. As Doreen kept going through the news, looking for any kind of feeds on this, there wasn't a whole lot to find. But of course back then ... She rose, locked up the animals and the front door, and then raced to the library.

A different librarian was on duty, one who just completely ignored Doreen's presence as she walked in the door, which suited her to a tee. She headed to the archives and quickly searched for anything relating to Henrietta Toko. She probably had reverted to her maiden name after Peter Hall's death.

Doreen found a wedding announcement some five years before the boys' shooting, saying that Peter Hall and Henrietta Toko had been married. After that there wasn't a whole lot of mention of Henrietta in the news, until Doreen fast-forwarded to find the news on Peter Hall's death.

After that, she caught a little bit more news on the "accident," but not a whole lot, just saying that it was a vehicular accident and that speed was considered a factor but so were the slippery roads. Those kinds of accidents made Doreen uneasy. Had somebody been cleaning up or something else?

On impulse she picked up her phone and called Mack.

"What do you want?" he asked in a distracted voice.

She chuckled. "*Hi, Doreen. How are you, Doreen? Do you*

*have any helpful tips for me, Doreen?* No, just *What do you want?*" she teased.

"Of course you want something," he replied. "You always want something."

"That's not true," she cried out. "I often give you something too."

After a moment's pause, and she heard the smile in his voice as he said, "Now that is quite true. So what do you want?"

"I want a phone number for this Henrietta Toko."

"Why?" he asked suspiciously.

"Because I have questions that I want to ask her," she stated, "but I can't find a phone number or an address."

"Well, that would make sense," Mack replied. "You know that, particularly given what's gone on in her life, I'm sure she doesn't want to be bugged."

"Well, being bugged is one thing," Doreen argued calmly, trying to be persuasive, "but having somebody ask questions about potential murders that her late husband could have been involved in might be a whole different story."

"And you could also stir up a hornet's nest."

"Are you trying to keep me away from her?" Doreen asked. "Or do I phone the captain and ask him for the contact info on Henrietta?"

"Oh, now that's interesting," Mack said. "I have no idea what the captain would do with your request."

"*Hmm.*" She pondered that and replied, "You know what? I think I'll go ask him." And, with that, she hung up on Mack, smiling as she heard him still spluttering when she disconnected. Then she quickly phoned the captain.

When he answered, his voice was distracted too.

"Sorry, Captain," Doreen said. "I'm not trying to bother you, but I have something else I want to follow up on. I'm looking for Henrietta Toko's contact information."

"Ah, that might not be so easy to find. It's probably unlisted."

"Do you have any idea where this lady might live at this point?"

"Well, she's a pretty big philanthropist in town, so I'm sure it's behind lots of guarded gates."

"Sure it is," Doreen agreed cheerfully. "But you never know, I might get in there."

"Maybe, I think she has an estate up in Southeast Kelowna."

She pondered that and muttered, "That would be a hard area to drive around and to find anything useful."

"It would," the captain confirmed. "Hang on a minute. I remember seeing something about her in our files."

She waited, hearing him click away on the computer.

"I don't have a phone number for her. I can tell you that she gets her mail in that general store off Spiers Road."

"Okay, and I suppose you can't give me Henrietta's address."

"Nope, sure can't, but, giving you where she gets her mail, I'm pretty sure you can figure it out."

"I'll do my best," she murmured. "Thanks." And disconnected the call.

Feeling buoyed by his vote of confidence and the fact that the captain didn't even ask her what she wanted Henrietta for, she put down her phone, looked at her notes, pondered what else she could try to find out, and then loaded up the animals. "Let's go shopping," she said to her crew.

Thankfully the reward money was in her account, and she did need a few groceries, so it wasn't out of the realm of possibility that she would buy a few things from a store she'd never been to before. And, when she got there, it was a quaint little corner store that looked frozen in time.

She wandered the store, until one of the clerks said, "I'm sorry. Animals aren't allowed in here. It violates health regulations."

She turned toward the clerk and apologized, looking down at Mugs and Goliath, both who were behaving themselves. "I didn't even think about it." She quickly snatched a loaf of bread and a gallon of milk and a block of cheese and the little bit of peanut butter that she had been studying in her hand and said, "Let me just grab these things, and I promise I'll take them away."

The clerk hesitated and then shrugged. "You're already here, so I guess it doesn't matter."

"And I am sorry," Doreen repeated. "I'm so used to taking them everywhere that I tend to forget when I shouldn't have them inside a store."

"That's all right," she replied, with a smile. "I mean, if I had animals, I'd want to take them with me everywhere too."

"They're such a blessing," Doreen noted, with a bright smile. "Particularly these guys."

At that, the other woman laughed. "They're definitely a collection." And then she saw Thaddeus, peeking through Doreen's hair, and she cried out, "Oh my. Now I know who you are."

Doreen stared at her. "What?"

"You're that—" And then the clerk stopped.

"Yeah, right." Doreen nodded slowly. "People call me the crazy lady."

"That's not what I would say," she stated, still smiling. "I would say, *You're that detective lady.*"

Doreen straightened proudly. "Yeah, that's me." She chuckled. "But most people are much less polite and call me the crazy lady."

"Well, you might be crazy," the clerk teased, "but you're my kind of crazy." At that, the woman cheerfully rang up Doreen's few purchases and asked, "Are you living around here now?"

"I was looking at property up here," she replied, trying to find a way to get the truth out without having to lie.

"It's really a nice area," the clerk said warmly. "People here are really friendly. Lots of people have been here all their lives."

"I understand some of the more prominent members of Kelowna live here too," Doreen mentioned, looking at the clerk curiously. "Is that your take on this area too?"

"Oh, there's lots of them," she replied. "Just look at all the wineries around Kelowna."

"And of course the mills too," Doreen noted.

"Right. Henrietta lives here," the clerk confirmed. "But we're used to her being here, so we don't even really think of her as being one of the old families. But she is. And that's the good kind of old family."

"I heard she was up here, but I've never seen any of these bigger estates. They all have big gates and security and big acreages."

"Yeah, that's Henrietta's place to a tee." The clerk laughed. "She's just up the road here. Great big, massively huge red metal gates that you can't miss, but, of course, you also can't get in. So she gets all her mail here."

"And does she come in herself or does she have, like,

hired help?" Doreen asked, with an eye roll. "I mean, as if I will ever have that kind of money."

"Right?" The clerk shook her head. "She doesn't come in all that often, not now. But she used to. After her husband died, she became a little more open, you know? I guess she needed to see people a little bit more. Yet, over these last few years, we haven't seen too much of her."

"She's also got to be getting on in age," Doreen noted.

"She is," the clerk confirmed. At that, she smiled and added, "But we all are."

Doreen chuckled. "Oh my, isn't that the truth." And Doreen accepted the bag of groceries from the clerk, with her thanks. "Much appreciated, and I am so sorry that I brought the animals inside."

The clerk smiled and shook her head. "Ah, don't worry about it. As long as nobody complains, we're all good."

"And the trouble with that is," Doreen noted, "just as soon as you figure nobody'll complain, you know somebody does." And, with a smile and a wave, she moved the animals back out to her car. She quickly got them into her vehicle and then watched as a few other people came and went—each buying a few groceries and picking up some mail and leaving.

With that, she looked down at Mugs. "What do you think? Shall we drive just around the corner here? Maybe we're better off going for a walk," she decided. At that, he woofed several times and got really excited.

She thought about it and nodded. "That would be a good idea. I mean, it's not as if we have any reason to be parking outside Henrietta's place anyway. So anything that gives us an excuse to get a little bit closer—because we wanted to walk the area—would certainly work."

And, with that, she put them on leashes and pulled them out of the vehicle yet again. As she looked up, the clerk appeared at the doorway to the convenience store, looking at her. Doreen shrugged. "He has to go for a walk," she said, with a smile.

"That's the thing about animals." The clerk smiled and waved.

"Always," Doreen replied, "but they're lovely and well behaved."

The clerk agreed. "That they are."

And, with that, and a nudge of the leash, she pulled Mugs in the direction the store clerk had mentioned, where Henrietta lived. As Doreen wandered, Mugs took his time, sniffed out everything. It really was a lovely day, so it was hardly a hardship to take them out for a little bit. And even Goliath, suspiciously so, seemed to be cooperating.

Doreen and her crew meandered down the road, smiling at passersby, a couple honked, and she just kept on trucking off to the side, doing her own thing. She wasn't bothering anybody, and nobody should be bothered by her presence. Still, it seemed like she was more than welcome here—or just basically ignored, as everybody else ignored people too. She smiled at that concept because there was a whole lot worse than being ignored.

By the time they had wandered down far enough to see the big red gates, she understood what the clerk had meant. They looked pretty formidable. But, oddly enough, they were also open, as if to say somebody who lived there was out and about.

Still, Doreen would have thought that they would have closed the gates behind them, if that were the case, but maybe tradespeople or somebody like that were working on the premises. Her ex had been specific about who was allowed on their property. Maybe this Henrietta woman was the same.

Doreen slowly let Mugs wander back and forth, and, when she looked up, a man stood at the driveway. She smiled at him. "Hey."

He nodded and asked, "What are you doing here?"

"Oh, I'm parked down at the general store," she explained, "but my dog here needed to get out and lift a leg. So we're just wandering the street." She frowned at him. "Are we disturbing something?"

He shook his head, looked at the dog, and noted, "You must be traveling a long way if you had to do that here."

"Not really, but it was too risky to wait," she told him.

She hoped Mugs would forgive the lie, but she had to have some excuse for being here. She looked at the gate and raised her eyebrows. "I've never seen a gate like that. Quite the color."

He nodded. "That's my grandmother," he stated, with a smile. "She's quite the artistic person and didn't want anything mundane that everybody else would have."

"Oh, I agree with her totally." Doreen stared at it as a marvel. "I mean, we don't see enough color. Traditionally all these big gates are black."

He nodded. "And black's fine. You usually don't have to paint it much. But, if anybody bangs into this gate and scratches it up, well, then it'll be fixed again, so it's a pain."

"I never thought of that," Doreen replied, "but you're right. Black wouldn't need to be repainted so often, right?"

"It depends what they've used as an undercoat," the man said. "Lots of times black's just an easily maintained color, and it doesn't require anything because all the undercoats are black too." And he pointed down at a small chip at the bottom that had lost its paint. "See? Like this. By rights this thing should get touched up again. I'll have to ask her if she wants to get it fixed."

"Not worthwhile then. Costly over time too."

"That is quite true, but I know that she loves it, so …"

Doreen burst out laughing. "And you know something? Depending on everything else going on in her life, maybe it's okay that she loves a red gate. Even if it is a pain."

He grinned at her. "So true." He looked at Mugs again, then he realized that Goliath was on the other leash. "I don't see many people with cats on a leash."

"Not many cats like leashes, and honestly this cat only likes leashes about 20 percent of the time," she shared. "The rest of the time I can't even get close to him with a leash in my hand. Yet today he was all over it."

"And why were you down at the store?" he asked curiously. "I don't think I've seen you around here before."

She shook her head. "I'm relatively new to Kelowna," she noted in that confiding tone. "And everybody keeps talking about how beautiful Southeast Kelowna is." She shrugged. "So I just wanted to come for a drive, stopped in at the corner store, and bought a few groceries, instead of going to one of the big box stores. It was kind of fun."

He just nodded absentmindedly. "Honestly I would be the opposite. I'd leave this area in a heartbeat."

"Why don't you then?" she asked, looking at him. "Surely there can't be much holding you here."

"My grandmother." He glanced back at the house in the distance. "Can't say I really want to leave her alone."

"Oh, now I understand that too. It's the reason I came to Kelowna—because of my nan."

"We're kind of attached one way or the other, aren't we?" he said, with that half smile.

"We absolutely are. I'd be lost without her," she admitted.

"I know what you mean," he agreed. He lit a cigarette, stood here for a few minutes, while she let Mugs wander. Then he added, "I'll go back inside. Have a nice day."

She smiled and waved. "You too."

And just as she turned away with Mugs, a sports car roared down the road and hit the brakes really hard. She looked up, and even the grandson stopped.

Sure enough, it was Bernard, the man who had given her the reward money.

He stepped out, looked at her, and said, "I didn't expect to see you here."

She repeated the spiel she had just given the young man and added, "And, of course, Mugs here decided that he needed a bathroom break."

Bernard chuckled. "Now this guy," he said, walking across the road and bending down to pet Mugs, who greeted him like an old friend, "he's quite the character." He looked over at the young man, standing at the gate. "How're you doing, Sean?"

"I'm okay. How are you?"

"Ah, I'm good. This is the young lady who helped solve my missing diamond problem," he stated, with a chuckle. "And I've been trying to get her to go out for dinner with me ever since."

The young man looked at him, then at Doreen, "Oh."

She shrugged. "Really, there's no *oh* about it. It was a lucky thing, that's all."

"Well, hardly," Bernard argued. "She's got a lot of

brains. More than that, she thinks differently. And believe me. I've never been so happy as to have that mess all over with."

"Hey, I was never so happy to get that reward money too," she replied, with a cheeky grin.

His laughter boomed out across the countryside. "May I take you for coffee?" he asked, then looked at her critters. "All of them for coffee?"

She smiled. "And what would you do if I said yes?" she asked in a teasing voice.

"Well, you can always come back down to the waterfront with me," Bernard offered, "and we can have coffee there."

She hesitated and then noted Bernard studied the young man with an odd expression. She decided a story was here. "Sure. Why not?" And, with a smile at Sean—who had never told her his name—she added, "Nice meeting you." She turned back toward Bernard. "I've got to walk back to the general store and get my car."

"Sure enough." He nodded. "Do you want me to give you a lift?"

She shook her head. "Nope, I'm okay to walk. That's what we're out here for anyway."

She hurriedly moved the animals down the road toward her car. She heard the two men talking behind her but couldn't hear enough to get the gist; she wished she were a fly in the road. That would enable her to buzz around and get all the information that she needed.

As soon as she was back in her car, and the animals loaded up, she wondered what was the best way to get down to his place.

He pulled up beside her and called out, "Just follow

me."

She nodded. "Will do." And, with that problem solved, she drove behind him.

Something was going on between Bernard and the young man, but she didn't know what. She wanted to ask him though, so, while she definitely didn't want to get any cozier with Bernard, she definitely did want to get information.

She sighed, looked at Mugs, and said, "Look at that? The things that we have to do in order to get answers."

He woofed at her several times. She smiled and finally pulled into the driveway behind Bernard. As she got out, she let the animals run free. Mugs immediately raced over to one of the gardeners, who gave him a big hello. She apologized to him. "Sorry, Mugs is friendly but a little rash at times."

The gardener smiled and said, "I love all dogs."

"It's obvious that Mugs knows that about you," she noted, chuckling.

Bernard smiled at her and motioned toward his front door. "Come on in." As soon as they got inside, with the door shut, Bernard whispered, "Now you can tell me what you're really doing up here."

She beamed at him. "And you can tell me about those people too."

"I can." He nodded. "Quite a few stories about them, that's for sure."

"I'm sure there are. Now whether any of that is useful, I don't know."

He stopped, stared at her, and asked, "Are you on another case?" She winced. He nodded. "Oh, this will get interesting." He rubbed his hands together. "Now what kind of a drink do you want?"

"Coffee."

He groaned. "Is there anything else you ever drink?"

"Tea," she replied immediately.

"That's not an improvement."

She burst out laughing. "That'll do just fine for now."

He sighed and nodded. "Fine." After ordering their drinks from his housekeeper, he led the way to the back patio. And, with the animals running loose, he sat down and asked, "Now, what's going on here?"

"I wanted to take a look at that interesting area," she murmured.

"Oh no, you don't." Bernard wagged his finger at her. "Much more is going on here than you're telling me."

"Yep, there sure is," she agreed, "but you tell me something about that family first."

"What do you want to know?" he asked.

"What was Henrietta's husband like?"

"Oh, he was a total jerk," he murmured. "I was pretty sweet on her way back then, but she was older than me, and it was one of those young crushes that thankfully didn't go anywhere."

"Why thankfully?"

"Because I don't think we would have been a good fit," he stated bluntly. "And the more I've watched her life fall apart, I realized what a good decision I made back then."

Doreen smiled. "You might have been a fling for her back then, but I'm not sure you would have been a long-term relationship."

"I wouldn't have been, indeed," Bernard admitted, "but my heart broke just at the thought of it."

She burst out laughing. "And the husband?"

He looked at her and grimaced. "A smarmy political

type, always pushing for something, always a little bit, I don't know, *off*, I guess. He wasn't my kind of a guy."

"Why not?" she asked immediately.

He thought about it, shrugged, and explained, "He was a ladies' man. I know that a lot of people see me as a ladies' man too, but I'm not out cheating on somebody I married nor with a bunch of other ladies while seriously dating somebody. In his case, I'm not so sure he ever committed to being with her."

"And that would be sad too," she noted quietly. "Nobody ever likes to think that they don't have the full love and attention of the person they care about."

"True. You're right," Bernard agreed, "and I never really got the feeling that their marriage was anything more than a business arrangement."

She stared at him. "Because of the Toko money?"

He nodded slowly, looking at her. "She's the only daughter, so stood to inherit everything."

"And she did, did she not?"

"She did, and then her husband died just around the same time as she lost her dad, so that caused her quite a bit of grief also."

Doreen considered that. "When was that?"

Bernard shrugged. "I don't have a time frame in my head, but her father died first, and, while they were still sorting through the will, the husband died too."

"Ah, how did the father and the husband get along?"

"I think they were great buddies." Bernard straightened up in his seat. "So now that you've been grilling me, what is it that you think is going on here?"

"I'm not so sure," she murmured. "Were there ever rumors about him having an affair?"

"Well, it certainly wouldn't have surprised me if there were, but I don't remember ever hearing any specifics. I definitely got the impression it would not be tolerated by Henrietta."

"No, I can't imagine that it would be," she said quietly. "That doesn't mean that the affairs didn't happen."

"And who do you think he had an affair with?"

"A teacher," she replied immediately.

"Oh, now that's interesting. … The only time I've ever seen a teacher with him was—" Then Bernard whispered the next part, mostly to himself, "Who was that young pretty little thing?"

The housekeeper arrived. Doreen just waited and thanked the housekeeper as she delivered coffee. The housekeeper never made a sound; she placed her coffee near Doreen and left almost as quickly, well-trained and silent. Doreen's ex-husband would have approved. Hating that she kept comparing things back to him, she waited for Bernard to answer her.

And finally he added, "I can't remember her name, but I want to say something like Shelley."

"Yep," Doreen confirmed. "Full marks to you. Her name is Shelley Brewster."

Bernard looked at Doreen in surprise. "Yes, that's her."

"Yep." Doreen nodded. "I want to know whether that affair ever became public and whether it had any impact on Peter's life."

"Well, if Henrietta ever found out or if her father ever found out, it would have been major," Bernard stated. "And *ugly* major."

She frowned at that and nodded slowly. "As in *murderously* ugly major?"

"What are you really getting at here?" He picked up his coffee and looked at her over the cup, waiting.

"Peter Hall was killed in a car accident some years ago," she began. "I guess I'm just wondering if it was a car accident or vehicular homicide."

He stared at her, sat back, putting down his cup. "Wow. You really do hit hard when you're up to bat, don't you?"

"Sometimes I have to," she said. "Most people don't really like answering questions."

"No, they sure don't," he agreed. "And why would that affair have any bearing on his death?" he pondered out loud. Then he shrugged. "Not that I can see anybody killing him over it, but it certainly would have affected his bottom line."

"Okay," she noted. "And what if Henrietta's father found out?"

At that, Bernard stared at her for a moment. "I don't think old man Toko would have disclosed anything to his daughter, but he sure would have had something to say to Peter."

She nodded at that. "Okay, and presumably whatever he was planning on saying wouldn't have been very nice."

Bernard burst out laughing. "Gosh, no, the old man was a stick-in-the-mud. It was one thing to have an affair—don't get me wrong. I mean in old man Toko's way of thinking, an affair wasn't serious—but it was *never* to be made public, and it was always expected to be highly discreet."

"So he would have been okay with the son-in-law's affair, as long as nobody knew about it?" Doreen asked to make sure.

"Toko did love his daughter, so maybe he wouldn't have been okay seeing her made a fool of like that, but old man Toko would have been more okay if it remained hidden. He was all about image."

"Would something like that affect the Toko bottom line?" she pondered.

"Well, the son-in-law was on the board of directors for the mills." Bernard considered that for a moment. "You know something? He was removed from the board around that time period." He looked at her and raised his eyebrows. "Do you really think somebody killed him?"

"I'm not sure if anybody killed him, but I can tell you that I'm investigating a shooting from a long time ago that never was solved and had something to do with Captain Hanson."

He stared at her. "Wow." He sank back into his chair. "That brings back an awful lot of unpleasant memories."

"What's that?" she asked, eyeing him curiously.

"You're talking about the captain's injuries from that drive-by shooting when he was a kid, aren't you?"

She nodded. "I suppose you were reminded of it fifteen years ago, when the investigation was revived, huh?"

"Nope, I heard about it like forty years ago," he stated, "because my dad used to warn me about getting into trouble with the wrong crowd and what it did to you."

"Paul was just ten, the captain eleven," she noted, frowning. "What kind of wrong crowd is that for them?"

"My dad was all about appearances too," Bernard noted, with a wry smile. "And appearances meant having the right friends. He always used events like that as a way to get me to understand the difference between the right and the wrong types of friends. My dad did that up to the day he died."

"And yet I know the captain would say that he may have been born on the wrong side of the tracks but to a good family."

# Chapter 20

LATER THAT EVENING, after Doreen had a sandwich out on her deck, she sat here, pondering the bits and pieces of information she'd gotten from Bernard today.

When she heard Mack walk through the front door, she called out, "I'm in the back."

He came outside to join her, and she turned to look at him. "Oh, ouch, you look tired."

"Yeah, it seems like a constant state of affairs these days."

She sighed. "I gather no good news?"

"It's not so much *no good news* as just not necessarily *any* news yet."

"Right, and that's the difference, isn't it?"

"Oh, it sure is," he murmured. "We're working on it though." He hesitated, then added, "I heard from one of the guys that you were out and about visiting today."

She frowned. "*Yeah.* That just means one of your guys tattled on me again."

He gave her a bright smile. "Maybe not see it as *tattling*," he suggested. "Maybe they're just concerned that you're getting in over your head."

"That's *tattling*," she declared immediately.

He chuckled. "So were you?"

"Getting in over my head? No," she stated. "Was I up in Southeast Kelowna, trying to get a lay of the land for Henrietta Toko? Absolutely. Did I run into Bernard while I was up there? Absolutely. Did I have coffee with him this afternoon? Yes." And she told Mack a little bit about what she had gotten from Bernard.

"Oh, interesting. So the father and then the husband."

"Exactly, but I'm not exactly sure what, if anything, that means."

He frowned and nodded. "And that's the trouble with this kind of information. You get a little bit here, a little bit there, but it doesn't really pull together, until you get that *one* piece of information."

"Right," she said, with a sigh. "And I haven't got it yet." She looked over at him hopefully. "Did you?"

"Nope, not yet. But you can bet the captain asked me to check in on you today. I think he was a little worried, after giving you the address or at least the store where Henrietta gets her mail."

"Oh, he told you about that, did he?" She laughed. "He didn't even think about it at the time. He just gave it to me."

"And I think that was where he wondered if he'd pushed the line a little bit."

"I didn't say anything to anybody about that," she stated. "I did talk to the clerk up there, and apparently Henrietta's a little bit of a recluse, and then I talked to her grandson, who mentioned that she's artistic and fairly free-form and loves her red metal gate—even though, if it were black, it would mean much less maintenance." Mack stared at her, and she shrugged. "You know that whole *people talk* thing."

"Yeah, I do know that whole *people talk* thing," he replied. "Can't say I expected that whole *people talk* thing to work so often with you though."

She glared at him.

"No, I should have known," he said, holding up a hand, "because people always talk to you."

"I'm easy to talk to," she declared, with a smile. "Something you should try to cultivate."

He just glared at her for that, and she burst out laughing. He gave her a reluctant grin and asked, "And what was your feeling about all of it?"

"I like the grandson," she shared. "He'd also be the type of kid who would have a truck like that." And then she stopped. "No, no, let me rephrase that. He's the type of kid who would have loved a restored truck like that, but I don't think he would drive it in that shape."

"In what shape?" he asked cautiously.

"With that horrible paint job, and I think he'd be the kind to have it spick-and-span, lots of chrome, lifted even, you know? The one with that big growl but a small truck bed, never sees the mud and never transports anything heavy enough to damage the truck."

He looked at her and then burst out laughing.

"Why the laughter?" she asked. "What was so funny about that?"

"Absolutely everything you said." Mack chuckled. "But you could be right. We don't often see that age group having *ugly* trucks," he noted. "The younger guys are usually pretty proud of their rigs."

"Exactly. So … I think it's connected to the will."

He let out a slow whistle. "You're still not making any sense."

"No, I just … You haven't connected the dots."

He rolled his eyes at that. "Well, I'm a little tired," he muttered. "So how about you don't make my brain work so hard that it hurts, and you connect a few of these dots for me and make sure that we have evidence and not just assumptions."

"But you know how I love assumptions," she stated, warming up to the topic. At his glare, she subsided and shot him a look. "Fine, but before evidence comes assumptions."

"And then we follow it up," he added, "to make sure that we're not just blindly guessing."

"That's your department," she quipped, with an impudent grin.

He sighed. "Talk to me."

"Okay. … I think Henrietta's father knew about the affair, and it was okay with him, as long as Peter didn't make a stink about it. Yet old man Toko probably did what he could to keep it all squashed. So, either old man Toko decided to cut his son-in-law out of the will or left him in the will but somehow told his daughter about the affair. If he cut Peter out of the will, then there's a possibility that Peter would have taken old man Toko to court over the will because, I guess, you know, in my head there's some sort of business agreement inherent with their marriage. Don't know whether there is or not, but it makes sense. And, if her father didn't cut Peter from the will, finding out about the affair would have been the last straw for Henrietta."

"But then what's that got to do with any of these … the drive-by shootings?"

"That's the problem," she agreed, "and I'm not exactly sure I have an answer for that yet."

"And we don't even know that Peter's car accident was

anything other than an accident."

"No, we sure don't, but do we know that it wasn't murder?" He glared at her. She raised her palms. "I know. I know. I know. We're back to this whole *proof versus assumption* thing."

"You're not even into an assumption yet," Mack nearly barked. "You're still wandering around in theory land."

"Sure," she admitted, "but you know that wandering around in theory land is how my brain works."

"I'll give you that," he replied quietly, then he yawned.

She looked at him and frowned. "Did you eat?"

He shrugged. "No, I don't think I did, not since lunch." He looked at her empty plate. "What did you have?"

"Just a sandwich, but I can make you one."

So much surprise filled his gaze that she felt guilty for never doing such a kindness for him before. "I can make you a sandwich," she repeated.

"I'm sure you can, but—Thank you. I would love a sandwich."

She nodded and then asked, "And coffee?"

"Always coffee," he said.

And this time she really heard the fatigue in his voice.

She hopped up and wandered back into the kitchen, put on coffee, and then made him a sandwich, doubling up all the inside stuff, so that it was hopefully big enough to hold him. As she took one look at it, she winced, then made a second one.

When the coffee was done, she carried out a cup to him, as he nodded off gently in the sun. She stood there for a long moment and then placed the cup near him and returned for his plate.

When she set down the plate, he looked up at her and

said, "I wasn't really sleeping."

"Seems like you should have been though," she replied in a quiet tone. "Look. If you need to just close your eyes for a few minutes, you know you can do that here."

"And I appreciate that. I really do. But I'm fine."

She wasn't so sure about that whole *I'm fine* thing, but, having used it a time or two on him herself, she knew that he wouldn't let her get away with it either.

She nodded. "Eat up. That might be just as good as a nap."

He stared at the two huge sandwiches in front of him and whistled. "Wow, your sandwiches have changed."

"Well, I learned to make them with a little bit more filling to make them a little more solid," she explained. "And, in your case, I just doubled everything."

He burst out laughing and then nodded. "You know what? That's not a bad way to do it," he noted quietly. He picked up the first half of the first sandwich and took a big bite and then smiled at her. "That's perfect, thank you."

She nodded self-consciously and said, "You shouldn't be … you should be doing a better job of looking after yourself."

Somehow, even while eating a sandwich, he managed to snort, and that was a talent all in itself.

She shrugged. "Hey, if you get to lecture me, I get to lecture you."

He didn't say anything to that; he just continued to eat. And she pondered what she had just told him about a possible connection. "I would like to know what Henrietta's grandson is driving. And I'd really like to see that truck that was following me yesterday."

"We still have the truck. It's in forensics. We have no

idea who was running into the mall, but you didn't recognize him as the grandson, right?"

She thought about that and shook her head. "I didn't get enough of a look at the mall," she replied regretfully. "That would have helped, wouldn't it?"

He nodded slowly. "It wouldn't have given us anything proof-positive obviously, but it would have given us a little bit more to go on."

She considered that, pulled out her phone, and called Nan. "Hey, Nan. You remember that guy who was following us and then ran into the mall?"

"Yeah, sure do," Nan said in a chirpy bird voice. "What can I help you with?"

"I'm just wondering if there's any way to identify what size he was. Did you get a better look at him when he got out of the truck at the mall?"

"You mean, like, jeans size or shirt size?" Nan asked in confusion.

Doreen grinned at Mack at that. "No, but like, six-two versus five-eight—something like that."

"Well, he was tall. He was a big man," she stated.

"And are you sure it was a man?"

"Yep, I'm sure it's a man," she declared.

Mack leaned forward and said, "Nan, it's Mack here."

"Oh, look at that," Nan replied, with pleasure in her tone. "You two are having dinner together."

"Your granddaughter made me a sandwich," he clarified.

At that, Nan tsk-tsked. "Doreen, is that all you could find to feed him? You'll never get a man that way."

Doreen face-palmed her forehead and then groaned. "Nan, can we get back to the discussion about this guy at the mall?"

"Sure," Nan replied, "but, boy, we'll have a talk later about what you are supposed to feed these guys."

"Sure, we'll have a talk about it later," Doreen repeated, glaring at Mack, whose grin was huge as he munched away on his sandwich. "Besides, he likes sandwiches," she muttered.

Nan sniffed. "You should at least keep cookies around."

At that, Mack's eyes widened, and he looked at Doreen hopefully.

She glared at him and stated, "No cookies for him." And his shoulders sagged, as if she'd broken his heart. She rolled her eyes at that. "Nan?"

"Fine, he was big. I told you that already."

"Yes, you did, and I'm trying to figure out what you meant by *big*."

"I would have guessed six-one, six-two."

"*Hmm*. Do you remember how he moved?"

"I don't know if I remember how he moved, but I'm sure video cameras are all around the mall, aren't they? I would say he was definitely that six-foot-plus kind of big."

"Maybe there are cameras," she noted. "I might send you a video later," she murmured. "Let me think about it."

"Anytime," Nan said in delight. "I'll have something to tell the others." And, at that, Nan rang off.

"Cookies?" Mack asked hopefully.

"No," she snapped, glaring at him. "You're just getting me into trouble all the time with Nan."

At that, his grin widened. "Then we're even."

"What trouble did I ever get you in?" she protested.

"Tons of trouble down at the office," he replied.

"Oh." Then she shrugged. "Okay, fine, you might have a reason for that one then."

He snorted. "*Might*?" he muttered. "You have no idea how many times I've gone to bat for you in the past."

"Maybe not," she admitted, "and you've obviously done a good job of it because the captain did ask for my help."

"And," Mack added, "he's also quite stunned that you've managed to get anything so far."

She looked at him. "And here I felt guilty because I wasn't managing to find anything."

"Well, you've certainly found more than we have. Although, I have to admit, I haven't even looked into this case. I hadn't even realized how involved the captain was in it actually."

"Yet I think that's part of the problem," she suggested. "Too often we aren't as aware as we should be, and we hug this stuff close, and we think everybody knows. Yet, over the years, what you know versus what someone else knows—say, Arnold for example—are two separate things."

Mack picked up another chunk of sandwich and didn't say anything but continued to eat. "Now what are you thinking?" he asked, looking at her in that strange assessing way.

"I'm wondering if the grandson is the guy we saw running into the mall."

He pondered that. "Didn't you say that you could hardly see him over the wheel in the cab?"

She shook her head. "No, Nan did." And then she looked at him. "The trouble is, Nan can barely see over the seatback, so, from the angle that she was looking back out of my car, I don't know that she would have seen very much of him while he was driving."

"And what about you?" he asked. "Did you get a look, even a quick one at the driver. I understood we were looking for somebody who was fairly short."

She thought about it and explained, "It's very deceptive, and I can't really say that I trust what I saw while I was driving because I was so focused on, you know, getting away from him."

"And that's a good point too. But why would the grandson have been in Vernon?"

"And that I don't know," she admitted. "I really don't know. Unless there's some connection."

"But then we're looking for ways to place him there and not necessarily any reason for him to be in Vernon."

She looked at him and then nodded slowly. "I guess for you that's a distinction, isn't it?"

"Of course it is. We always need these distinctions."

"But if I do find a connection of him having been there, would that help?"

"Sure, if we can put him in the same town, that's a start."

She thought about it. "You know something?" And then she stopped, shaking her head again. "No, I'll have to make a few more phone calls."

"And why is that?" he asked curiously.

She frowned. "No. I'm … I won't say anything, until I have a chance to check it out." He glared at her, and she shrugged. "Look. I know you don't like it, but sometimes some of this stuff just doesn't pan out, and I don't want to go off in one direction and find out that it's got nothing to do with it."

"Why not?" Mack asked. "You do that all the time."

She glared at him now, and he just laughed. She tugged a reluctant grin from her lips, and then she nodded. "I guess, *to you*, it seems like I go off half-cocked all the time, doesn't it?"

"Let's just say that I'm still trying to figure out how your brain works. And, so far, all these wild and wonderful avenues that you keep disappearing into don't really help."

"I guess I never thought of it that way."

"No, I'm sure you didn't." He chuckled. "The fact of the matter is, we don't always know what makes certain things make sense to ourselves and what other things completely make no sense. So, if you've got an idea that you want to rattle around in your brain, then I'll let you rattle it around. Just remember who needs to hear when you think you've got something that you want to kick back and forth."

"Oh, I like that idea. I'd be totally okay with that, once I get it locked down in my head." And, with that, she waited until he left. As soon as he was gone, she quickly called Nan back. "Nan, do you have anybody there who's related to Henrietta Toko?"

"Oh, *her*," Nan said, with a sniff. "That's a real snooty lady for you. You and your husband would have gotten along well with that family."

"No," Doreen disagreed. "My ex-husband would have."

"That's very true," Nan admitted apologetically. "I'm sorry."

"We keep making the same kind of innuendos about people and generalizations, but I have to wonder. Do you know anybody connected to them? Do you know anything about the grandson in particular?"

"*Grandson*?" Nan repeated. "I know Henrietta had a daughter, don't know if the daughter had any kids, but I don't think any other children were born to Henrietta."

"So then one daughter and the grandson."

"Well, at least one grandson—if that's who he said he

was."

Doreen stiffened at that. "He didn't. Bernard thought it was the grandson."

"Oh, you saw him today, did you?" Nan chirped, a wealth of meaning in her voice.

Doreen groaned. "Yes, I did, and I had coffee with him, and it's really not a big deal."

"Maybe not," Nan said.

"In particular, do either of them have any connections to Vernon?"

Nan stopped, and silence came from her end. "Are you thinking that grandson is the one who was running us off the road?" she asked, with a gasp.

"I'm not sure, and you don't get to talk to people about this," she warned her grandmother.

With a subdued voice, she replied, "No, I … I hear what you're saying, but that does give us a little bit of something to go on."

"No, at the moment, it doesn't give me *anything* to go on. That's the problem," she noted. "I need something to go on, and that's why I am wondering if there was any Vernon connection with the Toko family."

"I can ask a few people if they know anything about her," Nan offered quietly. "But, considering you had coffee with Bernard, you really should be checking with him."

"I think you're right," Doreen said. "You ask Richie and a few of your other cohorts, and I will ask Bernard." And, with that, Doreen hung up and quickly dialed Bernard.

His tone was jovial and happy as he answered. "Doreen, what can I do for you?"

"I'm wondering if there's any connection to the city of Vernon with Henrietta Toko and her grandson."

"Vernon, huh?" he replied. "Well, lots of people have business dealings in both towns. That wouldn't be in any way unusual."

"Right. And what kind of vehicle does Sean drive? Do you know?"

Bernard hesitated, then asked, "What's this all about?"

"A case," she said, "as you well know."

"Well, I do know some of what you're after," he confirmed, "but I would not like to think that the grandson was involved in anything."

"And I'm not sure that he is, but the sooner I can, you know, get him out of being involved, that's good too."

"Right, so you want to cancel him out of being somebody of interest."

"Exactly. So do you know what vehicle he owns?"

"*Hmm*, I'm not sure. I'll see if I can come up with something, and I'll get back to you here in a few minutes." And, with that, he hung up.

She stared down at her phone, wondering how investigations were ever done in the olden days. She sat here on her butt and made phone call after phone call to try and dredge up some information and then people would get back to her with another phone call. It was a fascinating process and just reminded her how much harder these investigations would have been years ago.

People must have been out walking around and maybe decided that some of these walk-arounds just weren't even worth it. It certainly made it a little easier to understand how much harder it was for information to pass back then. If people couldn't be bothered or were too tired or traffic was ugly or the weather was bad, maybe some of these questions just didn't get asked.

She considered that for a long moment, and, of course, it was hardly the captain's fault some forty years ago. He was a kid back then. And not only a kid but a young kid. He didn't come into the police force for many years afterward and certainly didn't get into a prominent position for decades.

As she continued to ponder this, Nan called her back and said, "Nobody really knows very much about Henrietta. She's kind of a loner."

"I thought she was the arty type."

"Oh, yeah, maybe," Nan agreed. "But you know how a lot of those people just cultivate the arty types."

"Maybe. Any idea if she would have had an affair?"

Nan huffed. "Her? No, not likely. But then we never really know what people are like, do we?"

"No, we sure don't," Doreen agreed quietly.

"I do know that her daughter was Philly," Nan shared, "and she got married and then was divorced not very long afterward. I think her daughter lives in England right now."

Doreen added, "Interesting that the grandson's here."

"Not necessarily, not if he's trying to stay close to Grandma Henrietta, who's got lots of money," Nan declared in a tart voice.

Doreen winced. "I really hate to think that everything's about money."

"Well, it is often about money," Nan said. "But, in this case, I really can't be sure. I don't know anything about them."

"Okay, that's good enough. Thanks for checking." At that, Doreen hesitated and then said, "You won't do anything foolish, right?"

"What could I possibly do?" Nan asked in a wry tone.

"An awful lot is going on around here that I don't know anything about," she explained to Nan. "I need information. I just wondered whether Henrietta was still living in that big fancy house or whether just the grandson lived there and maybe Henrietta was potentially in a home."

At that, Nan gasped. "But that would be terrible. She's got enough money for a private nurse."

"Maybe, but maybe she's lonely," Doreen suggested. "Like you, maybe she wanted to have a different kind of a life than being locked up in that home of hers all alone."

"I don't know," Nan replied doubtfully. "I think that's a big reach."

"Well, if it is, then it would mean that I'm going down the wrong path again," Doreen muttered, with a hard sigh. "But then what else is new? … I'll wait and see what Bernard comes up with."

"You do that," Nan replied, "and I'll keep pondering it here." And, with that, her grandmother hung up.

Almost immediately Bernard called her back. "I don't … I couldn't find any kind of a Vernon connection, until we went looking at her sister."

"Whose sister?"

"Henrietta's."

"I thought she was an only child," Doreen replied.

"She is, and yet she isn't."

"Okay, what's with that cryptic mess?" Doreen sighed. "Either she is or she isn't."

"*Daddy* had a child out of wedlock," he shared, with a note of humor.

"Oh, I see. So it's okay for Daddy to have an affair but maybe not okay for son-in-law."

"And that could very well have been something that the

son-in-law threw back in old man Toko's face too," Bernard noted. "Anyway, as far as the board membership goes, Peter Hall was asked to resign between his father-in-law's impending death and his eventual death."

"Oh, now that's interesting. Any reason given?"

"Lack of trust, I believe, was some of the information I got. Don't forget that old man Toko ran a big milling company. A ton of money was involved, and they had to be completely confident in their new CEO."

"And Peter resigned just because they asked him?"

"I doubt it," Bernard scoffed. "Business doesn't work that way. The request would have come with some heavy-duty *you're done* type of warnings."

"And so this sister, this other sister?"

"She lived in Vernon."

"And did she have a child?"

"She did, indeed," Bernard said.

"And I don't suppose that's the one who we met, right? Was that Sean?"

"As far as I know, Sean was Henrietta's daughter's son. The daughter goes by Philly. However, as I said, *as far as I know*, which means I don't know any of that for a fact. That would be an interesting take though, wouldn't it?"

"It's certainly an interesting thought to consider regardless. Maybe Sean is her grandnephew. Any chance of getting in to talk to Henrietta though?" Doreen muttered.

"Not likely, she lives as a recluse."

"And yet the grandson is out and about all the time."

"Yep."

"And what does he drive?" Doreen asked.

"According to my source, a fancy pickup truck."

"Right, and that's what I would expect."

"Sure, lots of young men have trucks around here."

"Have you ever seen one with flat-black paint all over, really dull and ugly-looking?" she asked.

"Not recently. I've seen odd ones over the years, but I can't say I've seen one in town here."

"Right, okay."

"Why?"

"The police picked one up outside the mall. We were chased home from Vernon by it."

"What?" he asked in shock.

And, with that, she gave a bare-bones version of what happened.

"Oh dear," Bernard said, "you're really rattling somebody's chain."

"Yeah, I just don't know whose," she replied quietly. "Yet everything keeps coming back to this affair." And, at that, she smiled. "Actually I do have something else that makes sense. I'll have to go."

"No, wait, wait," Bernard interrupted. "Tell me what you're thinking."

"No, not until I *know* what I'm thinking." She laughed. "For that, you'll have to stand in line because I don't even know myself." And, with that, she hung up quickly, before he could ask any more questions.

She reviewed what she'd learned and realized she had one more chain that had to be yanked. And, with that thought, she picked up the phone book and started searching for Brewsters. When she found three of them, she made several phone calls, until she found Shelley.

And when the woman answered, Doreen introduced herself. "Hi, my name is Doreen, I'm looking for Shelley Brewster."

"Yes, that's my maiden name. What can I help you with?"

"You're a teacher, I believe, an elementary school teacher."

"I was, yes. I haven't been that for quite a while."

"Right. Is there any chance that I could meet you for coffee or something, maybe tomorrow?"

Shelley hesitated and then asked, "What's this all about?"

Doreen worried that maybe she shouldn't say something because it's quite possible this woman would shut her right out. "I hate to even say over the phone," Doreen replied.

"Are you a reporter?" Shelley asked sharply.

"No, I am absolutely not a reporter. And I guess this probably feels very much like I'm being very intrusive, which is why I was trying to keep it fairly private for you. I guess—" And Doreen stopped again, not sure what to say.

"Well, you'd better spit it out now," Shelley snapped. "I don't quite understand why you're calling me, but now that you've disturbed me, the least you can do is address my curiosity."

At that, Doreen sat up straighter. "Do you know Captain Henry Hanson in Kelowna?"

"Of course. He was one of my students."

"Right, and it's his case from when he was a child, that drive-by shooting, that I'm looking into."

"You just told me that you weren't a reporter," she replied in an angry tone.

"And I'm not. I'm really not. I'm not a cop either."

"So why are you looking into it?" she asked in confusion.

"I know this will sound weird," Doreen began, "but the captain asked me to."

After a moment of silence on the other end, Shelley said, "I highly doubt that. He's got a whole police force."

"He does, and I'm sure you know that he has tried his best efforts to get to the bottom of this over the years, but, in some ways, there's a time limit for how many man-hours they can put into it, whereas I don't really have that same limitation," Doreen explained. "I've had some luck with this kind of thing, and, when I was talking to the captain, I told him that I would happily take a look because he's helped me out lots too."

Shelley was obviously confused. "I don't really want to go out anywhere for coffee," she stated, "but, if you want to come to my house tomorrow, we can meet here."

"That would be lovely, thank you," Doreen said. She quickly jotted down the woman's address and added, "I'll see you tomorrow morning."

"And make it early," she stated. "I'm not my best later in the day."

Setting it for a nine o'clock meeting, Doreen quickly hung up and sat here, thinking. Now if only she could shake loose this last little bit of information and have it make sense in her head. Because, right now, an awful lot was still going on in her head and yet wasn't quite formulated there. But she figured Shelley Brewster just maybe held the answer, whether she knew it or not.

And, with that, Doreen went to bed, her mind buzzing, and finally fell asleep.

# Chapter 21

***Friday Morning …***

DOREEN GOT UP the next morning, had a shower and coffee—just in case no coffee was offered or coming her way—and managed a piece of toast, while she fed the animals. She had woken up a little bit later than she'd expected, but, after a restless night, she'd finally fallen into a deep sleep, and now she was excited to get out of here.

She didn't even want to talk to Mack or the captain yet, but she hoped that maybe she would have something to give them soon enough. Trouble was, it didn't always work that way. She'd had a lot of hunches go sideways, and nobody had been able to do much about it. Especially her. And, with that thought in mind, she quickly packed up the animals in her car.

Maybe, just maybe, she shouldn't be bringing them.

She hesitated, looked at her crew, and said, "If she doesn't like it, I'll take you guys back and put you in the car, okay?"

Mugs woofed, and Goliath just gave her that *As if* look. Of course, from his point of view, everybody loved him. And he would be the one to choose whether he loved anybody else. Typical cat. She smiled at that, and, following the internet's directions, she made it to Shelley's house. It was a nice small home, what looked like a two-bedroom construction.

Doreen got out, hooking Goliath and Mugs to their leashes, as the front door opened.

A tall, slim, older lady, with salt-and-pepper gray hair, stood there. She looked to have aged very well.

"Hi," Doreen greeted her, while Shelley frowned. "I always bring the animals, so it didn't even occur to me but maybe you would prefer I leave them in the vehicle."

She looked at her and asked, "Are you Doreen?"

Doreen nodded. "Yes, I'm the one who called you last night."

She looked at the animals, back at Doreen. "Oh."

"Oh?" Doreen repeated.

"Yeah, oh." And then a note of humor crossed her face as she said, "You're *that* Doreen."

Doreen's eyebrows shot up. "*That* Doreen?"

Shelley nodded. "Come in. Come in," she said. "Bring the animals. I love animals." And, at that, the animals raced toward her, and she bent down to greet first Mugs and then Goliath. When Shelley saw the bird in Doreen's hair, she gave a happy sigh. "You are *that* Doreen."

Doreen winced. "Obviously you know something about me that I wasn't really expecting."

"You should by now, as you're getting quite a reputation."

"Well, I guess I am, and then there's all those cases that I'm afraid I'll never solve because I just can't get enough information out of people," she noted, with a wry sigh.

"And right now," Shelley noted, as she ushered them

into her living room, "you're looking into the captain's case?"

"Yes, it's something that's really bothered him all these years."

"With good reason," Shelley murmured. "It was a terrible time for all of us."

"Can you tell me anything about Paul, what was he like?" When Shelley's face turned sour, Doreen held up a hand. "I get it. Nobody wants to say anything bad about the dead."

The teacher looked at her in surprise and then nodded slowly. "I guess that's a problem too for you, isn't it?"

"It always is, until enough years have gone by that people are okay to talk about the deceased in more realistic references."

"Possibly," Shelley said. "I mean, of the two of them, I much preferred Henry. And I felt terrible at the time for that because, well, Paul was never given a chance to become a man. It wasn't fair that he should have died at such an early age."

"Exactly," Doreen agreed. "But there's also an awful lot of other issues that go into a child being who he was."

At that, Shelley looked at her sideways. "You've already heard quite a bit about him, haven't you?"

"I know that he had this nasty habit of following people, looking in windows when he shouldn't have been, gathering information for other people," Doreen shared, with a wry smile. "Whether you know about all that, I don't know."

The retired teacher stared at Doreen. "What do you mean about gathering information for other people?"

Doreen stared at her. "Paul's mother's boyfriend collected information for the guy he worked for. Some days there was work at the construction sites for him, and other days there wasn't. On those days he was trying to find information that he could get compensated for."

Shelley sat down with a hard *thunk*. "Good Lord. … After all these years it never occurred to me."

"You mean, the fact that your affair was something that the child knew about?"

She winced at that. "Oh, good Lord, and yet Paul wasn't even really old enough to understand anything."

"He understood that the information was valuable though," Doreen noted quietly.

The woman gave a shudder. "After all this time," she marveled.

"I know, and I'm so sorry because I know that dredges up an awful lot of your history that you'd like to forget."

"Except for Paul's murder," she noted. "That always bothered me."

"I need to ask you a few questions about the affair."

She nodded slowly. "Most people didn't even know."

"And yet, when I mentioned that Peter Hall had had an affair, they knew exactly who it was with."

Shelley stared at her in shock.

"Almost everybody I spoke with did. I just think nobody talked about it. For one, you were well respected. Two, it's connected to a child, whose death everybody was trying to avoid getting involved in."

"That's very true too," Shelley admitted in weary wonder. She shook her head several times, as if to clear it, and then added, "Wow, of all the things I considered that you might want to talk to me about, that's not it."

Doreen winced. "No, nobody ever wants to talk about it, so I understand that."

"The affair was foolish. I was young. I was stupid, and I didn't really realize in my own head that he was married. I mean, I knew. Don't get me wrong. I wasn't that stupid," she said. "I knew he was married, but I believed him when he said he would leave his wife." She shook her head. "There's this whole group of women who always want to believe what they're told. They try to convince themselves that what they're doing is okay, but it isn't. When I realized that he would never leave his wife and that I was just one of many, I was devastated. It was something I had to really sort through myself. I would never have thought I was *that* person, and yet here I was. I had become that person." There were tears in her eyes. "It took me a long time to get over it."

"I'm sorry for that," Doreen said. "Sometimes we want what we want, and we're fully prepared to justify our thinking that it'll be okay. And then, when we find out that it's not okay, coming back to earth is a hard landing."

Shelley gave a bitter laugh. "That's one word for it. It was rough. It was really rough."

"And was there any fallout for you at that time over the murder?"

She shook her head. "No, there wasn't. I mean, we broke up, and I didn't realize why at that time. I was pretty heartbroken, until I realized that he was involved with somebody else soon afterward. That showed me so much. I went through quite a state of self-examination at that point," she admitted. "But, at the time of Paul's killing, I just felt so guilty."

"Why?" Doreen pounced.

"I didn't have anything to do with the killing, if that's what you mean. But I also knew that he, Paul, had been looking into my bedroom window, and that made me feel terrible." She sighed. "Not only did it make me feel disgusted that somebody was a voyeur, but I also felt terrible because it was a child. I mean, regardless of who he was, I would not want anybody to see my behavior at that moment. And I also felt very ashamed and violated," she murmured. "Of course at the time, Peter told me that it was nothing and that I wouldn't have any repercussions. And he was right."

Doreen nodded slowly. "Did he ever say why there wouldn't be any repercussions?"

She looked at her in surprise. "Well, Peter couldn't afford to have any. I mean, it would have been terrible for him."

"Right. And do you know why?"

"Well, if his wife found out, it would have been horrific for him."

"And yet the wife didn't find out, if what I'm hearing is correct."

Shelley frowned at that and added, "I know he was still married years later, so I presume not. I also know that he didn't stop fooling around. One of the last times I saw Peter privately, his father-in-law had ordered him to come for a meeting, and Peter was pretty worried about that. Yet afterward he was calm. So obviously it was no big deal."

"Right," Doreen explained, "because the father-in-law had had a child out of wedlock himself, yet there were rules to follow when having an affair," she noted, with a darker tone.

At that, Shelley shook her head. "Exactly, such a different set of standards are there, one for the men, and one for the women."

"I know," Doreen murmured. "So you broke up soon afterward?"

She nodded. "Yes, and I never saw Peter again, not privately, not in that way. After Paul saw us together in my bedroom, I just, well, I couldn't. I felt so guilty that we had been seen in such a compromising position, and I was afraid I had traumatized Paul. Then Paul died suddenly, and it all became associated with the same thing in my head. He was also one of my students, and that just added to it." She reached for a tissue and wiped her nose. "Even after all these years, it still has the power to upset me."

"And so you didn't have anything to do with Peter afterward, is that what you're saying?" Doreen asked.

"No. Technically we were still, you know, the public part of whatever we were," she said, with a disgusted look. "But we weren't together. I didn't meet him in private anymore."

"And how did he take that?"

"In a way I think he was okay with it. He knew that I was pretty upset about Paul's death, and I guess he didn't want to deal with that. I was pretty teary about the whole thing."

"I'm sorry you went through that," Doreen said, "because it sounds very much like Peter couldn't deal with his own issues."

"No, he certainly couldn't," she agreed, with a wry look at Doreen. "But it didn't stop him from carrying on with other women."

And that Doreen could very well believe. "Okay, so that was the end of your affair then. And did you have any idea who would have killed Paul?"

She shook her head. "No, it was the gossip for so very long. Everybody had ideas, but nobody had anything specific that would help. I kept my ear out for a very long time because I knew that, in some way, I felt guilty about it all. Believe me. That was enough for me to toe the line and to become a very different person afterward."

Doreen's heart went out to the woman. "I'm so sorry. That would have been very tough emotionally."

"It was," she admitted. "I did finally get over it. I did finally marry. I had two beautiful kids," she noted, with a smile. "And, when I finally told my husband about it all, he was shocked that I was even that person back then."

"Right," Doreen noted. "And, even when you look back, you're probably shocked yourself."

"Oh, totally, but Peter was a very charismatic man, and, when I fell, I fell hard."

Doreen certainly didn't want to blame her for it. "And you have no idea who might have had anything to do with Paul's shooting back then?"

"Not at all. Paul's mom's boyfriend's son was around a lot, not that they were related or anything. He wasn't my favorite kid either, but I didn't have him in my class. I mean, every teacher has a teacher's pet, whether we're supposed to or not. You just automatically do. And, in Paul's and Jack's case, something was just off about both of them."

"Well, Sarah's boyfriend, Cleve Massey, was getting both of the boys—Paul and Jack—to snoop around and to get information for him because, you know, more ears and all that."

"That's just terrible," Shelley said, frowning. "So Paul went back to this guy and told him about our affair, huh?"

"Yes, and that's what the conversation between Peter and his father-in-law was about, I imagine," Doreen explained.

"And he was definitely worried beforehand, but then he seemed to be pretty laid-back about it later."

"Understood," Doreen noted. "Would be interesting to know what they talked about."

"I don't want to know," Shelley declared. "The thought that I was even the grist of any gossip is enough to make my stomach turn. I was so young and so foolish," she murmured. "God, you know you don't want to hate yourself for who you were back then, but sometimes it is really hard."

Doreen nodded. "And when Peter told you that he'd make sure that none of this would ever come back on you, you believed him?"

She nodded. "Yeah, I knew *Daddy* could fix it." She gave a nervous laugh. "And, of course, he did. None of it ever became public knowledge—although, according to you, a lot of people knew."

"A lot of people knew, but that's a whole different story than having the cops show up on your doorstep."

"Believe me. The cops did interview me, but all in the realm of being Paul's teacher," she noted. "So there was never any questions about my relationship with Peter, and …" She hesitated. "And honestly I was thinking my relationship with Peter didn't have anything to do with Paul's death. Yet the fact of the matter is, Paul had seen us together, and Paul had died not all that long afterward."

"So, in theory, Paul's murder could have had something to do with you."

Shelley closed her eyes and then slowly nodded. "And that's been my worst nightmare. Dear God, just the thought of that child being killed because of my having an affair?" She shook her head, opened her eyes, and looked at Doreen. "That would be the worst."

Doreen hesitated and then asked, "Did you ever suspect that Peter had something to do with Paul's death?"

At that, Shelley's eyes widened, and she shook her head frantically. "No, no." She bolted to her feet and raced about the room. "I didn't. And, even now, I don't. … I don't want to think about that." She stared at Doreen in horror. "*That* would be the worst."

Doreen nodded. "And, no, I'm not telling you that Peter did it. I'm just saying it's one of those things that I have to look at."

Shelley stared at Doreen fearfully. "It's possible though, isn't it?"

She winced. "Yes, it's very possible, but he's dead, so we'll never know."

"And that's the next thing." Shelley dropped back into her chair. "I know the police were taking a look into the car accident that killed Peter back then because of the timing. He died just after his father-in-law died." Shelley stared at Doreen for a long moment, then spoke again. "I don't know about his car accident," she began, "but honestly, in order for *Daddy* to be okay with Peter's affair, there must have been some sort of a meeting of minds."

"I know," Doreen agreed. "And what are the chances that the father would inform the daughter before he died, trying to protect his daughter from her adulterous husband, once Daddy was out of the picture?"

"That would have killed her," Shelley replied quietly. "It would have killed me to find out that my husband had been doing that all of our married life. So I can imagine the agony, the betrayal."

"And then Jack," Doreen added, "the other boy you didn't teach, Sarah's boyfriend's son, was also involved in finding out information. And he was killed in a car accident five years after Peter as well."

The retired teacher just stared at her. "That's … way too many deaths," she noted fearfully.

"And that's why I'm taking another look," Doreen murmured.

At that, Shelley started to cry. "A chain of events, … if only I had never been involved in this. Oh, my God." Shelley rocked herself back and forth in her chair.

Doreen winced. "I'm not saying it was you, but, if you think of anything that might add clarity to the scenario, please let me know. And it may not hit you now. It may not hit you for another few hours, even a few days. Or it may hit you in the middle of the night," she said, "but please, let me know."

After Shelley promised that, Doreen left, holding back her own emotions, especially with the new consideration floating around her own tears.

# Chapter 22

EVEN FOR DOREEN, the busy traffic in her brain was getting a little bit hard to manage, but still a kernel of understanding was hidden there right now. She wasn't sure if she was on track or this was completely off track, since she hadn't really clarified a few issues yet and wasn't even sure how to.

Back home, sitting outside on the grass by the creek, all of those theories ran around in her head. But an ugly one, a particularly ugly one, was rising about a little boy. But how could she confirm it? She questioned that for a long moment and knew there was no budget money for this, so she must find another way to accomplish it. Also doing an analysis like that would take time, time that she didn't really think they had.

She grabbed her pen and her notepad and jotted down the timelines, the people involved, the connections between those people, and who would be bothered enough by the words of a child. Everybody was focused on the secrets. Was a secret about an affair enough? Knowing she had to do it, she picked up the phone and phoned Paul's mom.

When Sarah answered and heard who it was on the other

end, she asked, her voice fearful, "Did you figure it out?"

"No, not yet," Doreen answered slowly. "But I'm close, I'm really close."

"Really?" she cried out. "Seriously?"

"Yes." And then she added, "Unfortunately."

A dead silence came on the other end. "What does that mean?" Sarah asked, but an odd note filled her voice.

"I guess the question really is something I must ask you. And I need an answer, and I need the truth from you," Doreen shared, trying to make her voice as gentle as possible.

"I've never lied," Sarah stated.

"No? Well, I can get the police to do a DNA test, if need be."

"Why would you need DNA?" Sarah asked in confusion.

Doreen stopped and then added in a very soft voice, "I think you know why."

And Sarah burst into tears.

When Doreen heard a *click* on the other end, she knew that either Sarah would call Doreen back or was too distraught to even go down that pathway. Doreen sat here for a long moment.

When Mack called a little later, he asked, "What's the matter?"

She stared down at her phone. "Why is something the matter?"

He paused. "I don't know. I just got the feeling that you're upset."

"Well, it's been an upsetting morning and afternoon," she replied quietly.

"You've got it, didn't you?" he cried out. "You've got it."

"No, I *think* I've got it," she corrected. "Remember? No assumptions. We need proof."

Mack snorted. "I think that's my line."

"Yeah, it is your line," she agreed, reaching up to rub her forehead. "And I'm really, really tired now," she said, her voice despondent and sad.

"I'll be right there. You sit tight. Don't do anything." And he disconnected the call.

She thought about that, wondering what she was even supposed to do. There wasn't a whole lot she could do. So many lives were lost. So many lives damaged. So many lives hurt. Over what? She didn't even know how to explain it. As she sat here, on the grass, with a cup of tea, her notepad in hand, her phone beside her, she just didn't even know what to say.

Mugs, as if understanding, came over and threw himself across her lap. She chuckled softly, wrapped her arms around him, and hugged him close. Goliath, obviously sensing exactly what was going on, came up and lay beside her, alongside her leg, stretching out as long as he could, almost reaching from her ankle to her thigh.

She gently rubbed his side and belly. "I don't know what I would do without you two guys," she murmured.

At that came a loud squawk, and Thaddeus came half-running, half-flying toward her, crying out, "Thaddeus is here. Thaddeus is here."

And Doreen burst out laughing. But with the laughter was tears. She wasn't sure whether she was exhausted or this case was just hitting her that hard. The fact that she was really close and just needed some way to prove it now made it that much harder. She could be wrong. She could be 100 percent wrong, and there would be even more lives damaged if she made accusations she couldn't prove. And yet, at the same time, in her heart of hearts, she knew she wasn't.

She picked up Mugs, the huge heavyweight that he was and just hugged him tight. When he started to wiggle in her arms, she let him go, and he got up and ran around her, barking. He ran in circles, until he started doing zoomies up and down the pathway. She smiled, enjoying the moment of freedom and almost innocence.

This moment right before confirming the truth? Well, it was, … it was special in a way. She could hold the hope of having solved the case, and yet the sadness of the truth would remain here for a while.

It would hit her when they finally confirmed all this. It would hit her. There was no doubt about it.

When she heard a vehicle door slam out front, she knew it was Mack. And when he appeared at the kitchen door, almost running through the house, he stopped when he saw her out by the creek and slowly walked toward her.

"Hey," he said, his voice soft, quiet. He sat down beside her. Seeing all the animals around her, Mack shifted behind her, one leg wrapped around either side of her, put his arms around her, and just held her tight against him.

She leaned back, her head up against his chest, and said, "The ending's not very nice."

He kissed her gently on the cheek. "Murder's never very nice."

"Especially in this case," she whispered.

And slowly, piece by piece, she laid it out for him. She felt his back stiffen, as he finally got it, and then he held her tight, buried his face against her neck, and just stayed with her. She felt something wet on her cheeks. She had been crying silently. She reached up to find tears dripping off her cheeks onto Mack's arms.

He pivoted her around so she was in his lap, and he just

held her, rocking gently. "That's one of the reasons I don't want you doing this," he shared quietly. "It hurts you too much."

"It doesn't hurt me any more than it hurt Paul's mother," she noted. "To lose a child and to not have any reason why and to wait all these years to get closure, only to realize how many other people were involved and died, it's heartbreaking."

"It absolutely is," he murmured. "And it's not your fault."

In theory she knew that. In theory it wasn't anything to do with her.

He rubbed his head along the top of hers and whispered, "You're also helping a lot of people find closure."

She nodded. "So why do I feel so sad then?"

"Because it's a sad business," he murmured. "There is no happiness in this. There's nothing there for any of us to reach out and to be happy about—not when you see that evilness."

"And yet an evilness borne from other pain," she added quietly.

He nodded. "I know that, and I get it, and I know that you'll see both sides of this and that you'll feel for all parties. At the same time you also know it doesn't make it right."

She sniffled in his arms and nodded. "I know it doesn't make it right, but it still doesn't make it easy."

His lips twitched, as he looked down at her. "You're the strongest woman I know. You will get through this."

She smiled. "You're becoming more like Nan every day." He stared at her in horror. And she burst out laughing.

Then he grinned at her and said, "I sure hope you'll explain that comment."

"Oh, I will." She chuckled. "Basically you're a cheerleader. You've always been my cheerleader," she noted. "And, no matter what I do wrong, you've always been there for me, and, for that, I'm very grateful." He looked at her worriedly. She gave him a sad smile. "It's just this case," she murmured. "I promise that I'll be back to normal tomorrow."

He nodded. "You better be. Otherwise no more cases for you."

"It's the one thing that I appear to be good at," she said, looking at him simply. "And I don't know how or why, but puzzle pieces? They go together in my head."

"And they go together in a very unique way," he replied quietly, "and I don't think you even realize how special that is."

"No, because it's my head."

He burst out laughing.

She grinned at him. "And, yeah, I'll be fine."

"You will be," he agreed. "Not only that, I managed to snag some pizza on the way over. I know we planned to make beef stroganoff but figured we could do that next time."

She stared at him. "You brought food?" She struggled to lean forward and to look up at the table on her deck.

He laughed. "Yes, I brought food. You worried me. And now I know why."

"Yeah, and we still have to do something about it."

"I know. What do you want to do?"

"Well, here's the question," she began. "I'm not exactly sure I have an answer for you, but I think I do."

"Of course we don't know who was the killer either, right?"

"No, but the options are pretty narrowed down."

He stared at her and then nodded slowly, a grim look on his face. "I guess. I guess it's always been that way, hasn't it?"

"Yep. And how sad is that?"

He just nodded. "It is sad, but we will sort our way through this," he muttered.

"Good, you do that. I'll go get pizza." And she bolted to her feet before he had a chance to grab her, and, with the dog and the cat running alongside her, she raced to the deck, where the boxes were. She sat down and opened them up and crowed, "Oh my, this one's just loaded with meat."

"Being around you as much I have," he noted affectionately, "apparently you need sustenance to keep going."

She looked up at him and nodded. "Yeah, I do. So this is all mine, right?"

He raised an eyebrow, his hands on his hips. "If I thought you could actually eat it all, I might be inclined to let you have it. However, as I need sustenance too, we'll share."

She burst out laughing and pointed. "It's yours. You go ahead and have the first piece."

"No, you're the one who's upset, so you get the first piece."

"Between you and Nan, it's food therapy all the way."

"It's a good thing we at least understand what this is," he teased.

"Yeah," she said, as she picked up the first slice. "Dinner."

# Chapter 23

DOREEN WAS HAPPY to have Mack at her side, as they tossed ideas back and forth. And finally she said, "We'll just have to face this head-on."

"Yeah, but then you're hoping for a confession," Mack replied. "That won't work so well."

"No, it won't, but I'm not exactly sure what else to do."

"We aren't sure who and what. I mean, we've got the kid driving behind you and Nan in that stolen flat-black vehicle. You're thinking it was the kid, right?" he asked.

She nodded again. "Right. It's only a thought because we didn't see him and because you don't have any forensic evidence on that vehicle. Or do you?"

"We have fingerprints," Mack noted, "but we don't have anything to check it against. And even then, remember. It was just a vehicle following you. They didn't touch you. They didn't do anything, except maybe act like a jerk of a driver."

"Exactly, and I'm wondering if that part wasn't more just to track me down. Maybe give me a good scare."

He stared at her. "Is that supposed to make me feel any better?"

"No, definitely not. No real way to know what was going on in Sean's head. Unless we talk to him about it."

"And I could," Mack stated. "I could go up there right now and ask the local authorities to set up a meeting with the kid and me."

"It still doesn't tell us why he was in Vernon. Or what our being in Vernon would have to do with him. But I do have an idea on that too."

"In what way?"

"Well, remember Graham Thurlow is in the seniors' home in Vernon. Plus, there was talk about Paige Thurlow's aunt being in Kamloops."

"And you think the kid, Sean, would have cared enough to be visiting the Thurlows?"

Doreen shook her head. "No, but I'm wondering if his grandmother Henrietta was in Vernon."

"So you think Henrietta's not living in her home here?"

"I don't know what I think yet because another part of me says nobody has seen Henrietta in Kelowna for quite a while."

He stared at her. "Meaning?"

"What if she's in the old folks' home herself? Or dead?"

He sat back, looked at her, and frowned. "Well, in a way that might make sense, particularly if she's not in great health."

"Yet, according to Nan, Henrietta should have lots of money to have private nursing if she needed it. So she could well be at her own home—and too ill to leave."

"Depending on who has her power of attorney, whether for financial matters or for her health care, that could be correct."

"Exactly. Maybe she's just declining. Maybe she doesn't

want anything to do with the bad memories. I mean, if she found out about her husband way back when, maybe it's just left a really bad taste in her mouth all this time. I mean, how do you deal with someone who is now dead, but you just found out he wronged you?"

He looked at her and added, "I feel like there's still something you aren't sharing."

"I'm sharing as much as I know," she stated quietly. "The rest is still up in that whole realm of supposition."

He stared at her. "I'm not even sure what to do with you when you're like this," he admitted. "Normally you're spouting off theories all over the place, and I'm the one telling you to hold back."

She grinned. "Yeah, you are normally. But, in this case, that's not quite the same thing."

"Nope, it sure isn't," he muttered. "So it's interesting to have the shoe on the other foot."

"Yeah, it doesn't feel so good, does it?" she asked, waggling her eyebrows. Then making a decision, she grabbed her phone and phoned the senior care home, where they had talked to Graham Thurlow. As soon as the receptionist came on the line, Doreen stated that she was looking for a Toko family member.

"We have two Tokos here," she replied, "two women."

"A Henrietta and …?"

"Yes, I have a Henrietta and a Philly," the woman confirmed. "Which one do you wish to talk to?" She sounded a little harried.

"How about Henrietta?" Doreen said. And, with that, she heard somebody calling out for Henrietta. Doreen looked over at Mack and nodded. He stared at her, as she put the phone on Speaker, so that he could hear.

When a querulous voice answered the phone, Doreen identified herself. "Hello, my name is Doreen."

A startled gasp came from the other end. "Yes? What? I don't know any Doreen."

"Ah, well, that's interesting. I thought maybe your grandson would have mentioned me."

"You know my grandson?" Henrietta asked.

"Kind of," Doreen said. "I guess the questions really are, how close you are to facing your maker, and is it time for you to talk?"

First, silence came. Then Henrietta asked, "What do you want?" This time she lost the querulousness and her voice was stronger.

"You can't hide forever," Doreen said. "A lot of people were affected by this."

"Nobody was affected," she stated in a hard voice. "And I don't want you calling here anymore." And, with that, she hung up.

Doreen set down her phone and looked over at Mack. He stared at the phone and asked, "Was that the same woman?"

"Yep, one who's trying to look like she's old and feeble, but, when confronted, then she gave up the ghost almost immediately. She doesn't do that acting part well."

"But why would she choose to live there?"

"Well, for one, she doesn't look like a suspect, does she?" she asked, looking at him.

He shook his head slowly. "No, you're right there. I'll have to phone the Vernon police and get them to have a talk with her."

"Or you get permission to go and interview her yourself," she suggested.

"It's not so much permission but a courtesy, since we're in different districts."

"Right, or you can wait."

"Wait for what?" he asked, staring at her.

She sighed. "I highly suspect we'll get a visitor.'

He looked at her and then all around and asked, "Tonight?"

She nodded. "I would expect so."

"You think the grandson's doing her bidding?"

"He's doing somebody's bidding, and it may be his own for that matter too," she noted. "According to everybody, a lot of Toko money is involved."

"She won't lose it, will she?"

"No, I don't think she'll lose it, but, depending on her age and what she might need healthwise, she could potentially spend all her money before it becomes an inheritance for anyone."

"And who would care? Only the grandson is left anyway."

"Well, there's Henrietta's daughter, Philly, then a half sister from her father's affair, plus Sean, who's a grandson or a grandnephew. I'm not sure whether Sean is her blood relative or not."

Mack stared at her. "Meaning, you don't think that Henrietta's daughter had a child?"

"I think her daughter, Philly, has been in a long-term care home for most of her life, and I think Henrietta goes there to visit with her. You notice that I didn't ask if Henrietta was a resident there, just if she *was* there." He looked confused for a moment. She nodded.

"When I phoned the home, I just asked for someone named Toko. The one who spoke to me then pretended to be old and infirm, but she gave up that act pretty fast. I think she's there visiting her daughter, with maybe the grandson driving Henrietta back and forth. I don't know. Or maybe she's living in Vernon now, to be closer to her daughter. Maybe that's why nobody's seen her around Kelowna very much. Maybe her daughter, Philly, took a turn for the worse."

"Okay. And then what difference does it make?"

"I highly suspect that potentially the grandson is her daughter's child, and …" She stopped and looked at him and added, "And Paul, the captain's childhood friend who was murdered, would have been Henrietta's husband's illegitimate child."

# Chapter 24

MACK STARED AT her in shock.

Doreen nodded slowly. "Remember? Peter Hall had affairs constantly, all over the place, and remember also the fact that nobody could find Paul's real father. That's because I'm pretty sure the name Sarah gave me is someone who doesn't exist. I phoned Sarah a little earlier tonight and told her that we had the option of doing DNA testing on Paul. She didn't like that one bit. And when she said she didn't know what I was talking about, I told her, *Yes, you do.* Then she hung up on me."

Just then her phone rang, and she looked down at the screen. "It's Paul's mother, Sarah." She put it on Speaker and said, "Hi, Sarah."

"Hi," she replied, and it was obvious that she was still crying.

Doreen told her softly, "I think it's time we told the truth."

"I think it is too," Sarah agreed. "I have to tell the police though."

"That's fine. I've got Corporal Mack Moreau right here, right now. Mack, say hi."

"Hi, Sarah. What is it you'd like to say?"

"My son, Paul, his biological father was Peter Hall," she confirmed, with a stifled cry. "I promised Peter that I would never say anything. And I loved that man. God, I loved that man. I ruined my marriage over him," she admitted. "But, as I found out, he didn't love me. I don't think he loved anybody, just the position he was in, and he wouldn't do anything to destroy that."

"And did he buy you that house?" Doreen asked her.

She sobbed again and then spoke. "He bought the house, and I lived there rent free, but that was on the condition that I never say anything."

"Of course. And then when your son died?" Doreen asked.

"Honestly I didn't think anything about it being connected to him. I mean, why would I? We'd already settled up our differences. I had a boyfriend at the time, and I still don't even know how this could possibly be related," she wailed. "But I am willing to state legally that Peter Hall is the father."

"And that's what I needed to know," Doreen noted gently. "I'm sure somebody will need to take a statement, something formal along that line. And thank you very much for telling us the truth tonight."

And, with Sarah sobbing gently, Doreen hung up the phone and turned and looked at Mack. "Now what do you think?"

He looked at her phone and nodded. "Wow. You know something? I think you're right."

"And that really narrows down the suspect pool."

"It does, doesn't it?" He stared off in the distance. "The captain will never believe this."

"It's not what we were thinking in the beginning, is it?" Doreen asked him.

"No, not at all. And it still doesn't really explain the second shooting. Why shoot at the captain too?"

"Yeah, it does explain it," she corrected, "but I was wrong. It's not so much because they thought the captain was Jack but because the shooter didn't know which child was who."

He looked at her in shock and then nodded. "That makes sense too, going to shoot them both. The shooter is thinking, *I only killed one but got lucky and killed the right one.*"

"Exactly. And a murderer went free."

A harsh voice spoke up. "She had to."

She stiffened and looked over at Sean. "You think so? It's your grandmother. Do you really think that that was something that she had to do? That boy was ten years old, with a whole life ahead of him."

Sean glared at her. "And you don't know what it's like to live in a family like that. My grandmother's a good person."

Doreen frowned at him. "I'm not saying she isn't a good person. I'm saying that maybe, at the time, she was quite misguided, either by jealousy or God-only-knows what other emotion." Doreen stared at Sean and the handgun he held. "It'd be divine justice," she said, pointing to the gun, "if that happens to be the same gun."

He stared down at it and almost winced.

"It is, isn't it?" Doreen asked. "Your grandmother asked you to come and to take care of things for her, didn't she? And, for that, you'll get her fortune. Because, of course, who else is there now to give it to?"

He stared at her and shook his head. "You don't understand."

"No, I don't. So why don't you explain it to me?"

Sean looked at Mack and asked, "Who are you?"

"Mack," Doreen replied quietly, "a friend of mine."

"Just like another male was in the wrong place at the wrong time forty years ago, I guess Mack is now too."

She looked at Sean, at Mack, and back at Sean. "Before I die, it'd be really nice if you explained it to me." She watched as Mack quietly hit Record on her phone.

Sean seemed to nod. "I don't even know the whole story, I just know that her husband couldn't keep his pants zipped. And her father, once he found out, thought it was hilarious. He never held Henrietta in high regard, and that made it worse. He'd laughed that she couldn't keep a man. He tormented her about it constantly, and she took it, ignoring it and burying herself in all kinds of other pursuits, artistic ones—and she's one awesome artist. But then her husband added to her misery. Peter couldn't hold back taunting Henrietta with the son that he'd given birth to and that this son was his blood and that maybe he should gain everything instead of her. After all, you know, *a grandfather needed a son, and a father needed a son,*" Sean parroted.

"Just some nonsense like that. Henrietta was devastated, and, when she realized that Peter was getting serious about claiming his illegitimate son and starting to bring in lawyers and seeing about DNA tests, et cetera, Henrietta decided to take things into her own hands. She's the one who shot Paul, as you know," he said, with a wry smile.

"Henrietta was never a wallflower. I think, in a symbolic way, she was shooting her own father and her husband. And when her own father died years later, she found out about all his affairs too. But that wasn't so bad, except that he was also planning on leaving most of the Toko money to her husband, the man who had ruined her life and who had made her so miserable all these years."

"So Henrietta then killed Peter?" Doreen asked.

"Yeah," Sean said. "She did. And I don't even know that that was on purpose or whether it was an accident. She told me how they had had a huge argument, and he raced off in his vehicle and tore down the road. She got into her truck and tore off after him, and he lost control and spun out and hit a rail. She said she walked over to check on him, but he looked like he was dying, so she sat there in the darkness and waited. When she checked on him the second time, he was dead."

Doreen stiffened at that. "Well, that's two murders for her."

"Technically she didn't kill Peter though," Sean protested.

"I think, if you don't render aid, it's the same thing," she murmured. "There was a good chance he could have survived, with proper medical attention."

"Maybe, but she didn't want him to. That was obvious. And, with him dead, that made things a lot easier for Henrietta."

"And what about Jack?" she asked.

Sean looked at her in surprise "Who's Jack?"

"The other kid involved in this somewhat, Paul's mom's boyfriend had a son, Jack Madison."

"Ah." Sean nodded slowly. "That kid. Yeah, that was her too, but that time she used the same truck that she used in the drive-by shooting—a ranch hand's truck. She bought it off him for a thousand bucks, and he had just painted it that ugly black, but it had streaks and stuff in it, so she grabbed some spray paint and painted over it to give it the same uniform look. Then she went and had a talk with Jack. But he was all about blackmail, and he knew exactly who the players were and why because he'd spent a lot of years trying to figure it out. And, once he figured it out, he went after Henrietta."

"That wasn't very smart of him, was it?" Doreen said, staring at him in fascination.

"No, I mean, you really shouldn't cross my grandmother."

"And is she your grandmother?"

He looked at Doreen and then shrugged. "I think so. We've never had DNA testing done. I assume so though."

"Why is that?"

"Because my mother, Philly, had an aneurysm during labor, and she was medically dead for many minutes," he explained. "They brought her back, but she was never the same. And I was with her for many years, but we always had nurses. My father did his best, but he couldn't stick around for that. And then my grandfather was no nursemaid himself, so I was raised mostly by strangers," he noted, with half a smile. "Except for her. Henrietta was always there."

"And she could never have more children, is that it?" Doreen asked.

Sean nodded. "Exactly. She tried so hard to get pregnant a second time, and, of course, that was just one more reason why her father bugged her all the time about not being able to keep a man, not being able to provide a male heir. Old man Toko was a heartless sexist who was emotionally and verbally abusive to his own daughter."

"A lot of those old guys from that generation are like that," Doreen noted sadly. "And, of course, with these three deaths, it all leads back to one person." She looked at Sean and asked, "Was that you or Henrietta driving the truck that day, following me out of Vernon back home?"

He stared at Doreen and said, "It was her driving. I was hunkered down in the passenger seat, so you would only see one of us."

"So why is she not here with you now?" Doreen asked. "And why would you even think to do something like this? Unless you've gone down the shooter's pathway for another reason."

He shook his head. "No, I've never killed anybody before." He looked down at the gun in his shaky hand and added, "Never fired a gun before."

"So why this time?" she asked curiously.

He looked up at her. "Because she's counting on me."

"She's perfectly capable of murder though, isn't she? She could do this herself, couldn't she?"

"Sure, but she knows that she'd get caught."

"So you'll get caught instead?" She stared at him. "Isn't that taking loyalty a little far?"

"I'm not getting caught," he argued. "Why would I?"

She sighed gently. "Just put down the gun, please. Let's not have any more unnecessary deaths."

"But that's the thing, according to her, this is very necessary."

"But it's not, and you won't get away clean," she told him. "I'm so sorry to ask, but has your grandmother's cognitive state declined at all?"

He winced. "If I were to say yes, and she heard me, she'd scream like a banshee. But, yeah, definitely. I've seen some signs. And I want to be there to make sure I get that inheritance," he stated. "Nothing like knowing your family is super wealthy, but you're not getting any of it until somebody dies."

"Yeah, I never understood that about wills," Doreen agreed. "Seems like money is the worst reason in the world to want somebody to die. In my opinion, we should share what we've got with those we love while we are all still on this planet."

"I'll get it all though," Sean said, "not just a payout here and there. Nobody else is left of the Tokos, except her."

"Right." Doreen smiled at Sean. "And how was she at trusting others?"

"Not good. I think her father and her husband made her very much wary of everybody."

"Exactly. So why would she let you come here to do this job? I guess it depends on whether she wanted the job done or whether she just wanted to see how you'd handle it."

At that, another voice, strong and strident, broke through the silence.

Doreen looked over to see a woman walking up from the creek. Mugs stiffened and growled at her.

Henrietta looked at him and sneered. "Dogs usually like me," she stated, then frowned.

"You were at my home yesterday, weren't you?" Doreen asked Henrietta. "Because he growled at you then too."

The older woman glared at her. "Yes, I was. And, yes, I'm the one who drove behind you, looking to find out where you lived and having a little bit of fun too," she stated. "I mean, if I could have killed you right then and there, I would have, but I couldn't find the right opportunity. You were a little too calm and controlled for my liking," she murmured, staring at her. "And who are you anyway?"

"I'm Doreen," she said, with a smile. "Nice to meet

you."

The woman snorted. "Good God, one of those always *going to be polite* types." She shook her head. "You know that it's a waste of time. People just take advantage of you when you're like that."

"Oh, I know," Doreen agreed. "Been there, done that, thanks." She looked over at Sean. "Really, Sean, you should just put down that gun. You've been misguided and all that, but your grandmother knows perfectly well what she's doing." Doreen looked over at her and asked, "Did you really have to kill that boy? He had his whole life ahead of him."

"He was a slimy, nasty little tattletale," she snapped. "And no way was Peter getting all my father's fortune," she muttered. "That was mine and mine alone. And now it'll be my grandson's."

"So why would you send him here to commit murder?"

"And that's why I'm here myself. I figured it wasn't fair to him."

"I'm up for the job," Sean protested.

She looked over at him, her face gentle. "No, no, you shouldn't have to be. This *Doreen* woman's right. This is my fight, my job to clean up." And, with that statement, she pulled another gun from her pocket. "Now there's two of us anyway."

"You think we'll just get shot without a fight?" Doreen asked.

"Sure, why not? You're both under a weapon right now. Not like you can do very much."

She smiled at her. "You do realize this is Corporal Mack Moreau, right? And once you kill a cop, then your life is forfeit."

The woman stared at Mack, and a slow fury built. "What?"

"Yeah," Doreen confirmed.

And Mack slowly nodded and stood. "Exactly."

She immediately swung the gun on him. "Don't move."

"Yeah? Or you'll kill me?" he taunted her. "I'll tell you what. My police captain asked Doreen here to look into the case of Paul's murder."

"What's that got to do with anybody?" she asked. "Why does he care?"

"Because he was the child that you shot and didn't kill, on that same day when you did kill Paul," Doreen explained. "That incident propelled the captain to the top of law enforcement here in town, and that case has never left him alone. You shot our captain in cold blood, and you killed his friend right beside him, and that's not something that anybody here takes lightly."

Henrietta stared at Doreen in shock. "Oh my." And then she laughed. "We really don't understand the webs we weave, do we?"

"No, you sure don't," Doreen agreed. "And right now you're at a crossroad. You get to decide if you're sucking your grandson into a life of crime. So far, it's just you on the hook. However, Sean would be allowed to have a life and to move on and to enjoy some of that money that apparently has brought you nothing but pain."

"That's money though, isn't it?" Henrietta stated. "It's the seed of evil."

"And yet here you are sending your grandson down into the same evil turmoil. Why would you do that?" Doreen asked her. "Here I thought you loved him."

"I do. That's why I'm trying to give him all my money."

"You could give him that money without you dying and without him having to do anything for it," Doreen stated. "That's just you stringing a line to somehow justify it. You don't have to justify anything. I don't know whether you would just hand it all over to Sean while you're still alive or at least give him enough to live off on, but to say that he has to commit double murder in order to get *an inheritance*, well, that's just a lie," she said. "If you really cared about Sean, you'd help him right now."

"Sure, but it's not help he wants. Sean wants it all."

"Everybody wants it all, but that doesn't mean that they want you to die beforehand in order to have it all," she explained *again*. "Stop projecting your values on Sean."

Henrietta stared at Doreen, and a mocking look came over her face. "And what? Who are you? Some kind of a philosopher or a psychologist that you can think through all that?"

"I understand people," Doreen declared, and she really did. *Particularly in this case.* "It's always been about money for you, money and control, and you never had any. So the minute you got control, you made sure you kept it."

Henrietta nodded slowly. "Well, that part's true. Nothing like *not* having control to show me the importance of having and keeping control in my life. I won't give that up anymore. And it's money that gives you control."

"It's also acceptance," Doreen added, tilting her head to the side. "It's also understanding your fellow man, finding compassion, and maybe guilt."

"No guilt in my world." Henrietta sneered. "And here's my understanding of my fellow man. You're the one who's poor. Look at the way you live." Henrietta winced.

"Yeah, but I've lived your way too," she murmured. "On

a much higher scale than you two," she added, with a chuckle. "And I'll tell you which I prefer. I prefer this."

At that, Henrietta said, "Then you're a fool." And she raised the gun, preparing to shoot.

Doreen quickly looked for her animals. Mugs growled low in the back of his throat. Goliath was sneaking up behind Henrietta. Thaddeus was quietly atop Doreen's shoulder. She told Henrietta, "If you do that, you'll be really sorry."

She stared at her. "Why? What will you do?"

"Me? Nothing," Doreen said. And she grabbed Thaddeus off her shoulder, looked at him, and said, "There you go, baby." And she flung him into the air. He soared up a little bit.

Henrietta laughed. "Your bird can't even fly."

"No, and he doesn't need to."

Thaddeus headed straight toward Henrietta, beak out, claws out, and grabbed hold of her shoulder and started pecking away at her face.

Henrietta screamed, "Get it off me. Get it off me." And her gun went off, then fell to the ground.

Meanwhile, the grandson tried to get the bird off his grandmother, but he tripped and fell to the ground, compliments of Goliath, with Mack on Sean in seconds. By now, Thaddeus flew back to Doreen, and Mugs took over, nipping at Henrietta's ankle, bringing her down now.

When a deep voice roared across the melee, Doreen looked up to see the captain standing there, a hard look on his face, and four other officers with him.

Henrietta shook off Mugs, looked at the new arrivals, and asked, "Who are you?"

Nobody was in uniform.

"I'm Henry Hanson, the police captain. So happy to see you now. It's been a long time coming," he murmured. "But I'll be very happy to put you behind bars for the rest of your life."

She glared at him. "I should have killed you."

He nodded. "You're right. You should have, but you didn't. So now it'll be my pleasure to make sure you pay for the rest of your life for murdering Paul." And his four officers quickly grabbed Henrietta and had her up on her feet again.

The captain looked over at Doreen and shook his head. "I don't know how this even makes any sense, but one way or another, somehow yet again, you did it. And I am forever in your debt." And he pulled out his handcuffs and snapped them on Henrietta.

Then the captain looked over at Sean. "I think I know you."

Sean looked at him and nodded. "Yeah. I don't know if I'm up on charges for this or not."

"No," Henrietta spoke up. "This isn't your deal. It's my deal. I made him come. I swore it's the only way he'd get his inheritance," she confessed quietly. She looked over at Doreen. "And that wasn't fair to him. This is my deed to make right."

"I don't know about that being left up entirely to you," the captain said, "but, Sean, you're coming down to the station, until we sort this out. If I find any charges against you, believe me. I will pursue them."

And, with that, the captain looked over at Doreen once more, and she saw the emotions working on his face.

She nodded. "I know. Go. Take care of them. We can talk later, and I'll fill you in on all the details."

"I feel like we need to fill them in now," Mack interjected.

She groaned. "It's a good thing you gave me some pizza because, if we have to go down to the station now …"

"We do," Mack confirmed. "This is how it works."

She glared at him, reached for the pizza box, hugged it up close, and said, "I'm taking this one with me."

Chester looked at her, rubbed his tummy, and asked, "Is there any more?"

She gave him a fat grin. "Sure there is. Mack brought it."

At that, the guys checked the other pizza box, snagged a few pieces each, before having to run.

Mack frowned at her. "I didn't even get any."

"Oops." She held out her box. "I'll share mine with you."

"Well, thank you," Mack said, with an eye roll. "Let's get the animals inside, and we'll go down to the station and take care of this. Then we can come back and just sit at the creek."

She smiled. "That sounds really nice."

And that's what they did.

It was perfect.

# Epilogue

*Not Quite a Week Later*

ALMOST A WEEK later, she sat outside, her face up to the sun, just enjoying having nothing to do—no killers to run down, no crazies to go after, just finding some semblance of normality in her world. The captain had been more than profuse in his thanks, and, as she had filled everybody in afterward, there had been several news announcements about the case being cracked finally.

As a lot of people already knew Doreen had been on the case, she had already received a lot of cheers and well-wishing.

She was due to head down to Nan soon, and Mack was coming with her for a postponed celebration. They were supposed to have the celebration a while ago, but then Mack had been shot. Since then they hadn't been able to set it up—until tonight. So, in about ten minutes, Mack would be here. She got up, brushed the grass off her dress, and slowly moved toward the house. She wandered through to the front door and found Mack standing outside on the front step by the hydrangeas.

He looked at her and said, "Wow, I don't think I've seen

you in a dress before."

She looked down, smiled, and replied, "I haven't had a whole lot of reason for wearing one."

He asked, "Are you ready to walk down to Rosemoor?"

"Yep. Are you?"

And, with his nod, they locked up the house and slowly moved toward the creek, all the animals coming as well. She had insisted because it wasn't fair to have a private celebration for Mack and Doreen in solving all these cold cases, when the animals were as much to thank for everything that she'd done anyway. And the Rosemoor management had finally agreed.

As she walked with Mack at her side, she noted, "It has been a crazy-busy summer."

"You think?" he quipped. "But the captain is chortling because of the cold cases you've closed, even though we had to open a couple new ones due to you," he added, with an eye roll.

"I think it is only fair to the families to explain their loved ones didn't die by accident and that we have the murderer behind bars."

"Absolutely," he agreed, squeezing her hand.

As they walked closer to Rosemoor, she looked at the houses on the opposite side of the creek. "Some really beautiful places are here."

"They truly are," he agreed.

"And I did finally connect with Scott at the auction house."

"Oh, good. Anything coming?"

She looked up at him. "Yeah, a pretty hefty check for the books. I haven't even told Nan."

"Is it enough to keep you in style for a little while? At

least in pizza?" he asked, with a grin. When she told him how much, he stopped in his tracks. "Good God, you can almost buy a house in Kelowna for that."

She shook her head. "I wouldn't want to."

"Why not?" he asked. "Are you not planning on staying?"

"Oh, I'm planning on staying, but I'm kind of partial to Nan's house."

He smiled, tucked her hand up close to him, and said, "At least now I won't have to worry about your not being able to feed yourself anymore."

She nodded. "*As long as I'm smart with it,* people keep telling me. I guess I'm not exactly sure what that'll mean though."

"And you will learn," Mack stated. "You're a smart woman."

She laughed. "Again there's that cheerleader."

"Nothing wrong with being a cheerleader." He gave her a hard glance. "Particularly when it comes from somebody who means it."

"I'm doing much better though, handling my money," she said, with a nod. "Never thought it would come to this, but really I am doing much better."

"You're doing fantastic—never meant to imply anything other than that."

"Good, because it's been a long hard summer in many ways, but it's also been very fulfilling."

"It has, indeed," he murmured. "For me too. … And I talked to my brother today."

"Oh, right. How's that move of his coming?"

"He said that he's tried to call you a couple times today."

She frowned, pulled out her phone, and winced. "Yeah, I

saw that earlier, and I just thought it was the one call."

"Are you avoiding him again?"

"No, not so much again," she admitted, "but I know my divorce settlement is going back and forth between him and my ex's attorney."

"They reached a settlement," Mack noted quietly.

"They did?" She stopped to look at Mack. "Nick didn't tell me."

Mack gave her a wry look. "You'd have to answer your phone for that."

She winced. "Okay, good." She hesitated, then asked, "Did he tell you the details?"

Mack shook his head. "It's not for me to know. He's your lawyer, and you have to deal with that."

"Do you think it'll keep my ex-husband off my back now?"

"I hope so," Mack said. "The question really is, if it'll be something that makes him feel threatened."

"Oh no, meaning that if my lawyer's happy, then my ex-husband won't be?"

"It's always a possibility," Mack noted. "Anyway, promise me tomorrow that you'll get in touch with Nick."

"I will," she said. He looked her straight in the eye. "I promise."

As they walked up to Nan's, she asked, "Have you got any new cases?"

"Meaning, *You don't give me enough cases*, right?"

"I don't know about that. However, the last one was *Silenced in the Sunflowers*, and that was a week ago."

"So, what does that mean?" he asked. "You must have a *T* case now?"

"Yes, that's what I was thinking, but I don't know what

it would be. I mean, what murder would involve a word beginning with *T*?" He came up with several words. She laughed at some of them. "I think *toes*," she suggested, nodding. "Toes in …" She stopped, saw headless tulips off to the side that hadn't been cut back, and said, "*Toes in the Tulips.*"

"And yet," Mack noted, "I don't have a case even similar to that."

"You didn't find any dead bodies recently?" she asked, with interest.

He stared at her and sighed. "Yes, … a young woman."

"Oh, I'm so sorry about that," Doreen said, sobering instantly. "It's always sad when it's a young person."

"I agree." And then he stopped and cursed.

"What's the matter?" Doreen asked.

He glared at her. "She was found in a garden."

She beamed. "Please, please, please, tell me that it was a garden with tulips."

"But tulips don't flower this time of year," he noted, shaking his head.

Her face fell.

"Except for the fact"—he stared at her, obviously with a terrible realization—"it wasn't really a garden. Flowers were thrown across her body. *Plastic* flowers."

She stared, her eyes wide. "And?"

He nodded slowly. "They were tulips."

She crowed immediately. "Yes, *Toes in the Tulips*, my next case."

He stopped, pulled her up close, put a hand on either side of her face, and murmured, "*My* next case is *Toes in the Tulips.*"

She reached up, kissed him hard and fast, seeing a glint

rise in his gaze before stepping away quickly. "My case," she said. "*Mine*." And, with that, she started to laugh and ran toward Nan.

Nan stood on her patio, and, when she saw the two of them, she opened her arms wide and called out, "There you are. At last you're here, and the party can begin."

This concludes Book 19 of Lovely Lethal Gardens:
Silenced in the Sunflowers.

Read about Toes in the Tulips:
Lovely Lethal Gardens, Book 20

# Lovely Lethal Gardens: Toes in the Tulips (Book #20)

A new cozy mystery series from *USA Today* best-selling author Dale Mayer. Follow gardener and amateur sleuth Doreen Montgomery—and her amusing and mostly lovable cat, dog, and parrot—as they catch murderers and solve crimes in lovely Kelowna, British Columbia.

**Riches to rags. … Time heals all wounds, … but old deeds still haunt, … even for the innocent!**

After helping the captain solve his long overdue case, Doreen's reputation is well and truly cemented in Kelowna. That's proven out when a young woman is murdered in her own apartment, and the police start looking at the boyfriend. With the town on edge, this young man seeks out Doreen's help to prove his innocence.

Corporal Mack Moreau is back to light duty work—

mostly keeping an eye on Doreen, if the captain has any say in it. It's hardly a hardship, as he loves being around her, when she's not dipping her toes in his active cases. And yet somehow she manages to find old cases that dovetail with his ongoing ones, giving her an exaggerated opinion of where her boundaries are.

What seems simple on the surface goes back into history to a case that was done and dusted, with the killer now out free, looking for revenge. But, of course, it's not that simple or that easy; and, by the time Doreen and her animal crew are done, the world has shifted for more than just one person in this case.

Find Book 20 here!

To find out more visit Dale Mayer's website.

https://geni.us/DMTulipsUniversal

# Get Your Free Book Now!

Have you met Charmin Marvin?

If you're ready for a new world to explore, and love ill-mannered cats, I have a series that might be your next binge read. It's called Broken Protocols, and it's a series that takes you through time-travel, mysteries, romance… and a talking cat named Charmin Marvin.

Go here and tell me where to send it!
https://dl.bookfunnel.com/s3ds5a0w8n

# Author's Note

Thank you for reading Silenced in the Sunflowers: Lovely Lethal Gardens, Book 19! If you enjoyed the book, please take a moment and leave a short review.

Dear reader,

I love to hear from readers, and you can contact me at my website: www.dalemayer.com or at my Facebook author page. To be informed of new releases and special offers, sign up for my newsletter or follow me on BookBub. And if you are interested in joining Dale Mayer's Reader Group, here is the Facebook sign up page.
http://geni.us/DaleMayerFBGroup

Cheers,
Dale Mayer

# About the Author

Dale Mayer is a *USA Today* best-selling author, best known for her SEALs military romances, her Psychic Visions series, and her Lovely Lethal Garden cozy series. Her contemporary romances are raw and full of passion and emotion (Broken But … Mending, Hathaway House series). Her thrillers will keep you guessing (Kate Morgan, By Death series), and her romantic comedies will keep you giggling (*It's a Dog's Life*, a stand-alone novella; and the Broken Protocols series, starring Charming Marvin, the cat).

Dale honors the stories that come to her—and some of them are crazy, break all the rules and cross multiple genres!

To go with her fiction, she also writes nonfiction in many different fields, with books available on résumé writing, companion gardening, and the US mortgage system. All her books are available in print and ebook format.

## Connect with Dale Mayer Online

*Dale's Website – www.dalemayer.com*

*Twitter – @DaleMayer*

*Facebook Page – geni.us/DaleMayerFBFanPage*

*Facebook Group – geni.us/DaleMayerFBGroup*

*BookBub – geni.us/DaleMayerBookbub*

*Instagram – geni.us/DaleMayerInstagram*

*Goodreads – geni.us/DaleMayerGoodreads*

*Newsletter – geni.us/DaleNews*

# Also by Dale Mayer

## Published Adult Books:

### Shadow Recon

Magnus, Book 1

### Bullard's Battle

Ryland's Reach, Book 1
Cain's Cross, Book 2
Eton's Escape, Book 3
Garret's Gambit, Book 4
Kano's Keep, Book 5
Fallon's Flaw, Book 6
Quinn's Quest, Book 7
Bullard's Beauty, Book 8
Bullard's Best, Book 9
Bullard's Battle, Books 1–2
Bullard's Battle, Books 3–4
Bullard's Battle, Books 5–6
Bullard's Battle, Books 7–8

### Terkel's Team

Damon's Deal, Book 1
Wade's War, Book 2
Gage's Goal, Book 3
Calum's Contact, Book 4
Rick's Road, Book 5

Scott's Summit, Book 6
Brody's Beast, Book 7
Terkel's Twist, Book 8

## Kate Morgan

Simon Says… Hide, Book 1
Simon Says… Jump, Book 2
Simon Says… Ride, Book 3
Simon Says… Scream, Book 4
Simon Says… Run, Book 5
Simon Says… Walk, Book 6

## Hathaway House

Aaron, Book 1
Brock, Book 2
Cole, Book 3
Denton, Book 4
Elliot, Book 5
Finn, Book 6
Gregory, Book 7
Heath, Book 8
Iain, Book 9
Jaden, Book 10
Keith, Book 11
Lance, Book 12
Melissa, Book 13
Nash, Book 14
Owen, Book 15
Percy, Book 16
Quinton, Book 17
Ryatt, Book 18
Spencer, Book 19

Hathaway House, Books 1–3
Hathaway House, Books 4–6
Hathaway House, Books 7–9

## The K9 Files

Ethan, Book 1
Pierce, Book 2
Zane, Book 3
Blaze, Book 4
Lucas, Book 5
Parker, Book 6
Carter, Book 7
Weston, Book 8
Greyson, Book 9
Rowan, Book 10
Caleb, Book 11
Kurt, Book 12
Tucker, Book 13
Harley, Book 14
Kyron, Book 15
Jenner, Book 16
Rhys, Book 17
Landon, Book 18
The K9 Files, Books 1–2
The K9 Files, Books 3–4
The K9 Files, Books 5–6
The K9 Files, Books 7–8
The K9 Files, Books 9–10
The K9 Files, Books 11–12

## Lovely Lethal Gardens

Arsenic in the Azaleas, Book 1

Bones in the Begonias, Book 2
Corpse in the Carnations, Book 3
Daggers in the Dahlias, Book 4
Evidence in the Echinacea, Book 5
Footprints in the Ferns, Book 6
Gun in the Gardenias, Book 7
Handcuffs in the Heather, Book 8
Ice Pick in the Ivy, Book 9
Jewels in the Juniper, Book 10
Killer in the Kiwis, Book 11
Lifeless in the Lilies, Book 12
Murder in the Marigolds, Book 13
Nabbed in the Nasturtiums, Book 14
Offed in the Orchids, Book 15
Poison in the Pansies, Book 16
Quarry in the Quince, Book 17
Revenge in the Roses, Book 18
Silenced in the Sunflowers, Book 19
Toes in the Tulips, Book 20
Lovely Lethal Gardens, Books 1–2
Lovely Lethal Gardens, Books 3–4
Lovely Lethal Gardens, Books 5–6
Lovely Lethal Gardens, Books 7–8
Lovely Lethal Gardens, Books 9–10

## Psychic Vision Series

Tuesday's Child
Hide 'n Go Seek
Maddy's Floor
Garden of Sorrow
Knock Knock…
Rare Find

Eyes to the Soul
Now You See Her
Shattered
Into the Abyss
Seeds of Malice
Eye of the Falcon
Itsy-Bitsy Spider
Unmasked
Deep Beneath
From the Ashes
Stroke of Death
Ice Maiden
Snap, Crackle…
What If…
Talking Bones
String of Tears
Psychic Visions Books 1–3
Psychic Visions Books 4–6
Psychic Visions Books 7–9

## By Death Series

Touched by Death
Haunted by Death
Chilled by Death
By Death Books 1–3

## Broken Protocols – Romantic Comedy Series

Cat's Meow
Cat's Pajamas
Cat's Cradle
Cat's Claus
Broken Protocols 1-4

## Broken and… Mending

Skin

Scars

Scales (of Justice)

Broken but… Mending 1-3

## Glory

Genesis

Tori

Celeste

Glory Trilogy

## Biker Blues

Morgan: Biker Blues, Volume 1

Cash: Biker Blues, Volume 2

## SEALs of Honor

Mason: SEALs of Honor, Book 1

Hawk: SEALs of Honor, Book 2

Dane: SEALs of Honor, Book 3

Swede: SEALs of Honor, Book 4

Shadow: SEALs of Honor, Book 5

Cooper: SEALs of Honor, Book 6

Markus: SEALs of Honor, Book 7

Evan: SEALs of Honor, Book 8

Mason's Wish: SEALs of Honor, Book 9

Chase: SEALs of Honor, Book 10

Brett: SEALs of Honor, Book 11

Devlin: SEALs of Honor, Book 12

Easton: SEALs of Honor, Book 13

Ryder: SEALs of Honor, Book 14

Macklin: SEALs of Honor, Book 15

Corey: SEALs of Honor, Book 16
Warrick: SEALs of Honor, Book 17
Tanner: SEALs of Honor, Book 18
Jackson: SEALs of Honor, Book 19
Kanen: SEALs of Honor, Book 20
Nelson: SEALs of Honor, Book 21
Taylor: SEALs of Honor, Book 22
Colton: SEALs of Honor, Book 23
Troy: SEALs of Honor, Book 24
Axel: SEALs of Honor, Book 25
Baylor: SEALs of Honor, Book 26
Hudson: SEALs of Honor, Book 27
Lachlan: SEALs of Honor, Book 28
Paxton: SEALs of Honor, Book 29
Bronson: SEALs of Honor, Book 30
SEALs of Honor, Books 1–3
SEALs of Honor, Books 4–6
SEALs of Honor, Books 7–10
SEALs of Honor, Books 11–13
SEALs of Honor, Books 14–16
SEALs of Honor, Books 17–19
SEALs of Honor, Books 20–22
SEALs of Honor, Books 23–25

## Heroes for Hire

Levi's Legend: Heroes for Hire, Book 1
Stone's Surrender: Heroes for Hire, Book 2
Merk's Mistake: Heroes for Hire, Book 3
Rhodes's Reward: Heroes for Hire, Book 4
Flynn's Firecracker: Heroes for Hire, Book 5
Logan's Light: Heroes for Hire, Book 6
Harrison's Heart: Heroes for Hire, Book 7

Saul's Sweetheart: Heroes for Hire, Book 8
Dakota's Delight: Heroes for Hire, Book 9
Tyson's Treasure: Heroes for Hire, Book 10
Jace's Jewel: Heroes for Hire, Book 11
Rory's Rose: Heroes for Hire, Book 12
Brandon's Bliss: Heroes for Hire, Book 13
Liam's Lily: Heroes for Hire, Book 14
North's Nikki: Heroes for Hire, Book 15
Anders's Angel: Heroes for Hire, Book 16
Reyes's Raina: Heroes for Hire, Book 17
Dezi's Diamond: Heroes for Hire, Book 18
Vince's Vixen: Heroes for Hire, Book 19
Ice's Icing: Heroes for Hire, Book 20
Johan's Joy: Heroes for Hire, Book 21
Galen's Gemma: Heroes for Hire, Book 22
Zack's Zest: Heroes for Hire, Book 23
Bonaparte's Belle: Heroes for Hire, Book 24
Noah's Nemesis: Heroes for Hire, Book 25
Tomas's Trials: Heroes for Hire, Book 26
Carson's Choice: Heroes for Hire, Book 27
Dante's Decision: Heroes for Hire, Book 28
Heroes for Hire, Books 1–3
Heroes for Hire, Books 4–6
Heroes for Hire, Books 7–9
Heroes for Hire, Books 10–12
Heroes for Hire, Books 13–15
Heroes for Hire, Books 16–18
Heroes for Hire, Books 19–21
Heroes for Hire, Books 22–24

## SEALs of Steel

Badger: SEALs of Steel, Book 1

Erick: SEALs of Steel, Book 2
Cade: SEALs of Steel, Book 3
Talon: SEALs of Steel, Book 4
Laszlo: SEALs of Steel, Book 5
Geir: SEALs of Steel, Book 6
Jager: SEALs of Steel, Book 7
The Final Reveal: SEALs of Steel, Book 8
SEALs of Steel, Books 1–4
SEALs of Steel, Books 5–8
SEALs of Steel, Books 1–8

## The Mavericks

Kerrick, Book 1
Griffin, Book 2
Jax, Book 3
Beau, Book 4
Asher, Book 5
Ryker, Book 6
Miles, Book 7
Nico, Book 8
Keane, Book 9
Lennox, Book 10
Gavin, Book 11
Shane, Book 12
Diesel, Book 13
Jerricho, Book 14
Killian, Book 15
Hatch, Book 16
Corbin, Book 17
Aiden, Book 18
The Mavericks, Books 1–2
The Mavericks, Books 3–4

The Mavericks, Books 5–6
The Mavericks, Books 7–8
The Mavericks, Books 9–10
The Mavericks, Books 11–12

### Collections

Dare to Be You...
Dare to Love...
Dare to be Strong...
RomanceX3

### Standalone Novellas

It's a Dog's Life
Riana's Revenge
Second Chances

## Published Young Adult Books:

### Family Blood Ties Series

Vampire in Denial
Vampire in Distress
Vampire in Design
Vampire in Deceit
Vampire in Defiance
Vampire in Conflict
Vampire in Chaos
Vampire in Crisis
Vampire in Control
Vampire in Charge
Family Blood Ties Set 1–3
Family Blood Ties Set 1–5
Family Blood Ties Set 4–6

Family Blood Ties Set 7–9

Sian's Solution, A Family Blood Ties Series Prequel Novelette

### Design series

Dangerous Designs

Deadly Designs

Darkest Designs

Design Series Trilogy

### Standalone

In Cassie's Corner

Gem Stone (a Gemma Stone Mystery)

Time Thieves

## Published Non-Fiction Books:

### Career Essentials

Career Essentials: The Résumé

Career Essentials: The Cover Letter

Career Essentials: The Interview

Career Essentials: 3 in 1

Made in United States
North Haven, CT
24 October 2022

25861919R00165